The Little Vampire of Counting House Lane

The Adventures of Trumper Gallant and Bingo Malloy

BOOK ONE

JP Gunby

MAOS
Publications

I0618901

Copyright © 2018 by JP Gunby

All rights reserved. No part of this publication may be reproduced, stored or transmitted in any form or by any means, electronic, mechanical, photocopying, recording, scanning, or otherwise without written permission from the publisher. It is illegal to copy this book, post it to a website, or distribute it by any other means without permission.

This novel is entirely a work of fiction. The names, characters and incidents portrayed in it are the work of the author's imagination. Any resemblance to actual persons, living or dead, events or localities is entirely coincidental.

JP Gunby asserts the moral right to be identified as the author of this work.

Designations used by companies to distinguish their products are often claimed as trademarks. All brand names and product names used in this book and on its cover are trade names, service marks, trademarks and registered trademarks of their respective owners. The publishers and the book are not associated with any product or vendor mentioned in this book. None of the companies referenced within the book have endorsed the book.

Published by MAOS Publications

First edition

ISBN: 978-1-7329657-3-7

For Tanisha and Reema

Contents

1   Counting House Lane   1

2   A Vampire in Dragonbutt!!!   10

3   The Beasley Mantra   19

4   No Ordinary Vampire   28

5   The Entwhistle Journals   42

6   Two Pairs of Feet   54

7   Entwhistles, Dooleys and Monsters   66

8   Roly Poly Remembers   78

9   It's a Little Vampire   88

10   Yet Another Victim   98

11   Buh! Buh! Buh!   114

12   Investigating Bertie   135

13   Back at Counting House Lane   148

14   A Band of Vampire Hunters   164

15   Setting the Trap   174

16   Don't Worry; I'm Not Going to Kill Him!   188

17   Behind Bars   200

18   The DWI   219

19   MAOS   241

Dragonbutt, the village where Trumper Gallant and Bingo Malloy lived with their aunty and uncle was really not just one village but two. In point of fact, it encompassed Greater Dragonbutt and the neighbouring yet smaller village of Lesser Dragonbutt. However, because so many houses had been built over the centuries, you can no longer see where Lesser Dragonbutt ends, and Greater Dragonbutt starts. So these days everyone just calls the two villages, Dragonbutt…

One

Counting House Lane

"Come on, Bingo," yelled Trumper, at the top of his voice. "Two whole weeks without school and Christmas is only five days away. Let's decorate the tree first, it looks like a six-footer, and after, Aunty J said we can each have a mug of hot chocolate and one of her freshly baked mince pies that are still warm from the oven, just the way you like them."

"That sounds great," replied Bingo, who had just entered the living room holding the stepladder. "I hope it's not the kind with that awful brandy she likes so much because I had one of those last year and really didn't like the taste, not one little bit."

"No, those are for the adults," reassured Trumper, laughing loudly. "These are the regular type that even kids like to eat."

Hot chocolate and warm mince pies are best enjoyed on cold winter days, and Aunty J knew the perfect way to make them both. Her hot chocolate was never made with the typical sugary powder found at just about every grocery store imaginable; instead, she always made hers from scratch with only the best chocolate from Bovington's Sweets and Chocolates, which was conveniently located on Dragonbutt High Street, in between Fanshaw's the Baker's and the Dragonbutt Arms Public House.

Their aunty's real name was Jemyma, although Trumper and Bingo preferred to call her Aunty J. She was pretty in an aunty-ish sort of way, with long dark brown hair that was often tied into a neat ponytail using a hair tie, the colour of which she liked to change from day-to-day. Her large brown eyes, friendly welcoming smile and easy-going manner meant she could get along with almost anyone, and this, despite the fact she was not Dragonbutt born, had over the years allowed her to become a popular resident of the village.

Neither fat nor thin was the best way to describe their forty-ish aunty and while still quite trim she claimed to be a good stone and a half lighter in her younger days, and by the look of her old photos, Trumper and Bingo could well believe it. And there was one more thing about their Aunty J; she always wore a pair of glasses with a thick black plastic frame that made her look like one of the boys' teachers, though teaching had never been her profession. Their aunty, in point of fact, was a dentist by vocation and ran the Dragonbutt Dental Surgery, along with her fellow dentist and close university friend, Azalia Blenkinsop, and their receptionist, Wenna Loopey.

"Ok, Trumper, I've finished hanging the last of the fairy lights on the tree. You can switch them on now," declared Bingo, before jumping to the floor, rolling over twice and then leaping to his feet as he waved his arms in the air.

"Bingo! I told you to be careful when using the stepladder or Trumper will have to hang the fairy lights in place of you," thundered Aunty J, in an exasperated voice that the boys had heard many times before.

"Don't worry, Aunty J," retorted Bingo, while flexing what he imagined to be his impressive muscles. "It will take a lot more than jumping a few feet to the floor to hurt me. Don't forget, I'm not a baby, in fact, everyone says that I'm big and strong for my age."

Trumper smiled and then switched on the fairy lights so that the Christmas tree was lit up in all the colours of the rainbow.

"Wow, the Christmas tree looks amazing. All I need to do now is place the star on the very top," stated Bingo, who started to walk towards the stepladder once again.

Meanwhile, Aunty J had carefully picked up the large silver star that was covered in glitter and had been in her family since before her grandmothers time and handed it to Trumper.

"Trumper, will you do us the honour of placing the star on top of the Christmas tree this year," beckoned Aunty J, as she smiled at him.

"Why does Trumper get to do it again? He put the star on top of the tree last year. It's simply not fair!" cried an annoyed-looking Bingo, stomping his feet on the carpeted floor.

"You should have thought of that before jumping down from the stepladder," berated Aunty J, who was in no mood for one of Bingo's tantrums. "Why don't you hang the stockings from the fireplace so that when Father Christmas slides down the chimney on Christmas Eve, he can fill them with lots of lovely presents?"

"I hope the stockings are bigger than last Christmas," grumbled Bingo, still irritated that Trumper had been asked to place the star on top of the Christmas tree. "Father Christmas didn't bring all the presents I asked for last year, although I'm sure he received my Christmas present list that I posted to him during the summer. It must have been the stockings, they were just too small."

Both Aunty J and Trumper laughed, and then she suggested he hang an extra stocking from the fireplace this year so that Father Christmas was sure to give him all the presents he had asked for. This cheered up Bingo somewhat and so he immediately pulled an extra stocking from the box that was labelled 'Christmas Decorations' and then marked it with a large letter 'B', just to make sure that Father Christmas would know the extra stocking was for Bingo and no one else.

Before Bingo could make any further objection, Trumper quickly climbed up the stepladder, all the way to the very top, and then placed the silver star on the highest branch of the tree before climbing down, taking each step as carefully as he could to please his aunty. The boys and Aunty J then looked up at the tree and all together they mouthed the word, "Perfect," while clapping their hands at the wondrous sight of the gleaming and very colourful Christmas tree.

Aunty J looked at Trumper and Bingo, and said in a soft-spoken voice, "Boys, there's only one more thing to do now."

They both knew what that was, although it was Bingo, who, with a big grin on his face, was the first to shout out the answer, "Hot chocolate and warm mince pies for everyone."

Trumper and Bingo always looked forward to Christmas, which happened to be the only time of the year they got to eat their aunty's delectable mince pies. Once out of the oven, they had to be patient for the pies to cool a little and then all it took was a sprinkle of icing sugar and a tablespoon of fresh pouring cream for Aunty J to make the best mince pies in the whole of Dragonbutt, or so the two boys believed.

Without saying a word, their aunty returned to the kitchen with Trumper and Bingo to make each of them a mug of hot chocolate. At first, she melted the rich sweet-tasting chocolate in a small saucepan and then slowly added her favourite extra-creamy milk that she invariably bought from Gribble's the Grocer's. Just as the chocolaty milk mixture came to the boil, she blended in a little honey from one of the most renowned stores in the county, Botters of Chelmsford, a noted honey purveyor to the Queen. This, she believed, gave her hot chocolate that extra something, much to the appreciation of the boys and anyone else who was lucky enough to experience it.

Once it was ready, Aunty J handed each of the boys a steaming mug of hot chocolate with one large marshmallow and a huge dollop of fresh whipped cream placed on top. Trumper and Bingo had learnt that the best way to avoid the marshmallow and cream from melting and falling into the delicious chocolate and milk concoction, was to eat the gooey marshmallow first, and then quickly spoon out the cream and drink the lovely sweet hot chocolate until the very last drop. And this is exactly what they proceeded to do.

By the time they had polished off the marshmallow and whipped cream, a plate of warm mince pies had been placed onto the kitchen table, and the boys promptly dived right in. When it came to mince pies, both Trumper and Bingo believed their aunty positively excelled. Where others cut corners and bought frozen pastry and jars of mincemeat from the grocery store, Aunty J made everything herself, including the mincemeat from an old family recipe that she had learnt from her mother.

For this, she used dried fruit, apple, citrus peel and spices, including nutmeg and a big pinch of cinnamon, and then mixed them all together in a large bowl with lots of brown sugar and divided the flavourful mixture into two. One bowl was for the adults and infused with a generous amount of good quality brandy, while the other had plenty of apple juice added for the children. The apple juice, she always liked to use, was called Braithwaite's and was produced at the Dragonbutt Cider Mill by Typsy Braithwaite.

Even though it was Saturday, their aunty's husband, Uncle P, the 'P' being short for Perygrin, was working in his office at the Dragonbutt Smoker, the weekly newspaper for Dragonbutt and the surrounding district, and wouldn't be home until later that afternoon. As its editor-in-chief, the Dragonbutt Smoker wasn't simply a job for their uncle, it was a passion. Not only was the newspaper owned by his family, but in all of its two-hundred-year history, one of his ancestors had always held the position of editor-in-chief.

Luckily for him, he did not have far to travel to work because the offices of Dragonbutt Smoker were located on Upper Dragonbutt High Street. If he took the short-cut along the muddy footpath that ran behind their house, it would only take him about twenty minutes or so to walk there, as long as he did not dawdle or break his short commute with a visit to the Dragonbutt Arms, both of which he was known to do, all too frequently.

Although Bingo was the younger of the two boys, he always ate faster and drank more hurriedly than Trumper, which he claimed was on account of his extremely high metabolism and unusually large tummy for a boy of his age. A trait that meant he often had to eat twice as much as anyone else, especially desserts and sweet snacks, which happened to be his favourite.

"Finished," announced Bingo, while wiping the pastry crumbs and chocolate stains from his face with the sleeve of his newly washed jumper. It was still only ten-thirty on Saturday morning, and even though Bingo was far from an accomplished reader, he had already mastered time and could read a clock without any help at all. "Only an hour and a half until lunchtime."

"Well done, Bingo," congratulated Aunty J, clapping emphatically and gently pinching one of his cheeks as she sipped her hot chocolate. "I'll be making your favourite for lunch today."

Trumper laughed, "Sausages again!" And Bingo, who was looking directly at his aunty, had a big broad smile on his face because it was true, sausages were his favourite.

It was not long before Trumper had finished his hot chocolate and took the last bite from his second mince pie. He then said, "Bingo, let's go upstairs to our bedroom so that we can play some games before lunch."

Bingo liked that idea and followed Trumper upstairs to the bedroom they shared. Both of the boys were not really into old-fashioned board games and instead preferred to play adventure and action games on Trumper's laptop, a birthday present from his aunty and uncle. Trumper always liked to be a detective in these games, looking for the bad guy, or better still, hunting for scary monsters. Bingo, on the other hand, simply liked the action games where he could dispatch all the monsters he could find, often in the most gruesome way possible.

"It's twelve o'clock and lunch is ready," yelled Aunty J, from the kitchen doorway, using a voice that was loud enough for Trumper and Bingo to hear over the noise of their game.

"Dispatching monsters always makes me hungry," uttered Bingo, laughing as he turned his head towards Trumper. The older boy agreed and closed his laptop before pulling Bingo up from the bedroom floor and running downstairs to eat the lunch their aunty had lovingly prepared.

Both of them had been given a large horseshoe of meaty Cumberland sausage, freshly prepared by Baverstock's the Butcher's, the finest Butcher in Dragonbutt, made of lots of pork and not too much spice. This was fortunate because although Bingo loved nearly all types of sausages, he really didn't like the taste of spicy sausages, or, for that matter, anything else that contained a lot of spice and made sure everyone knew it by frequently repeating the phrase, "I don't like spicy," which always made everyone laugh.

Sitting next to the Cumberland sausage was a hefty portion of their aunty's yummy and always satisfying bubble and squeak. This was made with locally grown potatoes that she had mashed with a little milk and butter, fried onion, lots of seasonal green vegetables; like roasted Brussels sprouts and fresh garden peas, and a generous sprinkling of Red Dragon, Dragonbutt's locally produced and award-winning cheese. She then fried this in an oversized non-stick pan and smothered everything in her tasty and always pleasing homemade onion gravy.

Trumper and Bingo had no idea why it was called bubble and squeak because when it was served to them, they never saw it bubble and not a squeak was ever heard, even when Bingo put his ear to the plate. Unbeknownst to the boys though, Aunty J had an ulterior motive to serve them what she knew was one of their most beloved of dishes, and that was bubble and squeak happened to be one of the best ways to get growing young boys to eat their greens.

Bingo always believed that a meal was never complete without something sweet and so for dessert, their aunty had prepared another of the boys' favourites. As soon as it had finished steaming, she brought out two large bowls of treacle pudding, made with lots of golden syrup and big juicy currants and raisins that had been soaked overnight in an ample quantity of Braithwaite's. And of course, treacle pudding could never be eaten without plenty of Aunty J's homemade creamy custard, which she liked to make with lots of luscious Dragonbutt milk that had been sweetened with a generous spoonful of Botters honey.

The boys lived in a little old house that had three bedrooms, although one of them was so small it was barely more than an oversized cupboard. Trumper and Bingo had always shared one bedroom and slept in bunk beds, with Trumper on the top bunk because he was the older of the two and Bingo always on the bottom. Aunty J and Uncle P also shared a bedroom; however, unlike the boys, they slept in one big bed. Bingo believed this was a really great idea because every morning when he woke like clockwork at five-thirty, he always ran into their bedroom and jumped into the bed so that his aunty would wake-up and prepare his breakfast.

Behind the little old house was a narrow but rather long garden that backed onto a footpath, the muddy one that was used by Uncle P as a short-cut to work that could only be reached by opening a small and always unlocked wooden gate. And at the very end of the garden was a sturdy red-brick shed with a roof made of slate, the colour of which could change from light to dark grey, depending on the weather.

No one would ever call the red-brick shed small, though it was not too large either. It had only one window that was blacked-out and a freshly painted white wooden door with a large padlock to keep out everyone but its key-holders. There were only three keys to the padlock, one held by their uncle and the other two hung from long silver chains around the necks of Trumper and Bingo, so that they could easily insert the key into the padlock without removing the chain from their neck.

The little old house was situated close to the centre of Dragonbutt at the far end of Counting House Lane, which was a dead-end, or cul-de-sac as the adults liked to say, so anyone going in had to go back out the same way. It was not very long, with less than two-dozen houses closely squished together and although the little old house was rather small, it stood out because of its bright red front door and a shiny brass plate with the number twenty-two clearly displayed for all to see, which, without fail, had been polished every week for years by their housekeeper and neighbour, Old Mrs Dingle.

Two

A Vampire in Dragonbutt!!!

⚜

The Royal Mail was always a little late delivering the post on a Saturday, and so it wasn't until after Trumper and Bingo had finished their lunch that they heard the letter-box in the front door open with a clank, followed by a small thud on the hallway floor.

"I'll get the post, Aunty J," yelled Bingo, as he raced against Trumper to get to the front door first.

Because the little old house only had a very short hallway, both of the boys arrived at the same time. It was Trumper though who picked up the small pile of letters, while Bingo snatched up the latest edition of the Dragonbutt Smoker that must have been delivered earlier that day. Out of habit, Trumper opened the front door to see the village post lady, Mad Tolly Butterworth, riding away on a shiny new bicycle that was painted an impressive Royal Mail red. An old faded red bag sat behind her, with the Royal Mail logo clearly printed in the centre and the word Dragonbutt written just underneath.

Everyone in Dragonbutt called her Mad Tolly Butterworth because every time anyone spoke to her, even to say good morning, she always laughed. And it was not a funny ha-ha type of laugh, rather, it was one of those crazy types of laughs which go on and on, the kind that you just knew, without a shadow of a doubt, meant she was utterly mad. In point of fact, one way or another, all the Butterworth's were a little mad. They had been for as long as anyone could remember and so it wasn't a surprise to any of the residents of Dragonbutt that Tolly Butterworth turned out to be as mad as the rest of the Butterworth family.

Aunty J and Uncle P's full names were Jemyma and Perygrin Entwhistle. Although their uncle had been given the name Perygrin Entwhistle at birth and had used it all his life, for some peculiar reason that Bingo could never fathom, their aunty only started to use the name Entwhistle after she married Uncle P. Why this was so, Bingo could not understand, and what her name was before, he could never remember.

Their uncle was Dragonbutt born, as were all the Entwhistles since the founding of the village. Uncle P never tired of telling the boys about all the monsters his ancestors had battled, which according to him were not simply stories but actual events, recorded in the Entwhistle journals and handed down through generation to generation of his family.

The boys loved to hear those stories that their uncle liked to tell so much and so barely three months ago Trumper and Bingo had been overjoyed when he gave them each a key to the red-brick shed. It was in the red-brick shed that Uncle P kept the Entwhistle journals he had cherished all his life, and now it was up to Trumper and Bingo to safeguard them for generations to come. This, as their uncle never failed to remind the boys, was not simply a family ritual, but part of the Entwhistle Oath to always protect the residents of Dragonbutt. In

11

actual fact, the oath was made because of an ancient prophecy by one of their uncle's ancestors on behalf of the Entwhistle family, during the dark days of Dragonbutt's history.

According to legend, the Dragonbutt prophecy, as it became known, came from the mouth of a dark witch, the Lady Eradorn Wyvern, who decreed that even if every monster was wiped from the face of Dragonbutt, one day they would come back to wreak their revenge. If ever the monsters were to return to the village, then it was the Entwhistle journals that held the key to stop them. It was for this reason that each generation of the Entwhistle family had protected the journals for the day when they would be needed. While still very young, that duty had now passed down from Uncle P to Trumper and Bingo, who, not yet fully understanding the importance of their task, had accepted the immense responsibility of taking the Entwhistle Oath and guarding the precious Entwhistle journals.

"Here's the post, Aunty J, and the Dragonbutt Smoker is here as well," announced Trumper, as he handed the letters to his aunty, yet kept the newspaper for himself so that he could read it aloud to Bingo. Of course, this was not just for the younger boy's benefit, but also for Trumper's, who, though now quite a strong reader, could always do with a bit more practise, especially when it came to some of the more complicated words.

Trumper then walked into the living room, accompanied by Bingo, who had picked up his toy sword or his training sword as he liked to call it and was pretending to fight a fire-breathing dragon, and by the look on his face, as always, it was Bingo who was winning.

On the front page of the Dragonbutt Smoker, Trumper read the title of the main story out loud, "Dragonbutt Vampire Claims Second Victim!" Bingo, after hearing the word 'vampire', immediately stopped fighting his imaginary dragon, dropped his sword to the ground and walked over to sit next to Trumper, who was perched on the sofa, to hear more of the enthralling story.

The older boy scanned through the first few lines of the article, reading quietly to himself at first and then he looked at Bingo. After clearing his throat, he began to read aloud the shocking story that like a bolt of lightning had momentarily grabbed their attention. "Last Thursday, at approximately eleven-thirty in the evening, Mr Shadwick Poly, a teacher at Dragonbutt Primary School, was walking home after leaving the Dragonbutt Arms and was viciously attacked and bitten by an unidentified assailant. Mr Poly, who is recovering at Dragonbutt Community Hospital, suffered the loss of approximately one pint of blood, although no trace of blood was found at the scene or on the victim's clothing. The only words uttered by Mr Poly, so far, have been 'Aaah! The eyes, those horrible glowing red eyes', which leads this reporter, Barry Beasley, to believe that Dragonbutt has experienced yet another vampire attack! Dragonbutt police detective, Heather Huntress, responded by saying 'Vampires simply don't exist and there is no evidence they ever have. Dragonbutt police are doing everything possible to apprehend whoever is responsible for these attacks and will keep the residents of Dragonbutt updated'."

"Dragonsbutts!" declared an excited looking Bingo, using a colloquial expression derived from the old Dragonbutt saying 'One dragon butt is bad, so a multitude of dragons' butts must be really bad!'. Although nowadays, it is more commonly used as a declaration of surprise, shock or simply utter amazement. "That's the second attack in just over a week. The same thing happened to the Reverend Pinkerton after bingo night, the one he runs every Wednesday evening at Dragonbutt Victory Hall. Old Mrs Dingle was there and told Uncle P all about it. The Reverend had left after everyone else and was attacked while walking back to Dragonbutt Vicarage at around eleven that evening. When he was found, he'd also been bitten and was mumbling something about seeing a pair of glowing red eyes, which can't be a coincidence."

"It has to be a vampire," announced Trumper, decisively, while carefully folding the Dragonbutt Smoker and placing it under his arm.

"Do you really think so?" asked Bingo, who could barely hide his excitement. "Dragonbutt police said that vampires don't exist."

Trumper, after several seconds of deep contemplation, finally replied, "I know, Bingo, but don't forget about the stories Uncle P has been telling us for years, regarding the monsters that roamed Dragonbutt during the dark days. Maybe the Dragonbutt prophecy has actually come true, and the monsters have now returned."

So do you believe they have come back, Trumper?" pleaded Bingo, who, if it had been left to him, would have run out of the house at that very moment to hunt for the vampire.

With a wry smile, Trumper looked at Bingo and announced, "That is exactly what we are going to find out and if we discover there is a vampire on the loose in Dragonbutt, then come hell or high water we will do whatever it takes to protect the residents of the village, just like it is written in the Entwhistle Oath."

Aunty J and Uncle P were not really related to Trumper and Bingo; rather, they were the boys' foster parents. This meant they looked after the two boys as if they were their own children; however, they were not Entwhistles and had last names of their own.

Both Trumper and Bingo always knew they had birth parents somewhere else, although, for some unexplained reason, they did not know who and had never been told where they were. In fact, the boys had often questioned whether they were Dragonbutt born, yet every time they asked, the same unsatisfactory answer was always given, "Boys, let's talk about that when you are a little older."

Trumper's full name was Trumper Gallant, a strong name and one the young boy was always fond of. He was already eight years old, with another birthday coming along soon, and almost everyone thought of him as clever, inquisitive and remarkably mature for his years. For a boy of his age, he was certainly quite tall, though his most notable features were undoubtedly his piercing deep blue eyes and his head of neatly combed hair, which could only be described as the blondest of blonde.

Bingo was not Trumper's birth brother, yet that did not matter because the boys always felt there was an unspoken bond between them, much stronger than just blood that they believed made them more than simply brothers. Bingo Malloy was his full name, only six years old but rapidly approaching seven.

Like Trumper, he had blue eyes, although they were a little lighter in colour and he had a mound of wavy yellowy-blonde hair that always looked quite messy, which was not surprising since Bingo never liked to comb it. He was taller than most of the other boys in his year at school, although he barely reached Trumper's shoulders and he was built as strong as a little Shetland pony, or so his aunty often liked to joke.

The boys had been fostered on the same day around five years ago, which was long enough for Trumper to remember very little of his life before moving in with the Entwhistles, and Bingo, too long to remember anything at all. For Trumper and Bingo, the Entwhistles and Twenty-Two Counting House Lane were the family and home they always wanted and so whatever had come before was not something they spent more than an occasional moment or two thinking about.

With the Dragonbutt Smoker under his arm, Trumper, accompanied by Bingo, strode into the kitchen. "They think it's another vampire, Aunty J," blurted out Bingo, still very excited about the extraordinary news.

"Dragonsbutts!" exclaimed their aunty, sounding somewhat alarmed and a little displeased. "Who told you that?"

15

"It's front-page news in the Dragonbutt Smoker," insisted Trumper, waving the newspaper vigorously at Aunty J. "Roly Poly was attacked and bitten by a vampire on Thursday night, and that's not the first attack, it sounds just like the one that occurred last week on the Reverend Pinkerton, and Barry Beasley thinks the same."

"By, 'Roly Poly', I assume you mean your teacher, Mr Poly," remarked Aunty J, while lifting her glasses and giving Trumper one of those 'telling-off' types of stares.

"Yes, of course, I meant to say, Mr Poly," replied Trumper, who in all the excitement had forgotten that Mr Poly's nickname, Roly Poly, was only used by the boys and girls at Dragonbutt Primary School and never in front of the adults.

At that moment, all three of them could hear the sound of a key turning in the front door before it opened with an excruciatingly long and rather loud creak. The boys froze and looked at their aunty sitting at the kitchen table, and then they heard a familiar voice, "Dragonsbutts! That door again, I only oiled the hinges last week." Everyone laughed all at once because it was only their uncle, who must have finished his work at the Dragonbutt Smoker and was returning home a little earlier than expected.

Uncle P was almost six-foot-tall with a thick head of wavy salt and pepper brown hair, however, the salt was rapidly overtaking the pepper as the years drifted away. He was only two years older than their aunty, though the boys thought the difference looked more like ten and he had a rather large protruding tummy that he claimed was on account of all the good food Aunty J loved to cook. Despite this assertion, nearly everyone in Dragonbutt knew that their uncle's girth was the result of his fondness for the homemade pies and local ale served at the Dragonbutt Arms, but that never stopped him from talking about his wife's delicious cooking to anyone that would listen.

"Hello, darling, and what are you boys up too?" asked Uncle P, with a smile on his face as he walked into the kitchen. At that point, he noticed the copy of the Dragonbutt Smoker in Trumper's hand. "Ah, I see you've read Barry Beasley's story about the vampire attack on poor Shadwick Poly."

"Yes, we were just talking to Aunty J about it, and then we heard the creak of the front door opening, and for a moment we thought a vampire was coming for us," replied Bingo, happy that his uncle had returned home.

Uncle P laughed and explained, "Bingo, vampires don't open the front door with a key, and besides, they only hunt for their victims at night. Our top reporter at the Smoker, Barry Beasley, is convinced we have a vampire attacking the residents of Dragonbutt and I for one have the inclination to believe him."

"Perygrin, don't say that. You'll scare the boys," pleaded Aunty J, who was never happy when her husband filled Trumper and Bingo's heads with tales of terrifying monsters. "No one has any idea what is behind these attacks, and I think you will find it is something far less sinister than a mythical vampire."

"That's why I have asked Barry Beasley to come over a little later, and I would like Trumper and Bingo to hear what he has to say," announced Uncle P, speaking as if it was his decision to make, but of course it was really Aunty J who would decide whether the two boys could listen to what the young reporter had found out.

After a short discussion between the two adults, in which their uncle could be heard repeatedly saying, "Yes, dear," and "Of course, dear," their aunty finally agreed that the boys could meet with Barry Beasley. To Aunty J, it was one thing for her husband to tell the boys tales of monsters that roamed Dragonbutt during its so-called dark days and an entirely different one to get them involved in, what he was now calling, an all-out vampire hunt.

Trumper and Bingo though were not perturbed in the slightest; as a matter of fact, they were positively thrilled with the opportunity to be involved in their first actual adventure to hunt down a bloodthirsty vampire and if the Dragonbutt prophecy was true, their first real live monster. However, this was not the only reason the boys were looking forward to meeting Barry Beasley again. Both of them knew that Barry had a weakness for Bovington's special lollies, or 'spollies' as they were locally known, and always carried a handful of them with him wherever he went, so at the very least, later that afternoon they would each likely receive one of their favourite yet notoriously tooth unfriendly sweets.

Three

The Beasley Mantra

A t four in the afternoon, the doorbell rang on the front door of the little old house. Bingo was the faster of the two and arrived first, although Trumper was close behind and was the one to open the door to see Barry Beasley waiting on the doorstep with a big friendly smile.

Barry was not only the Dragonbutt Smoker's best reporter, but he was also the youngest. At the tender age of twenty-five, he had worked for the Smoker, as the employees of Dragonbutt's weekly newspaper preferred to call it, for nearly four years. The young reporter was a slender six-foot-two, with inquisitive looking blue eyes and short ginger hair that he liked to spike with a little gel. Being Dragonbutt born, he was not only happy to be able to live in his revered village, but he was also thrilled to be working as a reporter for the renowned Dragonbutt Smoker.

"Merry Christmas, Trumper, and you too, Bingo," greeted Barry, as he shook the hands of the two boys. "I'm here to see your uncle and understand that both of you will be joining us."

"And Merry Christmas to you too, Mr Beasley," replied Trumper, using the polite term that Aunty J had taught him to say when addressing adults. "Just go through to the living room, you'll find him there."

"Call me, Barry, Mr Beasley is what they call my father," he laughed, while stepping into the little old house.

"Do you have any spollies for us, Barry?" requested Bingo, who was never what you would call shy.

"Of course, Bingo, you know I never go anywhere without Bovington's special lollies," answered Barry, while pulling out two colourfully wrapped spollies from his jacket pocket and handing one to Bingo and the other to Trumper.

"Thanks, Barry," acknowledged the boys in unison, as they unwrapped their spollies and without a moment's hesitation popped the much appreciated sweet treat into their open mouths.

Everyone in Dragonbutt knew why spollies were so special. It wasn't just the fact that they were crafted from three types of fruits and boiled for hours with a delicious sugary syrup. What made them so special was the rich sweet Bovington's chocolate that they were dipped in before being wrapped and sold to their always satisfied customers.

"Good afternoon, Perygrin, and Merry Christmas once again," announced Barry, as he walked into the living room and removed his heavy black leather jacket with its matching gloves that he often liked to wear during the winter months. "I hope that I haven't kept you waiting. There were a few more leads I was looking into, and I completely lost track of the time."

"Not at all, Barry, please take a seat, and you too, boys. Let's hear how Barry's investigation into the recent vampire attacks is coming along," stressed Uncle P, who looked eager to discover what the young reporter had found out.

Without delay, Trumper and Bingo walked towards their uncle and sat down on the big comfortable sofa that was conveniently located in front of the fireplace. Barry sat in the armchair where he had placed his jacket and gloves, and then without thinking, he stood up again and started to pace up and down the living room. This was something that Barry was well known for, although it was also the only thing that Uncle P could never abide about the young reporter.

"Barry, you're not in the office now. It would be much easier on us all if you sat down and told us what you have discovered," suggested Uncle P, rather firmly.

"Oh, yes, of course. My apologies, Perygrin," hesitated Barry, who had been so deep in thought he was unaware he'd been pacing.

Once more, Barry sat in the armchair and proceeded to tell the boys and Uncle P that he had been notified of the first attack by his long-time informer, Doris Clutterbuck. Doris was not just the office administrator at Dragonbutt Police Station and Barry's valuable source, but also a first cousin on his mother's side. They were only one year apart in age and had grown up together, living three doors away from each other in Old Privy Bottom, just off Lower Dragonbutt High Street. Every time Dragonbutt police had been presented with an interesting case, which in truth was never very often, it had always been Doris who tipped off her cousin. And so when she heard of the attack on the Reverend Pinkerton, it was Barry she contacted, even before the official police investigation had gotten underway.

On the evening of the first attack, it had been a typical night of bingo at Dragonbutt Victory Hall. Nothing out of the ordinary had happened, and only one fight had broken out the whole evening. This was considered a successful night as bingo evenings go, bearing in mind that most of the attendees were over seventy.

As everyone in Dragonbutt knew all too well, the oldies took their bingo very seriously. This is why the Reverend Pinkerton always insisted that walking sticks, walkers and any other potential weapon, including ladies handbags, had to be left in a locked room. And this, he liked to boast, had dramatically reduced the number of serious incidents since he had taken over bingo night from his predecessor, the Reverend Crankle.

Bingo night had finished around ten-thirty in the evening and, as usual, all of the attendees had quickly vacated the hall to walk the short distance to the Dragonbutt Arms, leaving enough time before its landlord could ring the bell for last orders. It was a tradition that the winner of the main prize should buy a round of drinks for all the losers and that night was no exception.

The winner on that particular evening was Bucktooth Tom Blewitt, so named because his two oversized upper front teeth precariously protruded over his lower lip. He had just returned after a two-week ban imposed on him for illegally calling 'bingo' when shamefully he still had two numbers uncovered on his card. Therefore, he was so delighted with his win; he bought two generous rounds of drinks for all the losers. Although the Reverend Pinkerton, he recalled, had been absent because he chose to stay behind and tidy the hall, which was to be used the following evening by the Dragonbutt Fire Eaters, for their bi-weekly members meeting to discuss the group's on-going charitable events.

"Yes, of course, Barry. I've been a Dragonbutt Fire Eater for years," interrupted Uncle P, who was not only a member of the prestigious club, for the past two years he had been its vice-chairman. "We met for our usual half-hour meeting at Dragonbutt Victory Hall and then moved on to the Dragonbutt Arms for the rest of the evening. That night is still a bit of a blur, but I do recall we ended up at the Dragonbutt Kebab House, the one that was opened last year by the Aimless twins, Shaz and Taz."

Trumper and Bingo giggled, while Barry simply smiled before

composing his thoughts and returning to the story. He recounted to them that a little before eleven, the Reverend Pinkerton chose to take the short-cut to Dragonbutt Vicarage and so he left Dragonbutt Victory Hall carrying a torch to light his way and walked down Bristletooth Lane to Pigswill Alley.

Pigswill Alley's real name was actually 'Pigs Willow Alley'. In the old days, it was used as a pig run so that the locally bred Dragonbutt pigs could be led to the village butcher's shop, Baverstock's, without having to mess up the lovely clean high street, which is what pigs were known to do. Its original name was 'Pigs Alley' and then 'Willow' was added to the name much later, after the residents of Dragonbutt decided to spruce up the alley, and line it on both sides with beautiful tall willow trees. Over the years, these grew so dense they formed a canopy that protected anyone using the alley from the sun and much of the rain. Henceforward, it was called Pigs Willow Alley, however, over the years this was shortened to Pigswill Alley, and that name is still used to the present day.

The Reverend Pinkerton's home of many years was Dragonbutt Vicarage, which was located a short distance from Pigswill Alley on Brimstone Close. This was a trek he had made on many an occasion, and if he walked briskly, it usually took him no longer than ten minutes. Yet on this particular evening, he never arrived at his destination. As a matter of fact, the Reverend had trudged barely a hundred yards down Pigswill Alley when something terrible happened.

"I know! I know! I know!" called out Bingo, rather loudly, while excitedly jumping up from the sofa and waving his spolly in the air. "It was a vampire, wasn't it, Barry?"

"Bingo, let Barry tell the story, and I am sure we will all find out what happened to the Reverend Pinkerton," asserted Uncle P, who had been listening to the young reporter's story intently and did not appreciate Bingo's untimely interruption.

After a deep breath, Barry went on to say that the Reverend Pinkerton was found on Pigswill Alley, sometime after eleven-thirty by Angus Hogswood, the owner of the highly acclaimed Hogswood Piggery, home of Dragonbutt's award-winning bacon, sausages and all sorts of other piggy things. Trumper and Bingo were big fans of Hogswood sausages and thick-cut smoky bacon. In fact, Bingo, if he had his way, would have eaten Hogswood bacon not once or even twice, but at least three times every day.

Angus had spent that evening at the Dragonbutt Arms, which is where he was usually found on most evenings and for that matter, many a lunchtime, standing at the end of the old familiar bar in a space reserved just for him. He left at around eleven-thirty and being in a particularly jolly mood, he sang songs from his favourite old bands, or to be more specific, the first two or three lines followed by mumbled words and incoherent humming. Bits and pieces were all he could remember, but that did not matter to Angus Hogswood, as he walked merrily onward, eager to return home for a good night's rest.

Just as Angus entered Pigswill Alley, he heard a noise in the distance coming from the opposite direction to his usual journey home. Curious to know what it was, he went to take a look and then tripped over what he imagined to be a large branch from one of the old willow trees. To his surprise, he could hear a groaning sound, and as he peered more closely at the object on the ground, Angus saw that it was actually a person. On closer inspection, he was able to see that it was the Reverend Pinkerton, his twisted body lying in the dirt with the left side of his pale face clearly visible and what looked like a tear in the backside of his always immaculately pressed black trousers.

Standing an impressive six-foot-four and weighing a hefty twenty stones in weight, Angus was not only a large fellow but also an extremely robust one. Since the Reverend Pinkerton was a small middle-aged man of five-foot-six, it was easy for him to toss the

Reverend over one of his strong shoulders and haul him to safety. This meant carrying the injured man the short distance along Pigswill Alley to the well-used opening between two old willow trees that bordered Bristletooth Lane. After ringing the doorbell of the nearest house, Angus dialled nine-nine-nine and asked for an ambulance and Dragonbutt police. Meanwhile, the homeowner, Wenna Loopey, gave what she thought to be basic first aid and a glass of water to the distressed and rather befuddled Reverend Pinkerton.

"So how is the Reverend Pinkerton doing now?" inquired Uncle P, who, although he was genuinely concerned about the Reverend's well-being, was really more interested in what the young reporter had found out about the bloodsucking vampire that had presumably been behind the attack.

To this question, Barry merely gave Uncle P a quick glance, as if to say, "I'm getting to that," and then continued with his story.

The Reverend Pinkerton was treated at Dragonbutt Community Hospital and was released after two days. According to his doctor, he was suffering from acute shock and had also lost about a pint of blood from what looked like a small but rather unusual looking bite. His only memory of the attack on Pigswill Alley was hearing someone's heavy breathing behind one of the old willow trees, and then he said that in the darkness he saw a pair of glowing red eyes. The next thing he remembered was opening his own eyes to see Wenna Loopey attempting to give him the kiss of life, which was quite an unpleasant surprise for the Reverend considering he had been breathing perfectly well at the time.

"Dragonsbutts! That's scary stuff," declared Trumper, who, like his uncle, was impatient to learn more about the attack. "But what makes you convinced the Reverend Pinkerton was attacked by a vampire and not simply a wild animal or an angry cat on the prowl late at night?"

"Well, Trumper, you may not know this, but I'm a bit of a Sherlock

Holmes fan," replied Barry, while glancing at Uncle P, who had the beginnings of a smile creeping across his face.

"That's putting it mildly," laughed Uncle P, as he turned his head to address Trumper and Bingo. "Barry is often seen working on a story at his desk, deep in thought, while wearing a deerstalker hat and pretending to smoke one of those old-fashioned curved pipes."

"Yes, it helps me think," disclosed Barry, wishing to return to the question Trumper had originally asked. "Anyway, according to Sherlock Holmes, 'Once you eliminate the impossible, whatever remains, no matter how improbable, must be the truth.'"

"At the Smoker, we call that 'The Beasley Mantra,'" interrupted Uncle P, chuckling to himself as if he had told a funny joke.

Trumper and Bingo had no idea what their uncle meant by the word 'mantra', nevertheless, they both enjoyed hearing about the exciting adventures of Sherlock Holmes, and Trumper, in particular, was keen to learn how the famous detective could help solve this mystery.

Once again, Barry resumed his story and said, "I started thinking about the loss of blood from the bite mark found on the Reverend Pinkerton and the glowing red eyes of his assailant. No person or animal that I know of has glowing red eyes, and any wound from a regular bite would have left a large bloodstain on the victim's clothing. Yet there was no blood found on any of the Reverend's clothes. Therefore, I deduced that a regular person or animal could not have been the attacker and so I eliminated these possibilities as thoroughly impossible."

"Good reasoning, Barry," interrupted Uncle P, yet again. "And how did you conclude we have a vampire in Dragonbutt?"

"That was elementary, my dear Perygrin," responded Barry, with a broad grin. "The attacker must be something we believe does not exist, or at least not since the end of the dark days. Vampires have glowing red eyes, and they bite and suck the blood of their victims. Although no one really believes that vampires exist in present-day Dragonbutt. So however improbable, it must be true that a vampire is responsible for the attacks on the Reverend Pinkerton and Shadwick Poly."

"Interesting, Barry, and I am with you one-hundred per cent in terms of your conclusion regarding the attack on the Reverend Pinkerton," nodded Uncle P, while leaning forward in his armchair. "But how do you know the attack on Shadwick Poly was by a vampire too?"

Barry smiled and confidently announced, "I obviously had my suspicions, though at first, I wasn't entirely sure because it could have been one of those copycat attacks you always hear about in the big cities like Chelmsford. That was until I interviewed Dr Banjani from Dragonbutt Community Hospital and Detective Huntress, the lead investigator with Dragonbutt Police."

Four

No Ordinary Vampire

I t was a quarter to five when Aunty J walked into the living room with a large plate of her mouthwatering mince pies that she had just taken out of the oven, which meant they were still a little too hot to eat right away.

"Yummy," yelled Bingo, who was always hungry between meals. "Can I have two mince pies, please?"

"Yes, Bingo, there are enough mince pies for all of you to have two each," replied Aunty J, pleased that her boys had a healthy appetite. "Good afternoon, Barry and Merry Christmas. I know it's going to be hot chocolate for Trumper and Bingo, but what about you, Barry? Would you like me to bring you a mug of hot chocolate or a nice cup of Earl Grey tea?"

"Merry Christmas, Jemyma. I'll have a mug of your homemade hot chocolate that I have heard so much about, please," replied Barry, who was eager to taste Aunty J's celebrated hot chocolate that Uncle P had lauded on many an occasion.

"You know me, dear, I'll have the same," announced Uncle P, with a reassuring smile.

Just as everyone was eating their mince pies, the ones containing the brandy for Barry and Uncle P and the non-alcoholic variety for the boys, Aunty J walked into the living room once again. This time she was carrying a tray containing four steaming mugs of hot chocolate, and naturally, all of them had a marshmallow and a huge dollop of fresh whipped cream floating on top.

"Thanks, Aunty J," cried the boys, and then they swiftly gobbled up the marshmallow and fresh whipped cream with the help of a dessert spoon.

"Merci beaucoup," proclaimed Barry, who often liked to show off his French language skills that he had acquired during a recent but rather brief liaison with a French exchange student named Désirée.

Finally, Uncle P slapped his large tummy, as he often liked to do after consuming something extra-special and exclaimed, "Thank you, darling, for the perfect hot chocolate and mince pies as always."

Once all of them had drunk every prized drop of their hot chocolate and eaten all the mince pies, Barry left the living room to thank Aunty J once again and to tell her that, in his opinion, she undoubtedly made the best hot chocolate he had ever tasted, which of course their aunty greatly appreciated. On his return, he continued with recalling the story of the second attack, the one where the schoolteacher, Shadwick Poly, had been the unfortunate victim.

"I think you know that Shadwick Poly, I mean to say, Mr Poly, teaches at Dragonbutt Primary School," conferred Barry, looking at Trumper and Bingo.

"Yes, I have him for science and Bingo knows him from the time he supervised detention," laughed Trumper, as he gently jerked his elbow into Bingo's ribs.

"It was only the one time," retorted Bingo, looking somewhat rattled.

"And it was Flitcher Jenkins fault that I got caught. He was supposed to be the lookout while I practised mixed martial arts with Bertie Bovington, but he let Dr Wimbish walk right into our classroom to catch us wrestling on the floor."

"Bingo, you were given detention because you and Bertie Bovington were playing instead of studying. And not because Flitcher Jenkins was too preoccupied to see that your headteacher had entered the classroom to find out what all the commotion was about and found that you were up to no good again," added a rather brusque, Uncle P.

"Fair enough," mumbled a sulky looking Bingo, as he looked down at the living room floor to avoid his uncle's harsh stare.

According to Barry, it had been eight days after the attack on the Reverend Pinkerton when the second incident took place. Dragonbutt police had been unable to come up with any leads and the case was simply floundering, with no immediate prospect of a breakthrough, or so Doris Clutterbuck claimed.

"And did the second attack take place on Pigswill Alley as well?" inquired Trumper, who was eager to ask a real detective type question, like the ones that Sherlock Homes would pose.

"Good question, Trumper," replied Barry, happy to answer Trumper's very pertinent line of inquiry. "Yes, the second attack took place not far from the first, on Pigswill Alley, and just like the attack on the Reverend Pinkerton, it happened late at night."

Shadwick Poly had been teaching at Dragonbutt Primary School for just over ten years, mostly science, though he occasionally taught sports and sometimes stepped in to teach maths when Millie Bender was unavailable. The Thursday of last had been a fairly typical day of teaching for him, in which one of his year three students nearly burnt down the science lab by substituting water for alcohol in an experiment. After the alcohol ignited, the flames set alight to a small part of the lab before being doused by the quick-thinking Mr Poly with one of the school fire extinguishers.

"Yes, we know all about that. The fire alarm went off, and the whole school had to line-up in the courtyard to be counted. It was nearly an hour before we could return to our classes," explained Trumper, happy that he could add a few more details to Barry's story.

"And then the fire engine came, and Dr Wimbish looked really angry again," added Bingo, eagerly. "Of course, it was Mad Maddox's fault, he's Mad Tolly Butterworth's little brother. If something crazy happens at Dragonbutt Primary School, it's nearly always Mad Maddox who's behind it. I'm just glad he's not in my year because sooner or later, anyone who hangs out with him gets into some sort of trouble."

By the time Mr Poly had cleaned up the mess in the science lab and finished writing the school incident report, it was around seven in the evening. So to calm his nerves, he decided to stroll down to the Dragonbutt Arms. This was the place used by most of the teaching staff at Dragonbutt Primary School for stress relief, after a long day of teaching their mischievous students. On this occasion, he had arranged to meet two of his close colleagues, Millie Bender and Austin Catliter, for a bite to eat and a few pints of something agreeable before returning home.

Bingo laughed out loud and blurted, "At school, we call him 'Mr Cat Litter', and every time he hears us calling him that, his face turns bright red."

"That's enough from you, Bingo," snapped his annoyed-looking uncle, while glaring at the young boy. "You should always respect your teachers, and you know as well as everyone, his name is pronounced 'Cat Lyter.'"

"Yes, Uncle P," groaned Bingo, who by now was accustomed to adults telling him off for all kinds of things. Most of the time he really did not know why, however, he had learnt it was better to simply agree with them or just nod his head.

When Mr Poly arrived at the Dragonbutt Arms, Ms Bender and Mr Catliter were already standing at the well-worn bar and diligently attending to their pints. Ms Bender was drinking the popular Butts Batch Cider, known by the residents of Dragonbutt as simply, Butts Batch. It was a rather strong brew made with locally grown apples and produced at the Dragonbutt Cider Mill by the acclaimed cider maker, Typsy Braithwaite. Mr Catliter, on the other hand, preferred the local favourite, Dragonstone Fire Ale, and Mr Poly gladly accepted a pint of this too. Dragonstone Fire, as it is more commonly called, was made in small batches at the Old Dragonbutt Brewery, which meant, regrettably for those poor souls that did not live in Dragonbutt, it was only ever available in the village and its surrounding district.

The three teachers swiftly downed their pints, and then Mr Poly ordered another round from the Dragonbutt Arms landlord, the ever jolly, Tad Dooley, who was always called Boosey Dooley by the residents of Dragonbutt. This was a name he had become rather fond of over the years, and whenever anyone asked him for his real name, he always replied that it was Boosey Tad Dooley, but just call me Boosey Dooley.

Pies had been the speciality of the Dragonbutt Arms since before Boosey Dooley had taken over as landlord from his father, who, by coincidence, was also called Tad Dooley. As Mr Poly and his colleagues were more than a little hungry after their eventful day at Dragonbutt Primary School, they decided to order right away. Everyone chose the Dragonbutt Arms most popular pie, which was Mr Poly's favourite, rabbit with a rich sauce made from Dragonstone Fire and a large spoonful of Oh My God! chilli sauce. This was made in Dragonbutt and so-named because once it touches your mouth, its main ingredient, fire-chillies, have such a kick, you are almost certainly going to shout-out the phrase 'Oh My God!'.

Although Boosey Dooley had offered Mr Poly and his colleagues a table, instead, the three teachers chose to eat their rabbit pies at the bar where they had been drinking their pints. For that reason, the landlord dragged three tall bar stools over to where they were standing, and then he walked back to the other end of the bar to give his best customer, Angus Hogswood, some much-needed company. And of course, share a pint or two of Dragonstone Fire with the big man.

Once dinner was over, and by tradition, the three of them had one more round of drinks, and then Ms Bender and Mr Catliter left the Dragonbutt Arms and returned to their respective homes in the village. Mr Poly then chatted to Boosey Dooley about his taxing day while drinking two more pints of Dragonstone Fire with the always congenial landlord, who, like most in Dragonbutt knew all too well, was rarely ever seen without a pint glass held firmly in his drinking hand, which happened to be his left.

At eleven on the dot, it was customary to call last orders and closing time was typically eleven-fifteen. On this particular evening, Mr Poly was about to leave when Boosey Dooley asked if he wanted 'One for the road'. Not wishing to offend the hospitable fellow, the teacher unwisely accepted a dram or two of Dragonsbreath, Boosey's infamous and extremely alcoholic homemade potato and acorn vodka that he illicitly and, to the most part, secretly distilled in the backyard of the Dragonbutt Arms.

It was not until eleven-thirty that Mr Poly was able to leave the Dragonbutt Arms to walk back to his house on Pucclechurch Crescent, which was located a short distance from the end of Upper Dragonbutt High Street. Feeling a little unsure on his feet, he decided to take the short-cut home and so he made his way to Pigswill Alley with the help of a torch that Boosey Dooley had lent him. Once he was in the dark alley, the Dragonbutt Primary School teacher had barely walked for more than a few minutes before he was startled by a noise originating from behind one of the larger willow trees. Now remembering, albeit a tad too late, that this was the same Pigswill Alley where the Reverend Pinkerton had been attacked the previous week, a feeling of fright and outright fear overcame him, and alas, he dropped Boosey's trusted torch on the ground.

"I bet that was when he saw the vampire," shouted out Bingo, as he jumped up and down on the sofa with excitement.

"Dragonsbutts! Bingo, calm down," snapped Uncle P, who had placed his right-hand over what he thought was the location of his heart. Trumper then proceeded to elbow Bingo in his ribs again, although a little harder this time, which resulted in a yelp of pain from the young boy and a retaliatory punch that made contact with Trumper's left arm.

After a short pause, Barry went on to say that only moments after Mr Poly heard the noise on Pigswill Alley, he asserted that a pair of glowing red eyes emerged from behind the willow tree, presumedly, the same red eyes that the Reverend Pinkerton claimed he had seen a week earlier. In the darkness, not knowing what was coming towards him, the teacher made the judicious decision to turn around and run back down Pigswill Alley in the direction of the Dragonbutt Arms. The next thing he remembered was being forcefully pushed to the ground by something with a considerable amount of strength, and then he must have fallen unconscious, as the next thing he remembered was lying in a bed at Dragonbutt Community Hospital.

"How did Mr Poly get to Dragonbutt Community Hospital?" asked Trumper, while rubbing his arm that was still aching from Bingo's rather forceful punch

"Well, he was quite lucky, because, on that particular Thursday night, Old Mrs Dingle was walking her dog along Pigswill Alley when she came across his unconscious body at sometime around midnight," answered Barry, as he unwrapped a spolly and offered two more to Trumper and Bingo, which they gladly accepted.

"Dragonsbutts! She must have scared the vampire away," commented Bingo, who was licking the Bovington's chocolate covering his spolly while keeping his eyes firmly positioned on Trumper, just in case the older boy tried to jab him in the ribs again.

"Yes, you might just be right, Bingo, or the vampire may have slipped away before the old lady arrived. All we know is that Old Mrs Dingle swears she saw absolutely no one at the scene of the attack, except the unfortunate Mr Poly slumped on the ground," nodded Barry, who, just like the boys, was now slowly sucking his spolly.

"Why was Old Mrs Dingle going for a walk on Pigswill Alley so late at night?" interrupted Trumper, thinking it sounded somewhat out of the ordinary for the old lady to be walking her dog at midnight, and not only that, she was doing it in the middle of winter.

"Good question, Trumper, I'll make a mental note to ask Old Mrs Dingle the next time I see her," promised Barry, as he threw his spolly stick into the fire.

"Is Shadwick Poly going to make a full recovery?" chimed in Uncle P, with a grave expression on his face as he looked intensely at the young reporter.

"He should do," assured Barry, nodding his head. "Although Dr Banjani wanted to keep him under observation for two or three days. As with the Reverend Pinkerton, he was treated for shock and had lost about a pint of blood from a small bite. However, the doctor told me that Mr Poly will be right as rain in no time at all and he did not expect there would be any lasting physical effects from the attack, nevertheless, mentally, it may take a little longer for him to recover from this traumatic event."

"So you have been able to speak with him?" asked Uncle P, pleased that Barry, in such a short amount of time, had already uncovered so much valuable information.

"Yes, I managed to have a few words with Mr Poly after he regained consciousness yesterday morning, but he really wasn't able to tell me much at all. Maybe if I had a little longer to interview him I could have found out more, unfortunately, Staff Nurse Fanshaw was on duty at Dragonbutt Community Hospital that day," groaned Barry, with a noticeable cringe.

"You mean Bone Cruncher Trudy Fanshaw, winner of the Dragonbutt arm wrestling tournament for the past three years?" cried out Uncle P, as he stood up from his armchair and put his hands behind his head.

"The very same," confirmed Barry, nodding his head vigorously.

"Dragonsbutts! I don't blame you for leaving, Barry. Do you know how she earned the nickname 'Bone Cruncher'?" exclaimed Uncle P, while smiling at the young reporter.

"Yes, of course," answered Barry, with a serious look on his face. "I was the lead reporter on the Smoker's sports section for nearly two years, so it was my job to cover the annual Dragonbutt and district sports day, and the arm wrestling tournament was one of the most popular events. After winning all her rounds against the women contestants, she went on to challenge the men, beating every one of them to get to the grand final with Angus Hogswood, who had been the reigning champion for the previous eight years."

"Oh yes, I remember it all, especially the grand final!" laughed Uncle P, as he leaned back in his armchair. "No one who attended that year could ever forget it. Everybody thought Angus would have an easy win, what with his immense size and weight and his massive arms that resemble tree trunks. Instead, Nurse Fanshaw just smiled at him, gritted her teeth and firmly held his hand. At first, their arms were locked and not moving, and then everyone could see the sweat running down Angus's brow, followed by a shocked expression on his face and a loud cracking sound. His arm hit the table, and Trudy Fanshaw was declared the winner, leaving the dumfounded Angus Hogswood with a fractured hand."

"I don't need to tell you, Perygrin, if she can do that to Angus Hogswood, it will take a braver man than me to confront Staff Nurse Bone Cruncher Trudy Fanshaw when she is on duty. If I need to speak to Mr Poly again, I will catch him when he is discharged from Dragonbutt Community Hospital, either at his home or when he returns to work," reported Barry, who was visibly grimacing.

"That's perfectly understandable, Barry," agreed Uncle P, laughing again as he thought about the young reporter encountering the fearsome Trudy Fanshaw, or the Bone Cruncher as she was most commonly called, though it was ill-advised to call her that particular name within earshot.

"In addition to the Reverend Pinkerton and Mr Poly, I was lucky enough to be able to speak with Dr Banjani, and he provided me with some additional medical information regarding the attacks. However, at the request of Dragonbutt police, I was inclined to leave some of the more sensitive details out of my story in the Smoker," explained Barry, with a serious-looking expression creeping across his face once again.

"That sounds rather ominous, Barry," responded Uncle P, eager to hear more.

Dr Banjani had told Barry that both the Reverend Pinkerton and Shadwick Poly sustained a mild concussion and each of them had been bitten, resulting in the loss of a small amount of blood. The doctor then went on to reveal the unusual bite marks found on the victims' bodies consisted of two small yet identical puncture wounds, and not only that, there was a significant amount of saliva surrounding the area of trauma. This was subsequently analysed, and the DNA was found to be a perfect match, proving that both men had been attacked by the same assailant, although strangely, the type of DNA was listed as unknown.

At this point in the story, Bingo jumped-up from the sofa and shouted, "Dragonsbutts! That means you were right, Barry, and everyone has to believe you. It's got to be a bloodsucking vampire because it attacks at night, has glowing red eyes and drinks your blood, and now Dr Banjani has confirmed that according to an analysis of its DNA, the fiend is not human."

"Yes, Bingo, everyone here acknowledges that we have a vampire in the village and I am sure that most of the residents will accept this fact too, or at least the ones who are Dragonbutt born and know about the prophecy. Nonetheless, in Dragonbutt, we now have many people who were not born here and do not believe in the old legends about monsters plaguing the village during the dark days, and they are the ones who are unlikely to accept the notion that we have a vampire living amongst us," cautioned Uncle P, who was now looking even more serious than Barry.

"So what does Dragonbutt police have to say about all this?" asked Trumper, completely absorbed by all that the young reporter had told them.

"Well, as I have already disclosed, Detective Huntress has been assigned to lead the case regarding the attacks on the Reverend Pinkerton and Mr Poly, which makes a lot of sense because we now know they were attacked by the same assailant," answered Barry, smiling once again.

"I hear that Detective Huntress is a highly regarded police officer," interjected Uncle P, who was stoking the fire that by now was looking a little tame. "She has only been here for a few months, and I understand she was transferred to Dragonbutt from the Metropolitan police in London, so I am sure she is more than capable of leading an investigation such as this."

"Detective Huntress, like most police officers, has a mind ruled by facts, and those facts are limited by her experience and what she believes to be real or mere fiction. She assumes vampires are pure fantasy, and so she will not entertain the idea that we have a vampire on the loose in Dragonbutt that can strike again at any moment," explained Barry, shaking his head.

"Yes, good point, Barry, she's also not Dragonbutt born and probably believes the Dragonbutt prophecy is no more than an old wives tale," acknowledged Uncle P, while raising his eyebrows to show his indignation.

"That means we really can't rely on Detective Huntress to solve this mystery," announced Trumper, who turned to give Bingo a sly wink. The vampire could literally be anyone living in Dragonbutt, with the exception of the Reverend Pinkerton, Mr Poly, the four of us, and of course, Aunty J.

Understanding what Trumper meant, Bingo jumped-up from the sofa again and yelled, "So Trumper and I need to find this vampire without delay and put an end to these vicious attacks."

"Really?" questioned Uncle P, wide-eyed and staring at Bingo. "And what about Barry and I. Don't you think this should be left to the adults and the professionals?"

"What professionals?" pleaded Trumper, looking a little agitated. "You've already said that Detective Huntress doesn't believe in the existence of vampires and you and Barry both work at the Dragonbutt Smoker and are therefore far too conspicuous to investigate a case like this. So that leaves Bingo and I. No one would suspect two boys from Dragonbutt Primary School are hunting for a vampire, and don't forget, we have been looking after the Entwhistle journals and preparing ourselves over the last few months for just this type of eventuality."

"I agree," howled Bingo, as he raised his right arm and thrust his fist into the air. "You're simply too old for this type of work, Uncle P, so we will capture this vampire ourselves, and I'm going to dispatch the foul beast. Don't worry, just leave it to us and this vampire's head will be served up on a plate to you by Christmas Day."

"Is that so," responded Uncle P, a little irritated that Bingo had called him old. "You may assist with Barry's investigation to establish the identity of this vampire; however, no one will be harmed, or as you most eloquently phrased it, 'dispatched'. Oh yes, and for your information, I am only forty-four."

"Yippee," bellowed Bingo, who was really not sure why his uncle disliked being called old, as anyone over the age of twenty seemed pretty old to him. "Let's start right now. You can formulate our plan, Trumper and I'll handle the weapons."

Just then, Aunty J walked into the living room and exclaimed, "What's that about weapons?"

"Oh, we were just talking about video games, Aunty J," responded the quick-thinking Trumper, knowing their aunty would not be happy that Bingo intended to hunt for Dragonbutt's troublesome vampire with a deadly weapon.

"I hope it was nothing," remarked a suspicious-looking Aunty J. "It's nearly dinnertime for you two boys. I'm cooking fish fingers and chips with mushy peas on the side, and for dessert, you can have the left-over treacle pudding from lunchtime."

"Yummy," shrieked the high-spirited Bingo, happy it was dinnertime at last. "Fish fingers are one of my favourites. Trumper, there's a change of plan. Let's eat now and start the hunt tomorrow."

A little distracted, Trumper simply nodded his head in agreement, while racking his brain to figure out what Sherlock Holmes would do to solve a perplexing mystery like this.

"Perygrin, it is Saturday, so I assume you will be eating at the Dragonbutt Arms, as usual?" asked Aunty J, who was looking at her watch, all too aware that her husband spent almost every Saturday evening at his favourite watering hole.

"Dragonsbutts! Yes, of course, darling," replied Uncle P, as he looked at his own watch to see that the afternoon had passed them all by and it was now almost six-thirty. "Would you like to join me, Barry?"

"Most certainly," confirmed Barry, not hesitating for even a moment. "A few pints of Dragonstone Fire and one of Boosey Dooley's hot pies would make the perfect evening."

"Good, then let's head over to the Dragonbutt Arms right away," affirmed Uncle P, who raised himself from the armchair he had been sitting in and proceeded to walk towards the living room door.

"Oh, before we leave, there is one more thing I learnt from Dr Banjani that Detective Huntress asked me to leave out of my reporting," revealed Barry, with a serious expression returning to his face.

"It sounds as if Dragonbutt police don't want the residents of the village to hear the full story," uttered Uncle P, who was eager for the young reporter to finish so that they could retire to the Dragonbutt Arms for the evening. "What was it, Barry?"

"Well, it was something about the puncture wounds," continued Barry, as he stood up and began to pace up and down the living room again. "What I mean to say is that the doctor revealed an important detail regarding the location of the bite marks on the victims' bodies."

"Oh yes, I was going to ask you whether the Reverend Pinkerton and Shadwick Poly were bitten on the same side of their necks. However, with all of the interruptions we had to contend with this afternoon it just slipped my memory," pointed out Uncle P, who was standing with one foot in the living room and the other in the hallway while making brief eye contact with Trumper and Bingo.

"That's the strange thing, they were not bitten on the neck," divulged Barry, as he shook his head.

"So where were they bitten?" exclaimed the boys and their uncle, with a baffled look on each of their faces.

Barry looked at the three of them standing before him and took a deep breath before solemnly announcing, "Both the Reverend Pinkerton and Mr Poly were bitten on the butt!"

Five

The Entwhistle Journals

"It's time to wake-up," shouted Bingo, as he ran into his aunty and uncle's bedroom, dressed in his pyjamas and, as always, brimming with energy.

"Oh, what time is it?" implored Aunty J, though she already knew what Bingo's response would be.

"Five-thirty, of course," answered Bingo, grinning from ear to ear.

"It's too early, Bingo," groaned Aunty J, sleepily. "Climb into the bed and let's sleep for another hour. Our bed is nice and warm so jump in, and we can snuggle up together. Your uncle didn't return home until rather late, so he is still out for the count."

Without hesitating, Bingo gleefully climbed into his aunty and uncle's warm bed and whispered into Aunty J's ear, "I was woken up last night when I heard someone struggling to get their key into the keyhole of the front door. Was that Uncle P coming home from the Dragonbutt Arms?"

"Yes, it was, and he woke me as well. He must have dropped his key at least three times and was making so much of a racket that I had to go downstairs and open the door myself and then guide the noisy sot up the stairs and into the bed," grumbled Aunty J, sounding more than a little displeased with her husband. "As you can see, he's still wearing his outdoor clothes."

"Ha-Ha-Ha," laughed Bingo, a little too loudly. Not that it really mattered though because by the sound of his uncle's thunderous snoring, most likely he would have been able to sleep through a hurricane. That is if Dragonbutt ever experienced one.

To his surprise, he fell asleep almost immediately, and it was not until seven in the morning that he woke to hear the familiar rumble in his tummy, signalling it was time to eat. Fortunately, Aunty J was also awake, and Trumper had just entered the bedroom, eager for his aunty to prepare their breakfast.

"Boys, it looks like it's going to be breakfast for three, let's leave your uncle to sleep off last night's festivities and go downstairs to the kitchen," whispered Aunty J, to Trumper and Bingo.

It was Sunday, and the boys already knew what they would be eating for breakfast because this was always the day of the week in the Entwhistle household that Aunty J made pancakes. Unlike the thin English pancakes that the boys loved to eat every Shrove Tuesday, with a squirt of lemon juice and a generous sprinkling of castor sugar, these pancakes were fluffy and invariably eaten with a large knob of Dragonbutt butter and a generous spoonful of Botters honey.

Breakfast was not really breakfast without something to drink, and so when the boys sat down at the kitchen table to feast on Aunty J's heavenly pancakes, she had one of their favourite refreshments close at hand. While their aunty preferred a cup of strong English breakfast tea, Trumper and Bingo always liked to drink a mug of hot chocolate or a bottle of Braithwaite's, and on this occasion, they were not disappointed in the least, as she placed a tall glass of Braithwaite's in front of each of them.

Both of the boys wasted no time at all in attacking the stack of pancakes that sat on the kitchen table. After smothering each of them in plenty of creamy Dragonbutt butter and lovely sweet Botters honey, Trumper managed to eat an impressive five, whereas Bingo devoured a monumental and record-breaking eight pancakes. Aunty J, on the other hand, took her time and ate a modest three, but as she told the two of them, that was more than enough for her.

"What are you going to do today, boys?" inquired Aunty J, as she started to clear away the dishes.

"We're going to hunt for the vampire that attacked the Reverend Pinkerton and Roly Poly," blurted out Bingo, without thinking and in a matter of fact sort of way, as if hunting vampires was something he and Trumper did every Sunday.

"Not right now, you can play later. Old Mrs Dingle is coming over in about an hour to clean the house, and I told her you boys would play with Baxter in the garden," replied Aunty J, who was not really listening to what Bingo had said, because if she had, the answer would have been a resounding, "Oh no, you're not!"

"Do we have too?" protested Trumper, thinking that hunting for the vampire, which had been terrorising Dragonbutt for the past couple of weeks, was far more important than playing with Baxter, Old Mrs Dingle's funny-looking dog.

"Yes, you do and don't forget to wrap up warmly because it's cold outside. I want to see both of you in your winter coats, woollen gloves and woolly hats," instructed Aunty J, as she loaded the dishwasher and wiped down the glass-topped kitchen table that was now smeared in sticky Botters honey and melted Dragonbutt butter.

"Come on, Bingo, let's brush our teeth and change out of these pyjamas and into our outdoor clothes, then we can go down to the red-brick shed and take a look at the Entwhistle journals before Old Mrs

Dingle and Baxter arrive," declared Trumper, while grabbing Bingo's hand and pulling him up the stairs and into the bathroom.

It could not have been more than five minutes before the two boys were dressed in suitably warm clothing and were pulling on their winter coats, a sky blue one for Trumper and a navy blue one for Bingo. Then came their woolly hats, both of them were maroon in colour, and each had the letters 'DPS' embroidered on the front in a golden-yellow thread that really made the letters stand out. DPS, of course, stood for Dragonbutt Primary School and was part of the boys' winter school uniform.

To ensure they would not get their feet wet during the long and notoriously wet winter months, each of the boys wore a brand new pair of black rubber wellington boots that covered their legs to just beneath the knee. The only thing for them to do now was to pull on their warm woollen gloves, a blue pair for Trumper and a red pair for Bingo, before leaving by the back door and running down the long garden path to the red-brick shed.

Standing outside the white door of the red-brick shed, it was Trumper who grabbed the key from around his neck and unlocked the door before entering and switching on the light. Bingo then followed and bolted the door from the inside with the heavy steel bolt that was meant to ensure its occupants would never be disturbed. Meanwhile, Trumper plonked himself down on the brown leather sofa that for many years had sat in pride of place at the editorial office of the Dragonbutt Smoker.

The brown leather sofa was not the only piece of furniture inside the red-brick shed. To the right of the white door was an extremely old and rather large chest of drawers, and attached to one entire wall, from the cold concrete floor to the ceiling, were several heavy oak shelves containing hundreds of volumes of the old Entwhistle journals. Each journal had been carefully placed in alphabetically order according to the type of monster (or even witch!) within its pages, and it was part of Trumper and Bingo's duties to not only look after every one of them but also dust each journal regularly.

Containing a solitary, and irrefutably invaluable artefact, the large chest of drawers held a two-headed battleaxe, which according to Uncle P had been used by his ancestors to fight monsters. The battleaxe had the letters 'M' and 'O' carved into its short yet solid wooden handle, and this, he had told the two boys, stood for 'Monster Obliterator'. Although it had not been used since the dark days, the fearsome weapon had been passed down through each generation of the Entwhistle family to the present day. Even after so many years, and for a reason that their uncle could never fathom, its blade had never rusted, and it always appeared to be as sharp as the day it had been forged.

It was Bingo, with his fondness for weapons, who took an immediate liking to the two-headed battleaxe. Its blade that resembled the shape of a flying bat was not too large or too small, and its short wooden handle was the perfect size for the young boy to grasp. As Monster Obliterator was undoubtedly a somewhat unwieldy name to pronounce correctly all the time, instead, he chose to call the intimidating and thoroughly lethal weapon, 'Little MO'.

As their uncle liked to joke, even with the brown leather sofa, the large chest of drawers and row after row of shelving containing the Entwhistle journals, the red-brick shed had more than enough space to swing one of the local tabby cats. That made it the perfect hangout for Trumper and Bingo and the ideal base for their first adventure, to hunt for the bloodthirsty vampire that had already attacked two of the residents of Dragonbutt.

Trumper wasted no time at all in attacking the Entwhistle journals, heading straight for the section that had been marked with the letter 'V' and looking for anything he could find regarding vampires. After a quick search, he managed to find three journals that dealt with vampires, which the Entwhistle's had hunted, fought and ultimately dispatched during the dark days in Dragonbutt.

The first journal was about an old Transylvanian vampire. Although this kind of vampire had been all too common during the dark days, Trumper knew that Transylvanian vampires were always extremely conspicuous. And so he was pretty sure he had not seen one in the village. Even Bingo agreed, telling Trumper his funny accent would have given him away by now. So the vampire menacing Dragonbutt, the boys concluded, was unlikely to be a Transylvanian vampire.

Another journal concerned a French vampire named François, who had travelled all the way to England to prey on the residents of Dragonbutt. The odd thing about François was that he actually liked garlic, which was truly unthinkable for most vampires because as everyone knows, vampires are supposed to hate the smell of that exceptionally potent vegetable. He was eventually captured and dispatched by Austol Entwhistle, a young boy of just eleven. Trumper and Bingo were both encouraged by this because a boy that was only a few years older than they are now had successfully tracked down and dispatched such a dangerous vampire.

François's downfall came after he passed out at the end of an evening in which he had eaten his way through five pounds of Mrs Minkjoy's black pudding, a dish she was quite renowned for during that time, and had drunk eight pints of Dragonstone Fire, which was even stronger in those days than it is today. Fortunately, this had allowed the young Austol to douse François in a copious amount of holy water from Dragonbutt Village Church, which had been supplied by the vicar of that time, the Reverend Muffle.

Even though holy water is harmless to ordinary people, being that it is no different than regular water, it can have a devastating effect on vampires. Not only does it burn, but it can also melt a vampire's body. And if enough holy water is used, it is possible to completely dissolve the entire vampire. In the end, all that remained of François the French vampire was his black beret and what was left of his rather long moustache, which, according to the custom of his native land, he always liked to curl up at each end.

The final journal that Trumper had picked out was about an old toothless vampire named Bill, who had traumatised Dragonbutt for four long years. Unusually for a vampire, he was unable to bite his victims and instead was forced to make a little prick in their neck using a thin but stout wooden straw, before he could suck out their blood to his heart's content. It was the wooden straw that eventually led to the demise of Old Toothless Bill, as he became known. While running from the scene of his latest, and as he would soon find out, his last victim, he tripped and impaled himself through the heart with his trusty wooden straw, so happily, that was the end of him.

"Did you find anything useful in the journals, Trumper?" inquired Bingo, who had been spending his time swinging Little MO back and forth, although thankfully, at a safe distance from Trumper.

"All the vampires that Uncle P's ancestors came across in the dark days liked to bite the neck of their victims. There was absolutely no mention of butt biting vampires in any of the journals, so it looks like this vampire we are hunting is no ordinary vampire," explained Trumper, while shaking his head. "What I've learnt is that vampires can only be seen at night and by day they look like perfectly ordinary people. Interestingly, none of them like holy water because it can burn their body and most, the exception being the French kind, hate the smell of garlic. And as far as I can tell, the surefire way to dispatch one of them is with a wooden stake through the heart, which always seems to do the trick."

"I like the idea of using holy water," beamed Bingo, while returning his Monster Obliterator to its home in the large chest of drawers. "We still have those two water pistols that Aunty J bought last summer. Why don't we ask the Reverend Pinkerton for some holy water from the font at Dragonbutt Village Church, so that we can use our water pistols to squirt the vampire with holy water?"

"Agreed," nodded Trumper, believing Bingo's idea was a really good one. "I can also ask Uncle P to cut plenty of stakes out of some strong wood because we can hardly hunt for a vampire without a good supply of sharpened wooden stakes."

"Great idea, Trumper, and we can borrow his mallet, the one he never uses and is always hanging from a hook in the garage so that when we find this vampire, we can hammer one of the wooden stakes through its heart," declared Bingo, who was obviously very keen to start hunting for the vampire. "What's more, I can use my backpack to carry all the weapons."

"You mean the one in the shape of a teddy bear?" exclaimed Trumper, while frowning at Bingo.

"No, of course not, that's just a baby bag. I mean my new school backpack, the big one that looks like Dr Who's TARDIS. Aunty J and Uncle P gave it to me when I started year two at Dragonbutt Primary School," rebutted Bingo, who was a big fan of Dr Who and really loved his backpack.

"Perfect! And I'll ask Aunty J for some garlic bulbs because garlic is going to be our best protection against the vampire," informed Trumper, with a smile on his face.

"Let's keep our fingers crossed that Dragonbutt doesn't have another French vampire," added Bingo, laughing uncontrollably and because it was so funny, Trumper joined in too.

It was then that the boys heard their aunty's shrill voice calling to them and so they immediately jumped to their feet and locked the door of the red-brick shed before running up the long garden path to the little old house, where Aunty J was patiently waiting by the back door with Old Mrs Dingle and Baxter.

For as long as anyone could remember, the old lady had lived at the entrance to Counting House Lane in a somewhat dilapidated house with a faded blue front door. Her husband, Old Mr Dingle, had passed away several years ago, though not before presenting the old lady with a little puppy that she promptly named Baxter, after the first name of her cherished and dearly departed other half. He grew to be barely two feet in height and was always a comical sight to behold on account of his unconventional breed that happened to have one rather unusual feature. This was because Baxter was a Bedlington terrier and instead of looking like a dog, he all too closely resembled a little black sheep.

"Merry Christmas, Old Mrs Dingle," greeted Trumper and Bingo, at almost the same time.

Barring their uncle, ordinarily, the two boys would have been extremely wary of calling an adult 'old'. That is if it had not been for the fact that all the residents of Dragonbutt addressed the old lady in this way. So Trumper and Bingo never once hesitated to call her, Old Mrs Dingle. At seventy-two, the old lady's short grey hair was usually hidden beneath one of the colourful silk headscarves she often liked to wear. And being somewhat short-sighted, she always wore a pair of wireframe glasses with lenses that were so thick they looked more like magnifying glasses, which invariably obscured her washed-out blue-grey eyes.

Standing barely five-foot-tall, Old Mrs Dingle was Dragonbutt born and had a lust for life that had not diminished with age. With no children of her own and only Baxter to keep her company, she kept herself busy by cleaning the Entwhistles' little old house, being an active member of the congregation at Dragonbutt Village Church and from time to time she looked after Trumper and Bingo. And if that was not enough, every week without fail, she attended two social evenings at Dragonbutt Victory Hall. One was the ever so popular bingo night that always took place on a Wednesday and the other, held every Sunday evening, was altogether quite secretive and something the old lady thought of as rather special.

"Merry Christmas, Trumper, and you too, Bingo," announced Old Mrs Dingle, while giving the boys one of her friendly and always welcoming smiles. "Baxter and I would normally be on our way to church at this time, but it's simply not the same without the Reverend Pinkerton. He's still recovering from that awful attack, and I have no idea when he will return to give the sermon at the Sunday service. Anyway, it shouldn't take too long to clean the house this morning because I know your kind aunty has already done half the work. Oh yes, and thank you for agreeing to take care of Baxter."

"That's no problem, Old Mrs Dingle, we love playing with Baxter," acknowledged Trumper, who, although he liked to spend his time playing with the old lady's funny-looking dog, on this occasion he would have preferred to use his valuable time more judiciously by hunting for Dragonbutt's elusive vampire.

"Boys, why don't you go and play with Baxter in the garden," suggested Aunty J, as she was impatient for Old Mrs Dingle to get on with her weekly cleaning. "Take his ball with you and let him run around because it looks like he needs the exercise."

While Baxter may not have been in total agreement with Aunty J, it was certainly true that the funny-looking dog had gained a little extra weight recently and so Trumper and Bingo led him into the garden to play a game of catch, something he always liked to win.

The boys knew that Baxter was very good at catching balls, especially when he jumped into the air and caught one in his mouth. Unfortunately, once the ball was jammed tightly between his teeth, he rarely liked to give it up and usually ran to the other end of the garden to hide it. This meant that every time Baxter caught the ball, Trumper and Bingo had to chase after him to retrieve it. On many an occasion, one of them would have to pry the ball from his teeth, while the other distracted him with one of the rubber bones that Old Mrs Dingle had left in the garden for the funny-looking dog to chew.

After about half an hour of playing catch with Baxter, it was not really clear who had exercised the most. The funny-looking dog that ran to catch the ball each time it was thrown, or Trumper and Bingo, who had to endlessly run after him. Trumper, a little tired from all the running, shouted over to Bingo, "Let's take Baxter for a walk so that we can visit Dragonbutt Vicarage to ask the Reverend Pinkerton for some of his holy water."

"Good idea, Trumper, but let's not dawdle because we need to return home for our lunch," replied Bingo, who was eager to fill his water pistol with the noxious holy water. In anticipation of coming face-to-face with the vampire that he believed the two of them would surely encounter before too long.

For Trumper and Bingo to walk from the little old house to Dragonbutt Vicarage, they had a choice of two options. The first and longer of the two, but decidedly less messy, was to make a left turn out of Counting House Lane and walk along the pavement that bordered Hunnickle Drive and then cross over the Old Dragonbutt Bridge to reach Lower Dragonbutt High Street. From there, it was just a short stroll to Brimstone Close, and the vicarage was located at the far end. This, the boys knew from experience, would take them something like twenty to twenty-five minutes to reach their destination.

Alternatively, if they chose to take the muddy footpath behind the little old house, it was only a short saunter to Dragonbutt pond and on the far side of this popular village landmark was a narrow path that led to Pigswill Alley. This conveniently ran all the way to the rear entrance of Dragonbutt Vicarage, which, if the boys walked at a brisk pace, would usually take them no more than fifteen minutes. The downside to this option was that at this time of year, Pigswill Alley tended to be even muddier than the footpath that ran behind the little old house. However, that did not deter Trumper and Bingo as they were both wearing their new rubber wellington boots, therefore, not surprisingly; it was the second option the two boys decided to take.

Six

Two Pairs of Feet

B axter could run much faster than Bingo, and it took all of his strength to pull on the lead and slow the funny-looking dog to a pace whereby the young boy could keep up with him. This allowed Trumper to catch-up with the other two, and within a few minutes, they emerged from the muddy footpath to see Dragonbutt pond directly in front of them. All they had to do now was traverse Hunnickle Drive using the somewhat rickety footbridge that had been built ages ago, though no one could remember exactly when, and then walk along the cobblestone path that bordered their much-loved village pond.

It was a very old pond that dated back to the founding of Dragonbutt, and it was rumoured to be quite deep. No one actually knew just how deep, because at each entrance, and there were two, signs were posted with the words 'SWIMMING IS STRICTLY PROHIBITED!'. At its centre was a small island, which was where the ducks and the swans that made their homes at Dragonbutt pond built their nests, hatched and reared their young and slept at the end of each day. On its far bank, standing beneath a sign that stated 'NO FISHING ALLOWED!', Trumper and Bingo could see two young boys wearing DPS woolly hats, and it looked as though they were fishing with a couple of long rods.

"Hey Bingo," yelled the tallest boy, while waving his arm in the air.

Recognising the two of them almost immediately, Trumper and Bingo walked with Baxter towards Bingo's close friends and classmates, Bertie Bovington and Flitcher Jenkins, who he had known since pre-school when they were both members of his now-disbanded gang.

Bertie Bovington lived on Counting House Lane at number eleven, only a handful of doors away from Trumper and Bingo's little old house. While Flitcher Jenkins home was located just a couple of streets over on Flamingo Crescent. Why it was called Flamingo Crescent had always been a bit of a mystery to the residents of Dragonbutt and Trumper and Bingo were no exception. This was because no one in the village could recall ever seeing a flamingo in Dragonbutt, nevertheless, this had not stopped the Jenkins family from painting their house a garish flamingo pink, to the consternation of their unfortunate and thoroughly discontented neighbours.

Flitcher was as tall as Bingo, and most would say he was not the brightest star in the sky, which meant, somewhat unkindly, he tended to be a little slow. Bertie, on the other hand, was considered quite short for his age and was noted for his cunning. While Bingo was solid yet still rather lean, Flitcher was unmistakably skinny and had dark brown curly hair with pale green eyes; and as for Bertie, he was kind of chubby with the distinctive straight black hair and dull blue eyes that all of the Bovington family seemed to share.

Both Bertie and Flitcher were Dragonbutt born, though it was Bertie that had the most recognisable name in the district. He was one of those Bovingtons that owned Bovington's Sweets and

Chocolates, which not only had a far-flung reputation for making first-rate chocolate and a number of top-notch sweets, it was also the only sweet shop in the village. A fact that had helped Bertie Bovington become an exceedingly popular and much sought after student at Dragonbutt Primary School.

"Merry Christmas, Bertie, and the same to you, Flitcher," called Trumper and Bingo, as they walked up to the two boys that were now pushing each other and giggling quite incessantly.

"Baa!" cried Flitcher, who pointed towards Baxter and burst out laughing.

Bertie joined in the laugher too and then asked, "Are you taking him for a shearing?" And this caused Flitcher to laugh even louder.

"No, we're not," snapped Bingo, annoyed that his friends were laughing at Old Mrs Dingle's funny-looking dog. "You know as well as I do that this is Baxter."

"Of course we do," replied Bertie, with a smirk on his face. "You can't blame us for laughing though because he really does look like a sheep. Anyhow, do you want to hang out with us and try to catch a few fish? We haven't had any luck yet, but you never know. I've also got a big flask of my mum's hot chocolate, and you are both welcome to have some."

"No thanks," responded Bingo, which was not at all like him to turn down a mug of Mrs Bovington's hot chocolate that he insisted was almost as good as his beloved Aunty J's. "We're too busy hunting for the vampire that attacked the Reverend Pinkerton and Roly Poly."

"Dragonsbutts!" exclaimed Bertie, the smirk on his face now gone. "My dad told me all about Barry Beasley's article in the Dragonbutt Smoker. So do you really think there's a vampire in Dragonbutt?"

"Can we help you hunt for the vampire?" interrupted Flitcher, his green eyes all ablaze. "My mum said that Dragonbutt police don't think we have a vampire, but she reckons we do and believes that everything

Barry Beasley reported in the Dragonbutt Smoker is true."

Before Bingo could usher even a single word in reply, Trumper stepped forward and answered, "That's alright, Flitcher, Bingo and I have everything under control."

Even though Trumper had nothing against Flitcher Jenkins and Bertie Bovington, he did consider them just kids, being that they were two years younger than himself, and besides, Sherlock Holmes managed to solve all of his mysteries with only Watson tagging along and so he was confident the two of them would do just fine on their own.

"Come on, Bingo, we still have work to do, so let's not waste any more time," yelled Trumper, who was already waving goodbye and hastily walking towards the narrow path that led to Pigswill Alley.

"Alright, Trumper. I'll see you later, Bertie, and you too, Flitcher," shouted Bingo, as he ran with Baxter to catch up with Trumper, who was a good twenty yards ahead of him by this time.

At the end of the narrow path, the boys turned left onto Pigswill Alley and walked speedily towards Dragonbutt Vicarage. Although not before Bingo had unclipped the lead from around Baxter's neck so that he could freely run ahead of them. By the time Trumper and Bingo had reached the vicarage, they had already caught up with the funny-looking dog, who, to the amusement of the two boys, had been generously watering one of the old willow trees. Without delay, the three of them walked up to the large solid oak door that in bygone times had served as a tradesmen's entrance and then Trumper leaned forward to ring the doorbell, while Bingo fastened the lead to Baxter's collar once again.

It was no more than a couple of minutes before Trumper and Bingo saw the Reverend Pinkerton's beady eyes peering at them through the small glass window that bordered the oak door. "Just give me a minute, boys," he croaked, and then slid its two heavy bolts to one side before unlocking the door with a rather large and very old brass key. "You can't be too careful during these troubled times when even a man of the cloth is not safe walking home, but enough of that, Merry Christmas to the both of you. It's too cold to stand around chatting in the doorway, so please come in and bring Baxter with you. I was just about to make some hot chocolate. Would you boys like some?"

"Yes please, Reverend Pinkerton," acknowledged Trumper and Bingo, who were both happy to accept a steaming mug of the Reverend's hot chocolate and if luck was on their side, a mince pie or two as well.

"Just take off your muddy boots and leave them by the door," requested the Reverend, while staring at Trumper and Bingo's wellingtons that were now thoroughly caked in mud from their walk along Pigswill Alley. "And there is a towel by the door you can use to clean Baxter." As the funny-looking dog had just as much mud covering his paws as the boys had on their boots.

Humphrey Pinkerton, or 'Humpy' as he was known to his family and close friends, had been the vicar of Dragonbutt for almost ten years, ever since Alastair Crankle, the previous vicar, had moved to the big city to become the Bishop of Chelmsford. He was a small man, softly spoken and always impeccably dressed, that unfailingly greeted everyone with a welcoming smile. Now in his early fifties, his fine head of dark wavy hair had long since waved him goodbye, and he had a little potbelly that only recently had begun to show. The Reverend was Dragonbutt born to a well-known family in the district whose ancestral home was in Fangorn, a small hamlet located around five miles from Dragonbutt. His family had resided at Fangorn Abbey since before the dark days, and it was even chronicled in the Entwhistle journals as being the haunt of a particularly unpleasant and rather unusual kind of monster.

After the pleasantries were over and now that Baxter's paws were passably clean, the Reverend led the boys and the funny-looking dog into the vicarage's perpetually cluttered study, the place where he often spent many a long hour writing his popular but notoriously lengthy sermons. Thankfully, it was comfortably warm due to the fire that his housekeeper had lit in the elegant Victorian fireplace on the far side of the room. The study was a fascinating sight to behold with row after row of books of all shapes and sizes that were haphazardly squeezed onto overcrowded shelves, which meant the study contained more books than the Reverend Pinkerton had ever bothered to count. Notably, these books had been collected by not just the present vicar, but all of his predecessors dating back to the founding of Dragonbutt Village Church.

"Please take your coats and woolly hats off, and I will be back with your hot chocolate in a jiffy," called the Reverend Pinkerton, as he walked towards the vicarage's expansive but somewhat old-fashioned kitchen. It was not long before he returned with a long rectangular tray containing three mugs of hot chocolate, a plate of warm mince pies that had a fresh coating of icing sugar sprinkled on top and a large bowl of water for Baxter. "Help yourself to the mince pies, boys, they're from Fanshaw's and were only baked yesterday."

Neither Trumper nor Bingo could ever resist a delicious mince pie, so without hesitating for even a split second, they both greedily dived right in. While store-bought hot chocolate and mince pies could never better the homemade kind that Aunty J made so well, it did not stop the boys from draining their mugs and eating their way through half a dozen of their favourite Christmas treat. Also, Baxter had not been left out, because along with the bowl of water, the Reverend had given him a mince pie of his own, which the funny-looking dog wolfed down so rapidly even Bingo could not help himself but look impressed.

"So boys, how are your aunty and uncle keeping these days?" inquired the Reverend Pinkerton, while beaming at Trumper and Bingo as he finished eating his second mince pie. "I haven't seen them in our little church for some time now, as a matter of fact, not since I performed their marriage ceremony some nine years ago."

"They're doing fine, Reverend Pinkerton, but lately they have both been really busy with the Christmas preparations," replied Trumper, who, although he could detect a disapproving tone in the voice of the smiling Reverend, he shrewdly chose to ignore it and instead gave Bingo a sly wink.

"Really, this morning I heard from my rector, Philipa Dibble, your uncle had quite the evening last night at the Dragonbutt Arms with Barry Beasley and Angus Hogswood," he continued, somewhat sarcastically. "Anyway, what brings you to Dragonbutt Vicarage? I only seem to get visits like this if someone has passed away or intends to get married and I don't think either of you is quite old enough to get married just yet."

The Reverend then chuckled to himself, and Trumper forced somewhat of a smile, while Bingo just looked alarmed at the mention of marriage.

"Never mind, boys, I was just pulling your leg. How can I help you?" asked the Reverend Pinkerton, who had clumsily spilt some of the hot chocolate over his new but thankfully black coloured trousers and was now blotting the chocolate stain with a clean white handkerchief that he conveniently kept in his pocket.

While keeping one eye on the clock in the study, Trumper explained how he and Bingo had read in the Dragonbutt Smoker that the Reverend and Mr Poly had both been attacked, albeit on separate occasions, by an unidentified assailant on Pigswill Alley. He went on to say that after meeting with Barry Beasley and Uncle P at their home the previous day, they had come to the irrefutable conclusion that a vampire was responsible for the dastardly attacks.

"Dragonsbutts! I have read Barry Beasley's articles, but do you really think we have a vampire on the loose in the village?" uttered the

Reverend Pinkerton, looking quite shocked by this time. "Although I am all too aware of our dark past that is steeped in legends, as an ordained minister for over twenty years, I'm not supposed to believe in the existence of any type of monster, and that includes vampires. Don't you think these attacks could be explained by somewhat of a less theatrical narrative?"

"According to the Entwhistle journals, we used to have all sorts of monsters and even some vampires living in the village, and don't forget about the Dragonbutt prophecy that tells us they will return one day," insisted Trumper, gazing straight into the eyes of the worried-looking Reverend.

"Trumper, I know all about the Entwhistle journals and the Dragonbutt prophecy," cautioned the Reverend Pinkerton, who was now looking a little pale. "My own dear family at Fangorn Abbey had a terrible monster that we Pinkertons rarely talk about. However, that was during the dark days, and it was eventually dispatched by one of your uncle's ancestors. If we truly have a vampire in the village, then that would mean the Dragonbutt prophecy has come true."

"Exactly," declared Trumper, while slowly nodding his head.

"And don't forget about the bite mark on your butt," added Bingo, rather enthusiastically.

"Bingo, if you mean the wound on my backside and the loss of blood, then I agree, that is a little strange," answered the Reverend, who shuddered as he thought about the night of his terrifying ordeal.

"Reverend Pinkerton, is there anything else you can recall about the attack that was not reported in the Dragonbutt Smoker?" probed Trumper, hoping the Reverend would be able to reveal something that not even Barry Beasley had discovered.

"I really can't remember too much about that night as it all happened rather fast. And don't forget I was unconscious after my head hit the ground," sighed the Reverend, who would have preferred to forget what befell him on that dreadful evening. "All I can recollect is walking along Pigswill Alley, and then I heard a small branch or twig snap, and that's when I could hear them running towards me. It was at that point I turned and saw a pair of glowing red eyes and then I ran. Regretfully, I didn't get very far before I felt a sharp pain in my backside and was forcibly pushed to the ground. The next thing I remember was Wenna Loopey trying to kiss me, though I hope that was just a bad dream. Then I woke up in a bed at Dragonbutt Community Hospital with Detective Huntress bombarding me with a whole bunch of asinine questions."

"You referred to 'them'," queried Trumper, thinking the Reverend had simply misspoken. "Surely you don't mean there was more than one attacker?"

"When I spoke with Barry Beasley, I simply told him I heard someone running towards me and then I saw those awful glowing red eyes that I can't seem to get out of my head. Therefore, he just assumed it was one attacker. The more I recall about that evening though, I do believe I heard two pairs of feet before I was knocked unconscious. So I guess there must have been two attackers," explained the Reverend Pinkerton, with a distant but fearful look in his eyes.

"But if you heard two pairs of feet then you must have also seen two pairs of glowing red eyes that night," remarked Trumper, thinking they could be onto something here.

"No, I'm quite sure about that," insisted the Reverend, speaking calmly but firmly. "I heard two pairs of feet but only saw one pair of glowing red eyes."

"Interesting," thought Trumper, without saying a word to the others. "Two pairs of feet but only one pair of glowing red eyes!"

"I'm getting confused," announced Bingo, who was looking a little restless by this time. "Do we have one vampire in Dragonbutt or two?"

Trumper smiled at Bingo because he knew they had uncovered

something about the attacks that neither Dragonbutt police nor Barry Beasley and their uncle was aware of. It was therefore imperative that the two boys visit the second victim, Roly Poly, and soon. To determine whether there was only one, or, as the Reverend Pinkerton had surmised, two bloodsucking vampires on the loose in Dragonbutt. That would have to wait though, as it was now getting close to midday and Trumper could clearly hear Bingo's tummy starting to rumble, which could mean only one thing, it was getting close to lunchtime.

"Thank you, Reverend Pinkerton, you've been a great help," announced Trumper, as he stood up and stepped away from the ornately upholstered chair he had been sitting on. "It's time for Bingo and me to return home for our lunch. Although before we go, would you mind if we help ourselves to a little holy water from the font in the church?"

"Yes, but what on earth for?" implored the Reverend, knowing that this was a rather strange request from a young boy.

"Holy water burns vampires, of course!" blurted out Bingo, as if the Reverend Pinkerton had just asked Trumper a ludicrous question.

"Well, I suppose you can't come to any harm playing with a little holy water. I will walk over to the church to get some. How much would you like?" asked the Reverend, who was slowly making his way to the study door.

"About a gallon should do," replied Bingo, while winking at Trumper.

With a bemused look on his face, the Reverend Pinkerton left the study and walked the short distance to Dragonbutt Village Church. Within a matter of minutes, he returned to the vicarage carrying an undeniably large yet sturdy plastic container. And to the boys' jubilation, it was filled to the brim with holy water.

"This should be enough holy water for at least half a dozen vampires," laughed the Reverend, as he handed the container to Bingo. "I managed to find an empty gallon container that previously held Bucktooth Tom Blewitt's fire wine, his homemade concoction that I use for communion. It's a little more potent than I would prefer for my parishioners, most of whom are quite elderly, so I always water it down to avoid the congregation falling asleep during the sermon."

Still laughing at his little joke, the Reverend led the boys and the funny-looking dog out of the study and along the hallway to where they had left their muddy wellingtons. Once they had pulled on their boots and retrieved their warm woollen gloves, they walked out of the vicarage and shouted, "Thank you again for everything, Reverend Pinkerton, and Merry Christmas."

"Come on, Baxter, it's time to walk home. I'm sure Old Mrs Dingle has missed you, and it's nearly lunchtime for all of us," pointed out Trumper, while he and Bingo waved at the Reverend one more time before entering Pigswill Alley. For a change, Trumper held Baxter by his lead so that Bingo could carry the large and rather heavy plastic container holding the precious holy water, which was not a problem for the young boy because he always liked to show off just how strong he was.

"I hope Aunty J is cooking sausages again," exclaimed Bingo, as the two boys and the funny-looking dog reached Dragonbutt pond. "My tummy is rumbling so much that I could eat at least a dozen of them, and then some."

"There's only one way to know for sure," yelled Trumper, who was already several yards ahead of Bingo. "Let's run all the way home and find out."

It was Trumper who arrived home first, and so he was the one to open the wooden gate before running with Baxter up the long garden path. After leaving the holy water by the white door of the red-brick shed, Bingo followed and by the time Trumper and the funny-looking dog had reached the little old house, he had all but caught up with them. Aunty J and Uncle P at this time were waiting in the kitchen with Old Mrs Dingle sitting beside them. She was already wearing her rather old and decidedly unfashionable coat, one of her colourful silk headscarves and a pair of woollen gloves, the colour of which could only be described as a particularly brazen looking hot pink.

"What's for lunch?" demanded Bingo, as he opened the back door and yelled at the top of his voice to get his aunty's attention.

"All three of the adults promptly walked out of the kitchen, and Aunty J announced, "Your uncle is treating the four of us to lunch at the Dragonbutt Arms."

"Yes, a little hair of the dog and a bite to eat is just what the doctor ordered," chimed in Uncle P, with a broad smile creeping across his somewhat haggard looking face.

"I may not be a doctor, but I can assure you there will be no Dragonstone Fire served this lunchtime. Braithwaite's is all you will be drinking, and that's final!" barked Aunty J, who was still a little annoyed that her husband had woken them all so late at night.

"Of course, dear," winced Uncle P, with one of those expressions on his face that made him look like a mischievous little schoolboy, the kind that had just been caught doing something rather naughty.

"Trumper, why don't you hand Baxter's lead to Old Mrs Dingle," beckoned Aunty J, as she was acutely aware of the time and knew they should leave for the Dragonbutt Arms right away. "Your uncle and I will be working until Christmas Eve. So Old Mrs Dingle has kindly offered to look after you and Bingo for the next couple of days, which means that the two of you will be seeing a lot more of Baxter."

"That's great, so we'll see you tomorrow, Old Mrs Dingle, and you too, Baxter," remarked the boys, while Trumper placed the funny-looking dog's lead into the old lady's outstretched hand.

"Hurry up, Trumper, I'm hungry," screeched an impatient Bingo, who was now running down the long garden path towards the muddy footpath at the back of the little old house. "I'll race you to the Dragonbutt Arms."

Seven

Entwhistles, Dooleys and Monsters

T he Dragonbutt Arms dated all the way back to the founding of Dragonbutt, although over the centuries it had been renovated, expanded and even modernised on several occasions. Even with all the changes, the Dragonbutt Arms would have still been recognisable to the residents of Dragonbutt who lived centuries ago, with its whitewashed stone walls and thatched straw roof, features that were still common to many of the buildings in the village and those of the surrounding district, even to this very day.

Standing outside this venerable Dragonbutt institution, in pride of place and hanging from a tall wooden pole, was the old Dragonbutt Arms sign. Although it had been replaced a multitude of times, the design had always remained the same. Two dragons, one large and the other small, who had been shot with what looked like an oversized crossbow bolt and were falling from the sky, before eventually crashing to the ground to form two deep hollows that in time would become the villages of Greater and Lesser Dragonbutt.

For the residents of Dragonbutt that were a little tall, the Dragonbutt Arms could be a tricky place to enter. With its low wooden beamed ceilings and undersized doorways, one had to always remember to heed the well-posted signs that stated 'MIND YOUR HEAD!'. And in particular, for those that were taller than a notable six-foot and wished to avoid a bump on the head when approaching the old bar, it was always wise to be mindful and pay close attention to the large sign that Boosey Dooley was so fond of, which simply said 'DUCK!'.

Once inside the Dragonbutt Arms, its age could clearly be seen. It had an expansive floor that was covered in large granite flagstones, many of which had become worn over the years and some had been repaired but never replaced. And its exposed stone walls always looked a homely touch along with a huge open fireplace with a big roaring log fire throughout the cold winter months.

Most of its patrons would have agreed that the Dragonbutt Arms was a sizeable establishment, with its long bar, comfortable brown leather sofas and extensive dining area filled with tables and chairs that could, at a pinch, seat fifty. Next to the bar were two doors. One that led to the backroom, which was typically only used by Boosey Dooley and a few select guests during what he liked to call his 'special occasions' and the other was to the kitchen, where his long-suffering wife, Flanna Dooley, laboured tirelessly to prepare a myriad of delicious culinary delights.

Sunday lunch had always been a busy time for Boosey Dooley because it was the only day of the week that his wife cooked her popular roasts. Beef, chicken, lamb or pork were all exceptionally succulent and always came with one of her famous Yorkshire puddings, which were so large they covered the whole plate and so all the meat and vegetables had to be placed inside. Every resident of Dragonbutt knew that Flanna Dooley cooked the best roasts in the village and it was for that reason the Dragonbutt Arms was always full every Sunday, from the time its doors were opened at eleven in the morning until the end of the lunch service at four in the afternoon.

By the time Aunty J and Uncle P arrived at the Dragonbutt Arms, Trumper and Bingo had been waiting a good ten minutes, which to the hungry boys seemed like an eternity. Loitering outside, yet close to the front door, the boys knew they were still too young to enter without an adult present and so unfortunately for Trumper, he had no other choice but to spend those long minutes listening to Bingo complaining and the loud rumblings of the younger boy's tummy.

Not wishing to prolong the boys suffering any longer, Aunty J ushered everyone towards the Dragonbutt Arm's front door that had been painted more times than any member of the Dooley family could remember and for some long-forgotten reason, always the colour green. It was nearly twelve-thirty and as to be expected the Dragonbutt Arms was almost full, although thankfully that was not a problem because earlier in the day, Uncle P had prudently called Boosey Dooley to reserve a table for four.

"Welcome, Perygrin, and Merry Christmas, Jemyma, and you too, Trumper and Bingo," boomed the thunderous voice of Boosey Dooley, as the four of them walked into the warm and welcoming Dragonbutt Arms. "I have a table near the bar for you that's not too close to the fireplace."

The landlord of the Dragonbutt Arms was a small man who was well-known for his rather loud and unmistakably deafening voice that somehow fit his unequivocally boastful nature and habit of telling tall stories. He had blue eyes and sandy coloured wavy hair and his robust frame, which was always plain to see, could easily support his ever-expanding waistline. As for his age, that had never been a secret, as those who had attended Boosey's last raucous birthday party knew all too well, he was now just one year shy of fifty.

"Merry Christmas to you too, Boosey," replied Aunty J, who had already taken off her gloves, tucked them into one of the pockets of her cream coloured winter coat and carefully placed it over the back of her chair. Uncle P did the same with his black coat and the boys followed with theirs, although not before placing their woollen gloves and DPS woolly hats beside them on the table.

After another round of Merry Christmas and a polite chorus of praise for the colourful yet pitifully small Christmas tree that stood close to the bar, Boosey Dooley handed everyone a copy of the Dragonbutt Arms Sunday lunch menu, to the gratification of everyone sitting at the table.

"What's it to be, Perygrin, a pint of Dragonstone Fire or would you prefer Butts Batch?" cackled Boosey Dooley, knowing that Uncle P was probably quite the worse for wear after his rather unrestrained evening with Barry Beasley and Angus Hogswood.

"Thank you, Boosey, he'll have a bottle of Braithwaite's," interrupted Aunty J, sounding terribly stern. "And if you don't mind, the boys and I will have the same."

"Coming right up," acknowledged the landlord, who had taken four bottles of Braithwaite's out of the fridge behind the bar and was placing them, along with two tall glasses for the adults and a couple of long bendy straws for the boys, onto the table. "Now, what would you all like to eat today?"

"Beef for me, please Boosey," declared Aunty J, who had known what she wanted to eat even before opening the menu.

"I think the lamb with some of your delightful mint sauce would go down a treat," announced Uncle P, who was looking rather famished after missing out on his breakfast. "And boys, how about the same for you? The locally reared lamb at the Dragonbutt Arms is always quite exquisite."

Both Trumper and Bingo looked at each other and shook their heads from side to side. "No way, Uncle P, every time we see lamb, we just can't help thinking of Baxter," objected Trumper, and Bingo nodded his head in agreement. "I don't think either of us could ever eat lamb again."

Everyone laughed including Boosey Dooley and then Bingo bellowed, "I'll have the pork with one of Baverstock's big juicy chicken sausages."

"And I'll have the same," nodded Trumper, believing that Bingo had made an excellent choice for Sunday lunch.

"Boys, how is your special project coming along?" inquired Uncle P, while slowly sipping his Braithwaite's and discreetly winking at Trumper and Bingo, hoping that Aunty J would not notice.

"We've already found some useful information about vampires in the Entwhistle journals, although there was no mention of vampires that bite their victims' butts," shrugged Trumper, thinking his aunty could hardly object to them hunting for a vampire that she believed did not exist. "We also met with the Reverend Pinkerton this morning at Dragonbutt Vicarage and he is certain that just before he was attacked, he heard two pairs of feet running towards him."

"Dragonsbutts! Do you mean to say that we now have two vampires in Dragonbutt?" asked an astonished looking Uncle P.

"Perhaps. However, what I don't understand is that although the Reverend Pinkerton heard two pairs of feet, he only saw one pair of glowing red eyes. And not only that, Barry told us the DNA from the saliva found on both of the victims came from the same assailant," recalled Trumper, making direct eye contact with his uncle. "That's why Bingo and I will need to meet with Mr Poly, to find out what he can remember about the night he was attacked."

"Boys, I know that most of the residents of Dragonbutt would not agree with me. Nonetheless, I don't like all this talk of vampires and simply find it hard to believe they are anything but pure fantasy. So I am sure there must be a more rational explanation to these attacks," cautioned Aunty J, looking downright unamused.

Uncle P looked at Aunty J and told her, in a rather sympathetic tone of voice, that it was difficult for those who were not Dragonbutt born to believe in the Dragonbutt prophecy and the old legends, though undeniably, they were all true. In the end, to avoid a scene, their aunty agreed that she would simply disagree with her husband until the day came around when a real live vampire knocked on the front door of their little old house.

"Aunty J, can we have some garlic?" requested Bingo, almost casually, as if he was asking for an ice cream or something like that.

"And why do you need garlic?" queried Aunty J, guessing his request had something to do with vampires.

"Vampires hate the smell of garlic, so it can protect us from being bitten," asserted Bingo, who by now was so hungry, if his aunty had given him a garlic bulb at that very moment, right there and then he probably would have eaten it raw.

"The Reverend Pinkerton has already supplied us with holy water and all we need now is lots of garlic and some wooden stakes," added Trumper, hoping that the mention of wooden stakes would not scare his somewhat squeamish aunty.

"Oh my," shuddered Aunty J, at the mention of wooden stakes. "I suppose you can't do any harm with holy water and garlic, however, I'm not sure you should be roaming around Dragonbutt with wooden stakes. I can buy some garlic bulbs from Gribble's the Grocer's, as Emblyn Gribble always opens her shop every Sunday afternoon."

"And I can make some wooden stakes for you this afternoon. There is a long wooden rod stored in the garage that I can saw into smaller pieces, which should work admirably. Don't worry, dear, I'll make sure the wooden stakes are blunt at both ends," promised Uncle P, while turning towards Trumper and Bingo to give them a discreet wink.

"Perfect," acknowledged the boys, each of them now displaying a big

71

broad smile.

"Ah, lunch at last," announced Aunty J, as Boosey Dooley placed their roasts onto the table. "Now, enjoy your lunch and let's have no more talk about vampires until everyone has finished eating."

On each large round plate sat one of Flanna Dooley's giant Yorkshire puddings, and inside every pudding was the roast meat, along with an enormous chicken sausage for Trumper and Bingo, just as they had requested. What came next was the roast potatoes cooked in plenty of lard from the Hogswood piggery, followed by a hefty portion of gourmet Red Dragon cauliflower cheese and a selection of seasonal vegetables. Naturally, everything had then been smothered in a generous quantity of Flanna's acclaimed Butts Batch infused onion gravy.

For once, it was not Bingo that finished first, but Trumper, who proceeded to slap his tummy to show that he had been more than satisfied with the outstanding meal. Bingo was next, although only because he had saved the best for last and so all that remained on his plate was the chicken sausage, which he finally polished off with three enormous and rather gluttonous bites.

"Anyone for dessert?" asked Aunty J, a question she already knew the answer to because no Sunday lunch at the Dragonbutt Arms was ever complete without eating a prodigious helping of Flanna Dooley's sticky toffee pudding, made with a little Butts Batch and a lot of love, as Flanna always liked to say.

"Me! Me! Me!" uttered Bingo, with the last piece of his chicken sausage still in his mouth and waving one arm in the air.

"Me too," seconded Trumper, as he was never one to say no to a bowl of sticky toffee pudding.

"And me," confirmed Uncle P, who, by the size of his ample tummy, looked as if he had already eaten one too many of Flanna Dooley's rich desserts.

"We'll have four helpings of sticky toffee pudding, please Boosey," ordered Aunty J, as the landlord cleared away their dishes, not in the least surprised they had requested his personal favourite, Flanna's heavenly sticky toffee pudding. "And while you are in the kitchen, please give our compliments to the chef."

"Flanna will be pleased that you enjoyed your lunch," nodded Boosey Dooley, as he disappeared into the kitchen.

Flanna Dooley was rarely seen by the customers of the Dragonbutt Arms, preferring instead to spend her days doing what she liked best, which was to cook her delicious roasts, pies and desserts. She was not only the backbone of the Dragonbutt Arms and responsible for much of its success, but in reality, Flanna was the one who really ran the business. As she was always cooped up in the kitchen, her husband could usually be seen behind the bar, often with a pint of Dragonstone Fire in his well-used drinking hand. However, once Boosey heard the familiar cry, 'Tad', he would always come running to his beloved wife.

While the four of them were waiting for their dessert, the mountainous figure of Angus Hogswood strolled into the Dragonbutt Arms and immediately propped himself up against the bar. Standing in his favourite well-trodden corner, just beside Uncle P, he was already thirty-four with pale blue eyes, a fine head of thick black hair and a big bushy beard.

"Good afternoon, Angus," greeted Uncle P, who was smiling at the big man with his arm outstretched to shake his hand. "Here for Sunday lunch as well?"

"Just a liquid lunch for me, Perygrin. Merry Christmas, Jemyma, and you too, Trumper and Bingo," he bellowed, with a boisterous laugh and then turned to see Boosey Dooley returning from the kitchen. "A pint of your finest ale, please landlord."

"Certainly, Angus, one pint of Dragonstone Fire coming right up," answered Boosey Dooley, grinning from ear to ear. "I haven't seen you in the Dragonbutt Arms for some time. Not since you left here around midnight, last night!" Uncle P proceeded to laugh at this, followed by the landlord and finally Angus, who, naturally, had the loudest laugh of them all.

"Sausages and bacon are very popular at this time of year, so I've been busy working up at the piggery since early this morning," roared Angus, as he slammed the palms of his giant-size hands down onto the bar. "I have to say that these vampire attacks have begun to worry me because you never know who will be next. If Dragonbutt police don't find this vampire soon, then it just might drive me to drink." This time it was Boosey Dooley who laughed nearly as loud as Angus and Uncle P felt obliged to join in too.

"Yes, it was a terrible thing that happened to the Reverend and I was standing right here at this very bar chatting to Shadwick Poly last Thursday night, only minutes before he was attacked walking back home along Pigswill Alley," sighed Boosey Dooley, while pulling a pint of Dragonstone Fire for Angus. "Luckily for everyone, there is still a Dooley in Dragonbutt to hunt down this vampire and dispatch the bloodsucker, just like in the dark days."

"Dragonsbutts! A Dooley!" exclaimed Uncle P, his face turning an unflattering shade of red. "I believe you mean an Entwhistle. It was the Entwhistles and not the Dooleys that dispatched all the monsters during the dark days and I have the journals to prove it."

"Here we go again," laughed Angus, impatiently waiting for his pint of Dragonstone Fire. "They were arguing about this for two whole hours last night, right up until closing time."

"Were they now," interjected Aunty J, rolling her eyes and yawning because she had heard the same argument between the Dooleys and the Entwhistles many times before.

"While the Entwhistles were writing their journals, it was us Dooleys that were out dispatching all the monsters," barked Boosey Dooley, as he finally handed Angus his pint of Dragonstone Fire. "It was only the other week when I reminded the Reverend Pinkerton about the time a Dooley saved the Pinkertons over at Fangorn Abbey. As everyone in Dragonbutt knows, my ancestor was the one who heroically dispatched the beast that had been terrorising them for years."

"That was an Entwhistle who dispatched the beast of Fangorn Abbey, not a Dooley," snapped Uncle P, who felt obligated to defend his family legacy.

"Does it really matter who dispatched the monsters during the dark days," pleaded Angus, as he picked up his pint of Dragonstone Fire and emptied it almost at once, leaving a line of froth on his big bushy beard. "Another pint of Dragonstone Fire, please landlord."

"Angus, did you see or hear anything on the night that you found the Reverend Pinkerton on Pigswill Alley?" inquired Trumper, who thought it would be an opportune moment to change the subject from Entwhistles, Dooleys and monsters, to their present concern, the mysterious vampire that had been attacking the residents of Dragonbutt.

"Nothing out of the ordinary, Trumper," acknowledged Angus, while picking up his second pint of Dragonstone Fire that the landlord had placed beside him on the bar. "I don't remember hearing anything and only really saw the Reverend Pinkerton after I tripped over him. It wasn't until I had the Reverend inside Wenna Loopey's house that I saw he had been injured and that's when I called for an ambulance to take him to Dragonbutt Community Hospital."

"It was lucky the vampire didn't attack you, Angus," added Bingo, who was eagerly awaiting the arrival of his sticky toffee pudding.

"No need to worry about that, Bingo. We Hogswoods are made of strong stuff you know," beamed Angus, with a chuckle. "And besides, after eight pints of Dragonstone Fire all I needed to do was breathe over this vampire and he would have soon changed his mind about biting me."

Angus Hogswood always liked to joke like this, and, as usual, everyone roared with laughter. Just then, they all heard the ear-piercing voice of Flanna Dooley calling her husband's name and so Boosey Dooley hurriedly ran into the kitchen, only to quickly reappear carrying four large bowls of steaming hot sticky toffee pudding with a large dollop of fresh whipped Dragonbutt cream on the side.

"Yummy," declared Bingo, as he rubbed his bloated tummy. "I was beginning to think our dessert would never get here."

"Flanna's sticky toffee pudding is so popular today that she had to make a fresh batch and this one has just come out of the oven, so be careful, it will be hot!" smiled Boosey Dooley, who was already walking back to his regular haunt behind the bar.

Sticky toffee pudding was the absolute perfect dessert. It was not only sweet and sticky, as the name suggests, it was also yumingly chewy, as Bingo often liked to say. The chewiness came from the chopped dates that Flanna Dooley liked to soak overnight in plenty of Butts Batch, which always enhanced their flavour and helped make her sticky toffee pudding, unquestionably, the best in Dragonbutt.

As Bingo placed the last spoonful of his sticky toffee pudding into his gaping mouth, he slapped his tummy and exclaimed, "Finished." Although none of the others at the table slapped their tummy, they all agreed that Sunday lunch had been truly splendid and no one, except for Bingo, of course, could contemplate eating another bite, at least, not until dinnertime.

Knowing that it was time to go home, Aunty J paid the bill and Uncle P left a tip of two pounds, one pound for the waiter and one pound for the chef. 'Just enough to show appreciation, but not too much to make it look like you are showing off', as their uncle was fond of saying.

"Thank you for the excellent lunch and Merry Christmas once again,

Boosey, and you too, Angus," declared Aunty J, as she rose from the chair she had been sitting on to retrieve her coat before the four of them left the warmth of the Dragonbutt Arms for the cold wintry Sunday afternoon. Uncle P, on the other hand, was still a little annoyed at Boosey Dooley and so he simply nodded his head while pulling on his own coat and heading for the door.

"Have a good Sunday and a Merry Christmas," shouted Boosey Dooley, with a grin across his face as he walked to the kitchen with the four sticky toffee pudding dishes that had all been licked clean.

"Perygrin, you take the boys home while I pop over to Gribble's to buy some garlic bulbs and a few other groceries," announced Aunty J, who was about to cross to the other side of Dragonbutt High Street using the village's one and only yet well-used zebra crossing.

"Alright, dear, see you a little later," acknowledged Uncle P, as he and the two boys walked slowly down Dragonbutt High Street towards Counting House Lane.

"Uncle P, so are you really going to cut some wooden stakes for us this afternoon?" pleaded Bingo, somewhat enthusiastically.

"Certainly, but what will you boys be doing for the rest of the day?" inquired their uncle, while clapping his hands together in an earnest attempt to stay warm.

"I think it's time that Bingo and I visit Mr Poly at Dragonbutt Community Hospital," answered Trumper, as he turned to walk in the opposite direction.

"Oh, I forgot to tell you that Barry called this morning and said that Mr Poly has already been discharged and is now recuperating at home," recalled Uncle P, rather absentmindedly. "Give him my best wishes and make sure you arrive home before dark."

"That's even better," exclaimed Trumper, while turning towards Bingo and smiling. "Come on, Bingo, Roly Poly lives on Pucclechurch Crescent, and it's number seven if I'm not mistaken."

Eight

Roly Poly Remembers

❦

The boys knew that the quickest way to get to their teacher's home on Pucclechurch Crescent was to take the shortcut along Pigswill Alley, and so to ensure they were home before dark this was the route they decided to take. After saying goodbye to their uncle, who preferred to take the longer and far less muddy journey home, Trumper and Bingo cut through Bristletooth Lane and then strode past Dragonbutt Victory Hall before entering Pigswill Alley through the opening between the two old willow trees.

Walking briskly, it wasn't long before they arrived at Pucclechurch Crescent, which conveniently bordered Pigswill Alley. From there, it was easy for the boys to find the house they were looking for with the number seven painted onto its rather unsightly and tired looking olive green door.

It was Bingo who reached up to ring the doorbell; however, unlike the regular doorbells that simply make a boring ding–dong type of sound, this one played the first few verses of the William Tell Overture by Rossini, or so the boys had been told. Trumper and Bingo had never heard of Rossini and only knew of William Tell as a man from long ago who had shot an arrow into an apple that was sitting on top of a young boy's head. They did recognise the tune though, as the theme music to an old television show with a masked man on a horse who liked to yell 'Hi-Yo Silver!'.

As Bingo was humming the popular tune with a smile on his face, the door suddenly opened and to the boys surprise it was not Roly Poly looking down at them. Instead, standing on the other side of the door was Millie Bender, who, without hesitating, said, "Oh, hello Trumper and Bingo, I wasn't expecting to see you boys until the new school term. Is there anything I can do for the two of you?"

"Hello and Merry Christmas, Ms Bender," greeted Trumper, happy to see the teacher of his favourite class at school, which happened to be maths. Bingo, on the other hand, looked a little dismayed as he always detested maths and liked her class the least. "We heard about the attack on Mr Poly, so Bingo and I came over to wish him a speedy recovery."

"Well, Merry Christmas to both of you and come in out of the cold," insisted Ms Bender, while giving the boys a welcoming smile. "Mr Poly is in the living room. It's the first door on the left, but please take your muddy wellingtons off first so that you don't dirty his carpet."

Millie Bender was rather pretty for a maths teacher and claimed to be around five-foot-six whenever she wore high heels. She was already thirty-nine and by all accounts had never been married. Her bright auburn hair, that many said was far too long for someone in her profession, was the colour of autumn, and her matching eyes, which had been described by some as overly pleasing, were often obscured by a pair of dark-framed glasses that she was rarely seen without.

Trumper and Bingo, followed by Millie Bender, walked from the small porch at the front of the house into the hallway and then opened the first door they saw on their left. Sitting on what looked like a very comfortable armchair and wrapped in a blanket was Roly Poly, who, apart from seeming a little pale, appeared to look very much like his usual animated self.

Shadwick Poly, the perpetual bachelor, as he often liked to call himself, was now in his early forties, though he still clung to the youthful face of his younger years. He had blue eyes and straight blonde hair, which he invariably liked to part, although, alas, his parting had grown more pronounced as the years passed away. Standing a mere five-foot-eight, he was known to the boys and girls at Dragonbutt Primary School as the always cheerful, Roly Poly, on account of his last name and his substantial and ever-expanding girth.

Sitting directly across from Roly Poly on a matching armchair, was the ever so serious-looking, Austin Catliter, who, along with Millie Bender, had been a teacher at Dragonbutt Primary School for the past five years. As all three teachers were around the same age and none of them had been fortunate enough to be Dragonbutt born, they had quickly become close friends in the village they now called home. While Ms Bender was the head of maths, Mr Catliter taught English and sometimes sports. Most people suspected the two of them were romantically involved, however, unbeknown to almost everyone, it was Roly Poly that Millie Bender actually had her heart set on.

The living room the boys had just entered, with its patternless blue carpeted floor and old cast iron fireplace containing the dying embers of what presumedly had been a roaring fire, would be considered minimalist at best. Apart from a sofa, two armchairs, a coffee table and a large bookcase containing dozens of rather dusty and worn-looking science books, the room was all but bare. The only personal touches that Trumper and Bingo could see were what appeared to be a silver-framed photo of a relatively young Roly Poly and an ageing Christmas tree with several broken fairy lights, which by the look of it had long since seen better days.

"What a pleasant surprise," uttered Roly Poly, as he offered the boys his hand. "I wasn't expecting to see you, Trumper, until the New Year, and I see that you have brought Bingo as well. You've gained quite a reputation at Dragonbutt Primary School, young man, and I understand you are only in year two. Except for detention, we really haven't met yet, although that will all change in year three when you'll be taking my science class. Please take your outdoor clothing off and throw everything over the back of the sofa because it's far too warm in here for woolly hats and winter coats."

"Certainly, Mr Poly, and Merry Christmas," smiled Trumper and Bingo, who then sat down on the sofa next to Millie Bender.

"And you too, Mr Cat Litter. Oh, I mean Catliter," corrected Bingo, almost at once and with a smirk on his face as the mistake he had made was by no means an accident.

Austin Catliter's face reddened a little at Bingo's insult and then, with a disapproving glare, he glanced at his young student before replying, "Yes, Merry Christmas, Bingo, and you too, Trumper. Anyway, I have to be on my way now. Millie, will you be coming as well?"

"Not just yet, Austin, I'll stay with Shadwick a little longer to ensure he has something nice and hot to eat for his dinner tonight," replied Ms Bender, with a hint of a blush and a half-formed smile.

Teaching English, sports and chasing after Millie Bender were all that Austin Catliter was really interested in. Like Roly Poly, he was in his early forties; however, that was where their similarity ended. Twice divorced with no children of his own, he had grey-blue eyes and stood a quite respectable five-foot-eleven with a well-earned muscular physique and a completely bald head that he liked to shave at least twice a week. And unlike his fellow teacher and friend, who was habitually jolly and rarely could be seen without a smile, he was often considered too serious and rather slow to pick up on a joke.

Trumper and Bingo were undeniably a familiar sight to Austin Catliter, who took both of the boys for English and occasionally sports, during those times when the head of sports, Puffer Hendrick, as he was customarily known because of his fondness for vaping, was unavailable. While Trumper was the model student, being that he was always attentive and consistently received straight A's, Bingo was somewhat of a troublemaker in his class with a reputation for being a little cheeky. Because of this, instead of receiving a B plus, which the young boy always believed he deserved, he often had to make do with a disappointing, and, in his opinion, rather unfair B minus.

Once the English teacher had said his goodbyes and left Roly Poly's house to return to his home, which was conveniently located only two streets away, Ms Bender smiled and asked, "How about a nice mug of hot chocolate for everyone?"

"I'll have one," screeched Bingo, rather loudly and drowning out poor Trumper, who, instead, had to nod his head.

"Oh, yes please, that would be lovely and I think there are some mince pies in the cupboard beside the fridge," declared Roly Poly, because, just like Trumper and Bingo, he was rather fond of mince pies and most other kinds of Christmas treats.

"Perfect, I'll warm up a plate of mince pies as well," exclaimed Ms Bender, as she stood up and walked towards the kitchen.

While everyone waited patiently, all except Bingo that is, because he was eagerly awaiting the arrival of the hot chocolate and warm mince pies, Trumper looked over at Roly Poly and asked, "Mr Poly, Bingo and I are working on a project, and if you are feeling up to it, we would like to ask you a few questions?"

"Of course, boys," responded Roly Poly, looking quite intrigued. "But what sort of project is it that you have to take time out of your Christmas holiday?"

"The vampire sort," blurted out Bingo, before Trumper could even say a word. "We're hunting for the vampire that bit you on Pigswill Alley."

"Dragonsbutts! A vampire," exclaimed Roly Poly, looking somewhat alarmed.

"That's right, Mr Poly, we're investigating the attacks on the Reverend Pinkerton and yourself. After talking with Barry Beasley, we believe that at least one vampire is responsible," explained Trumper, looking very serious now that they were on the subject of vampires. "We have already spoken to the Reverend and so Bingo and I would just like to ask you some questions to confirm or deny what we have already uncovered."

"Oh my!" gasped Roly Poly, while shaking his head. "It was only this morning that I read Barry Beasley's article in the Dragonbutt Smoker in which he claimed both the Reverend Pinkerton and I were bitten by a vampire, but I just put that down to journalistic exaggeration from a rather young and exuberant reporter. Of course, although I am familiar with the old Dragonbutt prophecy and those ancient myths regarding monsters, don't you think there is a less fanciful explanation to these attacks?"

"They are not myths, they're legends, and the Dragonbutt prophecy has come true!" shrieked Bingo, as he was none too pleased with Roly Poly. "You're not Dragonbutt born so you won't believe what is happening until it's too late and a vampire bites you on the butt again."

"Well, to tell you the truth I really don't know what attacked me. All I can remember are those horrible glowing red eyes," insisted Roly Poly, who had been quite taken aback by Bingo's forceful comments and was now taking his time to compose himself.

"That's exactly what the Reverend Pinkerton told us he saw, just before he was attacked, a pair of glowing red eyes staring at him in the darkness," stressed Trumper, eager for his science teacher to reveal more. "Can you remember anything else about your assailant?"

"Nothing at all, unfortunately, I dropped my torch and it was simply too dark on Pigswill Alley to see anything because even though there was nearly a full moon last Thursday evening, the canopy from the willow trees managed to block out most of the light," explained Roly Poly, racking his mind for anything else he might have seen on that fateful night.

"What about the glowing red eyes. Did you see only one pair, or maybe two?" probed Trumper, secretly thinking what questions Sherlock Holmes might have asked at a time like this.

"It was definitely just one pair, that I'm certain," trembled Roly Poly, as he thought about those terrifying glowing red eyes.

"And how many pairs of feet did you hear on Pigswill Alley that night?" inquired Trumper, cleverly switching Roly Poly's recollection of the attack from what the frightened teacher saw to what he heard, an artful move that even Sherlock Holmes would have approved.

Roly Poly paused while he thought back to the night of the attack; although this time he tried his best to recall what he had heard. "Now you mention it, I do remember hearing something as I was attempting to flee and it sounded like two pairs of feet running very close together, which means, if I am not mistaken, there must have been two attackers on Pigswill Alley."

"Interesting," proclaimed Trumper, though he was still rather puzzled as to why the Reverend Pinkerton and Roly Poly had both heard two pairs of feet but only saw one pair of glowing red eyes before they were attacked.

"Oh, I nearly forgot. There is one more thing that I can remember," shared Roly Poly, as he looked directly at the wide-eyed boys. "When I saw those glowing red eyes, I do believe they were quite close to the ground."

"You mean to say your assailant was short?" responded Trumper, unsure at that moment what this new piece of information could mean.

84

"Yes, very short," confirmed Roly Poly, while slowly nodding his head.

As Trumper and Bingo thought about what Roly Poly had just revealed, Millie Bender walked in with an old battered silver tray containing four mugs of steaming hot chocolate, a pile of serviettes and a large plate of warm mince pies, which to Bingo's trained eye looked as though they had been bought at Fanshaw's.

"It's been an hour and a half since we ate lunch and I'm hungry," declared Bingo, who was the first to pick up one of the mince pies and happily take a bite out of the delicious treat.

"That long!" laughed Ms Bender, as she sat down on the sofa between Trumper and Bingo. "You must have a very high metabolism, Bingo."

"Our aunty says that Bingo has a bottomless tummy," sniggered Trumper, while reaching for a mince pie himself.

"You can eat as many mince pies as you like, boys, and drink your hot chocolate, it's full of calcium and will help you grow up big and strong, just like Angus Hogswood," chuckled Roly Poly, as he helped himself to a mince pie. "And please take a serviette."

"I heard the three of you talking about the terrible attack on Mr Poly while I was in the kitchen and something about vampires. I assume the two are not connected?" commented Ms Bender, who was laughing, oblivious to the fact that Trumper and Bingo believed Roly Poly's attacker was actually a real live vampire, or maybe even two.

Before Bingo had a chance to give his maths teacher the same lecture concerning the existence of vampires and monsters in Dragonbutt that he had given to Roly Poly a little earlier, Trumper interjected, "We were just comparing the attack on Mr Poly with the identical one that took place the previous week in which the Reverend Pinkerton was the victim."

"Millie, Trumper has just helped me recall something about the night I was attacked, which leads us to believe there were two attackers.

What concerns me though is that they have already struck twice and may well do so again, but the question we need to ask ourselves, is when and where?" stressed Roly Poly, with a serious-looking expression on his face. "Unfortunately, I don't have a great deal of faith in Dragonbutt police as Detective Huntress doesn't seem to have a single lead in this case and is no closer to catching who is responsible than the night the Reverend Pinkerton was attacked."

"Both of the previous attacks took place late at night and in the same location, so that means Pigswill Alley is where Bingo and I will focus our investigation," pointed out Trumper, who had just finished his hot chocolate and was now enthusiastically biting into his second mince pie.

"But what if you bump into them, Trumper?" asked Roly Poly, not at all sure the boys should be looking for his attackers, though he was certain, whoever they turned out to be, bloodsucking vampires they definitely were not.

"Don't worry about that, Mr Poly," assured Bingo, as he took the last bite out of his third mince pie and grinned. "We've got some special equipment back at our house that will make mincemeat out of this sort of thing."

"Boys, I think you need to leave this to Dragonbutt police," chimed in Ms Bender, who had no idea that the 'sort of thing' Bingo was actually referring too, were none other than bloodthirsty vampires.

"I couldn't agree more," added Roly Poly, nodding his head as he reached for another mince pie. "I will contact Detective Huntress tomorrow morning and let her know that I heard two pairs of feet just before I was attacked on Thursday night, which may help with her investigation. Or so we can only hope."

"Well, thank you for your time and the lovely hot chocolate and mince pies, Mr Poly, and you too, Ms Bender. We need to be on our way home now," announced Trumper, who was looking at Bingo and shaking his head to deter him from eating a fourth mince pie. "I hope you have a Merry Christmas and a Happy New Year."

With a smile, Roly Poly returned their seasonal greetings and then Millie Bender escorted Trumper and Bingo to the front door. As soon as the boys had pulled on their wellingtons and were wearing their coats, DPS woolly hats and warm woollen gloves, they left the house yelling, "Merry Christmas and Happy New Year, Ms Bender." Once the two of them were outside, they quickly waved her a farewell goodbye and then hurriedly stomped to the end of Pucclechurch Crescent before making their way home by way of Pigswill Alley.

"Come on, Bingo, it's going to get dark soon and we both know what comes out at night in Dragonbutt," remarked Trumper, as he urged the younger boy along with the chilling thought of running into a couple of ferocious and undoubtedly blood-hungry vampires. "Let's run all the way home to Counting House Lane."

Nine

It's a Little Vampire

‑‑‑‑‑‑

"Hello, boys," greeted Aunty J, who was sitting at the kitchen table and reading the Dragonbutt Smoker when Trumper and Bingo noisily entered through the back door of the little old house. "I bought a large bag of garlic bulbs at Gribble's and after I joked to Emblyn that you needed the garlic to protect yourselves from Barry Beasley's imaginary vampire, she just shook her head and handed me a dozen complimentary garlic lollies before wishing the two of you good luck. It's funny because I never thought of Emblyn as the sort of person who would believe in the existence of vampires."

"Thanks, Aunty J, that's perfect and just what we needed," acknowledged Trumper, who, along with Bingo, had taken his muddy wellingtons off and deposited them on an old copy of the Dragonbutt Smoker, which had been placed in the hallway by Uncle P to avoid dirtying their new and only recently laid beige coloured carpet. "I'm not at all surprised about Emblyn Gribble though, she's Dragonbutt born, so she must believe in the old legends about monsters, and of course, the Dragonbutt prophecy."

While Trumper and Aunty J were talking, Bingo was busy rummaging in his aunty's shopping bag for the garlic she had brought back from Gribble's the Grocer's. Without difficulty, he found the garlic bulbs in a large brown paper bag, which must have numbered at least two dozen. Although he was pleased to see so many, it was the garlic lollies that the young boy was most interested in, as he was impatient to try one before his eagerly anticipated dinner.

"Ah, here they are," exclaimed Bingo, holding a small white paper bag full of garlic lollies.

"They're not for you to eat now, Bingo. Let's take them down to the red-brick shed along with the garlic bulbs," stressed Trumper, rather forcibly as he wanted to prevent Bingo from squandering one of their precious garlic lollies before they even had a sniff of a vampire.

"You can take these wooden stakes as well," called out Uncle P, who had just opened the back door and was standing outside with a shopping bag full of the homemade wooden stakes he had just cut. "I made a dozen and one more for good luck, so I hope that's enough."

Their uncle was chuckling to himself as he stepped into the little old house and handed the shopping bag to Bingo. He had cut his long wooden rod into thirteen pieces and each one of them was about twelve inches in length. Contrary to his promise to Aunty J though, during their Sunday lunch at the Dragonbutt Arms, he had carefully sharpened one end to create the perfect wooden stake. This, he was sure, would certainly strike fear into the cold heart of absolutely any type of vampire the boys could possibly encounter in Dragonbutt.

"Uncle P, can we borrow your mallet as well?" pleaded Bingo, still a little annoyed that Trumper would not let him have one of the garlic lollies.

"Of course, it's in my toolbox on the lower shelf in the garage, right next to my old set of golf clubs," revealed Uncle P, happy that the mallet he had bought so many years ago might actually prove to have a use.

"Thanks, Uncle P. I'll go and find the mallet while you, Trumper, can go upstairs and get my Dr Who backpack and the two water pistols that are in our bedroom," instructed Bingo, who, after his disappointment with the garlic lollies, felt like ordering Trumper around for a change. "I keep the water pistols hidden in my underwear drawer and the backpack is under my bed, just beneath the pile of dirty clothes I wore yesterday."

"If I must," sighed Trumper, with a less than enthusiastic look on his face, because delving into Bingo's underwear and touching his dirty clothing was not something he relished doing at any time of the day or night. "I'll meet you in the red-brick shed with the water pistols and your backpack. Just make sure you bring everything else."

"Remember that dinner is at seven tonight, boys," added Aunty J, hoping Bingo could last that long before eating his next meal. "And don't forget to wrap up again before you go outside. I want you to wear your coats and woolly hats, and remember to put your muddy wellingtons on when you are outside the back door because I don't want mud on my nice new carpet."

"What are we having for dinner?" demanded Bingo, hoping that his aunty was going to cook one of his favourite meals again.

"Your friends, Bertie Bovington and Flitcher Jenkins, dropped by while you were visiting Mr Poly and gave me some fish they had caught," answered Aunty J, with a smile. "Bertie said they had caught so many that his mum, who knows just how much you like to eat fish, told him to give a few of them to Trumper and Bingo, and so I accepted and will be making fish pie tonight."

"Goodie," shrieked Bingo, as he jumped up and down. "Fish pie is one of my favourites." And with that, the two boys went their separate ways.

By the time Bingo had located Uncle P's mallet at the far end of the garage, placed it in the shopping bag containing the wooden stakes and carried them along with the bag of garlic bulbs and the garlic lollies, all the way down the long garden path, Trumper had already reached the red-brick shed and unlocked the padlock, switched on the light and was standing next to the large chest of drawers with the water pistols, Bingo's Dr Who backpack and the sturdy plastic container of holy water.

"Dragonsbutts! You stink of garlic," sniffed Trumper, looking suspiciously at Bingo as he entered the red-brick shed and bolted the door behind him.

"Of course, I don't want to be bitten by a vampire," laughed Bingo, who quickly stuck the garlic lolly he had been holding in his hand back into his open mouth. "You should try one, Trumper; they're nearly as good as a spollies."

Trumper shook his head and thought; at least they still have the remaining eleven garlic lollies and the bag of garlic bulbs to ward off vampires, and then he muttered to himself, "I just hope that will be enough."

The two boys sat down on the brown leather sofa, which meant Trumper, at last, had time to contemplate and discuss with Bingo everything that had been baffling him about this case. Firstly, although every vampire in the Entwhistle journals had bitten their victims on the neck, for some unknown reason, the Reverend Pinkerton and Roly Poly had, rather strangely, been bitten on the butt.

"What about Old Toothless Bill?" interrupted Bingo, who, while sucking his garlic lolly, was patiently listening to Trumper. "He stabbed his victims in the neck with a wooden straw and then sucked out their blood."

"That's true, Bingo, however, I think we can assume that with modern dentistry, vampires of the twenty-first century are more than likely going to have a full set of teeth," laughed Trumper, and Bingo couldn't help himself but laugh too."

Once the boys had stopped laughing, Trumper went on to say that he had hoped Roly Poly would have been able to refute the Reverend Pinkerton's contradictory recollection of the night he was attacked. Namely, that he saw one pair of glowing red eyes on Pigswill Alley, yet he claimed to have heard two pairs of feet running towards him. Unexpectedly and rather astonishingly, their science teacher confirmed that during his brutal attack, he too had heard two pairs of feet but only saw one pair of glowing red eyes. Unfortunately, this meant Trumper was still no closer to answering the all-important question, does Dragonbutt have one vampire on the loose or two?

"Maybe there is only one vampire, but he has a sidekick that helps him out. Just like Dr Watson helped Sherlock Holmes," shrugged Bingo, thinking Trumper would likely as not just laugh at his suggestion.

Even though Trumper did not believe the vampire they were looking for had a sidekick, at least not in the way Bingo had implied, he did recall reading something about a vampire's accomplice in one of the Entwhistle journals. For that reason, he leapt from the brown leather sofa and made his way over to the heavy oak bookshelves to retrieve the journal he had read earlier that day about a troublesome Transylvanian vampire. After a few minutes of searching for the section he was interested in, Trumper looked towards Bingo and told the younger boy that, for once, he could be right.

Trumper revealed that the Transylvanian vampire who had plagued Dragonbutt so long ago was known to have some kind of special psychic power. This enabled him to control certain people, although they had to be the weak-minded type and foolish enough to peer into the vampire's glowing red eyes. These individuals were not vampires themselves, yet they were under the control of a powerful vampire who could force them, against their will, to do his evil bidding. This could explain why the Reverend Pinkerton and Roly Poly had both heard two pairs of feet but only saw one pair of glowing red eyes when they were attacked. So, Trumper announced, Dragonbutt may only have one vampire after all, and if this is true, it probably has a rather dim-witted sidekick tagging along as well.

Bingo, brimming with confidence because he had helped solve a crucial piece of the puzzle, proclaimed to Trumper, "Hey, you've forgotten something."

"Really, and what's that?" hesitated Trumper, who, somewhat overconfident, was quite sure he had remembered everything.

"Roly Poly told us that his attacker must have been very short because the glowing red eyes he saw staring at him on Pigswill Alley were close to the ground," explained Bingo, looking quite pleased with himself.

"Oh yes," shrugged Trumper, unwilling to admit he had forgotten about that lone fact. "I was going to bring that up next."

"No need," grinned Bingo, while rubbing his hands together. "I know why."

"You do!" exclaimed Trumper, with a bewildered look on his face.

"Yes, it's obvious," replied Bingo, looking confidently at Trumper. "It's a little vampire."

Trumper was quiet for a few seconds and then said, "Good work, Bingo, once again I think you might just be right. That would explain why our vampire never bites the neck of its victims, and instead, bites them on the butt."

It was Bingo's turn to look a little confused and then being quite curious, he asked, "Why is that, Trumper?"

"Because if it is a little vampire, then it cannot possibly reach its victim's neck, so the next best place to bite someone and drink their blood, that is soft and close to the ground, is their butt," disclosed Trumper, happy that this mystery was at last beginning to unravel.

"Dragonsbutts! So who do you think it is?" pleaded Bingo, who was jumping up and down with excitement.

"I have no idea," admitted Trumper, as he shook his head. "But tonight, after Aunty J and Uncle P have gone to bed, we are going to head over to Pigswill Alley, and with a bit of luck, we might just find out."

To ensure they were well-prepared for their adventurous night ahead, Bingo picked up his Dr Who backpack and placed the remaining eleven garlic lollies in the pouch at the rear of the bag, so that he could easily retrieve one at a moment's notice. He then took a dozen or so of the garlic bulbs out of the large brown paper bag and stuffed them into the two side pockets. Next, he grabbed hold of the mallet and half a dozen of the sharpened wooden stakes and deposited them in the main compartment of the backpack. Meanwhile, Trumper had filled the two water pistols with holy water and handed one of them to Bingo, who, knowing he should keep it on-hand, ready for a fight, promptly slid the water pistol into his coat pocket and urged Trumper to do the same.

"From now on, I'm going to call this a 'holy water pistol'," chuckled Bingo, as he pulled the water pistol out of his coat pocket and pulled the trigger, just to make sure it worked. "I still have plenty of space in my backpack for Little MO, so stand back, Trumper, while I take a practice swing."

"You won't need to bring Little MO with you tonight," insisted Trumper, who was quite sure the two of them already had everything they required to confront the little vampire. "It's nearly seven and Aunty J will be serving dinner soon. So just leave everything here and let's go back up to the house."

Whether it was breakfast, lunch or dinner, everyone knew that they never had to ask Bingo twice. Without saying a word, he placed his Dr Who backpack on the floor, unbolted the door and then ran out of the red-brick shed, all the way up the long garden path and into the little old house, leaving an unsurprised Trumper to lock-up behind him.

And by the time he entered the house, Bingo had already removed his outdoor clothes and was sitting next to Uncle P at the kitchen table, impatiently waiting for his dinner.

"Please wash your hands, Trumper," called out Aunty J, as he marched into the warm kitchen after taking off his wellingtons and placing them on the already muddied copy of the Dragonbutt Smoker. "Dinner will be on the table shortly."

As Trumper sat down at the kitchen table with newly washed hands smelling of fresh lavender, Aunty J placed his dinner in front of him and Bingo's, to his relief, came next. She then walked back to the oven and quickly returned with a plate of piping hot food for Uncle P and the same for herself.

"Yummy," yelled both of the boys, with their customary smiles that they always wore at mealtimes.

Fish pie was another of those dinners that their aunty made exceedingly well. She had covered the freshly caught fish in a creamy cheese sauce and then topped everything with a delicious leek and onion mashed potato. This, in turn, had been coated with a handful of grated extra-strong Red Dragon cheese; the kind that was only ever sold at Gribble's the Grocer's. Finally, she had cooked each pie in its own oval terracotta dish and served them hot and sizzling straight from the oven, though not before placing each one on a large earthenware plate to avoid burning the precious table mats she was so fond of.

While the boys blew frantically on their fish pies, Uncle P, with a rather serious look on his face, inquired, "So how is Shadwick Poly?"

"He looks pretty good considering he was bitten by a vampire," responded Trumper, who was still waiting for his fish pie to cool down so that he could take a bite. "I'm sure he will be back at school in the New Year."

"I don't want any talk of vampires at the dinner table!" snapped Aunty J, who would have slapped Trumper's hand if he had been sitting closer to her. "Boys, don't forget that Old Mrs Dingle and Baxter will be coming over at eight-thirty tomorrow morning. Oh yes, and today is Sunday, so that means it's bath night for the both of you. After we have finished eating dinner, I'd like you to go upstairs and wash all that mud and grime away, and next time I see you, there should be two clean and sweet-smelling boys wearing their pyjamas and ready for bed. Is that clear?"

"Not bath night again," groaned Bingo, while hurriedly eating his fish pie. "I don't see why I need to have a bath because I'm only going to get dirty again.

"Don't forget, Bingo, a clean boy is a good boy," smiled Aunty J, as she pinched his cheek.

"Whatever," responded Bingo, while shaking his head. "Anyhow, I'd like to know what are we going to have for dessert?"

"I have some nice fondant fancies that I bought from Fanshaw's," smiled Aunty J, knowing this would please the two boys. "They're the ones you like that have the lemon buttercream filling and white fondant with chocolate swirls."

Once Trumper and Bingo had licked their dishes clean so that there was not even a smidgen of fish pie to be seen, they started on the fondant fancies and polished off the whole plate in absolutely no time at all. After dinner, as their aunty had instructed, they trudged upstairs for the Sunday night bath that Bingo always loathed, although funnily, he was the one who rushed into the bathroom first, only to reappear in hardly any time at all wearing his favourite blue and white striped pyjamas.

"Finished," he shouted to his aunty, who was standing watchfully at the bottom of the stairs.

"I mean a full bath, Bingo," yelled Aunty J, as she was all too aware of the tricks the young boy would use to avoid having a bath.

"Not my hair as well," cried Bingo, knowing what his aunty's answer would be, even before he heard it.

"Yes, all of you, and I will be checking," barked Aunty J, somewhat exasperated. "And that goes for you too, Trumper."

Dragging his feet, Bingo headed back into the bathroom and this time Aunty J could clearly hear him splashing about in the bathtub. A good ten minutes later a rather irked looking Bingo appeared in his pyjamas once again, although this time his hair was dripping wet.

"I've finished, Aunty J," bellowed Bingo, while sniffing to make it look like he had caught a cold. "It turns out I didn't need a bath after all because the water only turned a little brown."

"Dry your hair and then come into the living room," called back Aunty J, happy that Bingo was clean once more, at least until the next day. "It's your turn now, Trumper."

Unlike Bingo, Trumper quite liked bath night. After draining the younger boy's dirty water from the bathtub, he turned the tap on full to fill his bath with plenty of hot water and even dropped in a sachet of his aunty's eucalyptus bath salts. Now that he was clean and dressed in his black and grey trimmed pyjamas, he ran downstairs and into the living room to see Bingo sitting on the sofa and drinking a mug of Aunty J's always satisfying hot chocolate.

"Ah, Trumper, I'll bring you a mug of hot chocolate as well, although you will need to drink it quickly because it's getting close to your bedtime," urged Aunty J, as she opened the living room door to return to the kitchen. "Oh yes, and don't forget to brush your teeth before you go to bed. And that means you too, Bingo."

After finishing their mugs of hot chocolate, both Trumper and Bingo said goodnight to Aunty J and Uncle P before climbing the stairs and brushing their teeth. Knowing they would be hunting for a bloodthirsty vampire later that night, the two boys eagerly jumped into their beds, and with no intention of sleeping, they patiently waited for their aunty and uncle to retire for the evening.

Ten

Yet Another Victim

❧

It was just after ten that Trumper and Bingo heard Aunty J and Uncle P climb the stairs, brush their teeth and finally switch the lights off on the landing before heading to bed. Fortunately, the boys' bedroom was never completely dark because of the streetlight that stood directly outside their window, and so after waiting another ten minutes, Trumper swung down from his bunk to see that Bingo was already out of bed and taking off his pyjamas.

"Leave your pyjamas on, Bingo, and you need to be very quiet," whispered Trumper, afraid Bingo, being the noisier one, may inadvertently wake their aunty and uncle. "Just pull your clothes over your pyjamas because it's bound to be cold outside."

Bingo, excited that the two of them were embarking on an adventure, looked at Trumper and stuck his thumb in the air to indicate he understood. After tiptoeing down the stairs, each boy quietly finished dressing for the cold night ahead by pulling on their winter coats, DPS woolly hats and warm woollen gloves. Wisely, Trumper remembered to take Uncle P's torch that always hung on one of the hooks by the front door and after slipping into their wellingtons, which their uncle had kindly cleaned, they unlocked and without a sound hurriedly left by the back door.

Into the garden, the two intrepid vampire hunters crept and down the long garden path they silently ran, only to reach the red-brick shed in no time at all. Without delay, Trumper unlocked the padlock, while Bingo held the torch so that he could see the keyhole. Once inside, the boys turned on the light and closed the door, and this, thankfully, permitted them to talk more freely.

"I'm glad that you brought Uncle P's torch," remarked Bingo, as he walked over to his Dr Who backpack, which was now crammed with everything any respectable vampire hunter would ever need when hunting for a dangerous vampire.

"Yes, I thought that even though the sky is clear tonight and the moon is out, it will be pretty dark on Pigswill Alley and I wouldn't want that little vampire creeping up on us. And with a torch, if we do come across him, we might just be able to identify who this vampire really is," disclosed Trumper, while checking the time on his phone. "Anyway, both of the previous attacks took place between eleven and twelve, so let's not dawdle, we should leave right away."

"Alright, Trumper," acknowledged Bingo, who, despite the late hour, was wide awake and raring to get on with their vampire hunt. "If we see the little vampire, I want to be the first to squirt him with holy water."

As they silently departed the red-brick shed, Trumper closed the door and turned his key in the padlock once more to ensure the precious contents inside would remain secure. Bingo then noiselessly opened the wooden gate, and with Trumper leading the way, they confidently marched up the muddy footpath to Dragonbutt pond.

Once the boys had walked to the end of the cobblestone path that bordered Dragonbutt pond, it only took them a minute or so to reach their destination. Trumper had been right about bringing the torch, because as soon as the two of them entered Pigswill Alley, despite it being the height of winter and the tall willow trees had lost most of their leaves, the dense canopy of branches that had grown so thick over the years only allowed for a few rays of moonlight to penetrate the ground beneath. In normal times, this may have sufficed for walking, but not for hunting a formidable adversary that was likely, if they were not exceptionally careful, to bite one of them on the butt.

Without uttering a word, Trumper pulled the torch from his coat pocket and shone its powerful beam up and down Pigswill Alley. This was to ensure their path was clear and they were not about to receive an unpleasant surprise so early on in their vampire hunt.

"So which way now, Trumper," hesitated Bingo, as he pulled out the holy water pistol from his coat pocket, ready to shoot at anything that moved. "Shall we head towards Dragonbutt Vicarage or Pucclechurch Crescent?"

"Good question, Bingo," confirmed Trumper, who, to be honest, hadn't really thought that far. "How about we toss a coin to decide the direction we should go. Do you have a coin I can use because my trouser pockets are empty?"

"I'm afraid not, they're all in my Hogswood piggy bank that is sitting on the bookshelf in our bedroom," answered Bingo, after checking his own trouser pockets for any errant coins and finding none.

For several minutes the boys contemplated how they were going to solve their dilemma, and then Bingo shrieked, "I know, let's decide by playing Rock-Paper-Scissors."

"Shush!" hissed Trumper, while placing his hand over Bingo's mouth in the hope of silencing him. "Alright then, if I win, we head over to Pucclechurch Crescent, and if you win, we'll walk towards Dragonbutt Vicarage."

"You start, Trumper, but let's make it the best of three," urged Bingo, with a great deal of enthusiasm because this was one of his favourite games, which of course he always liked to win.

As the boys were quite good at playing Rock-Paper-Scissors, the first game went on for some time, until Bingo finally won with a rock blunting Trumper's scissors. Fortunately, the second game was a little quicker with Trumper's paper smothering Bingo's rock, and this, not surprisingly, infuriated the younger boy enormously.

"Bingo, it's all down to this last game," cautioned Trumper, who had momentarily forgotten the reason they were standing in the middle of Pigswill Alley at such a late hour of the night, and instead, was thoroughly engrossed in their rather juvenile game.

Although both of the boys were pretty serious about winning games, in the end, it was Bingo who triumphed with his scissors cutting into Trumper's paper, which compelled the younger boy to jump into the air and yell, "Winner!"

"Shush!" snapped Trumper, yet again. "So it's decided, we head towards Dragonbutt Vicarage. And Bingo, let's talk quietly from now on. If you need to say something, then just make sure you speak in a whisper."

"Will do, Trumper," muttered Bingo, as he pulled off his Dr Who backpack and placed it on a large willow tree branch that must have only recently fallen to the ground. "But first, let's have a garlic lolly; it will give us some much-needed protection if we are attacked by the little vampire."

"Good idea," agreed Trumper, who gladly accepted one of the garlic lollies from Bingo.

Knowing they should be on their way, the boys stealthily walked along Pigswill Alley in the direction of Dragonbutt Vicarage. Trumper shone the torch to light their way, while Bingo firmly clutched onto his holy water pistol. As the night was cold and probably near freezing, it meant that the ground was hard and therefore nowhere near as muddy as it had been during the day. The only thing that could alert anyone of the boys' presence on Pigswill Alley was the sound coming from their mouths as they sucked the garlic lollies. Naturally, Bingo was by far the louder of the two, being well-known for his skill in sucking through an entire lolly within a little under three minutes.

"What's that noise?" remarked Trumper, a little too loudly as he held up one of his hands, already forgetting that he was supposed to whisper.

"What noise?" asked Bingo, who had been too busy enjoying his garlic lolly to listen for any unusual sounds.

"The squeaky noise that seems to be getting louder, which means it's coming this way," replied an impatient Trumper, while looking in the direction they had just come.

"Yes, I hear it now," confirmed Bingo, pointing his holy water pistol into the darkness. "Do you think it's the little vampire?"

"It could be, so hurry up and get behind that big willow tree, and be ready to squirt your holy water pistol on my command," cried Trumper, as his heart began to race.

On a bend in Pigswill Alley, the boys stood behind the biggest willow tree within arm's reach. Trumper, like Bingo, had drawn his holy water pistol, while the remains of their garlic lollies had fallen to the ground. Bingo rummaged in his Dr Who backpack for a few garlic bulbs and some of the wooden stakes which he placed beside the willow tree. At that point, Trumper switched off the torch and dropped a couple of garlic bulbs into his coat pocket, as did Bingo. Then, with a holy water pistol in one hand and a wooden stake to the ready, the boys listened as the squeaky noise grew louder and got closer by the second.

Just before the squeaky noise was upon them, Bingo grabbed one of the wooden stakes, and not waiting for Trumper, he leapt from behind the willow tree and into the path of whoever was approaching, pulling the trigger on his pistol and squirting the holy water for all he was worth. Blinded by a bright light, a screech that sounded like brakes and then a crashing thud barely a few feet away, "Aaah," squawked a shrill voice, yet Bingo bravely stood his ground.

Still holding his holy water pistol in one hand and a wooden stake in the other, he screamed at the top of his voice, "I'll get you, you bloodsucking vampire," and then he charged at the body that was now lying on the ground.

"No, it's only me," screamed a familiar voice, which luckily stopped Bingo's advance, dead in his tracks.

"Dragonsbutts! Is that you, Flitcher?" inquired Bingo, who was foolishly asking a redundant question, because by now, Trumper was shining the torch to reveal a somewhat ruffled looking Flitcher Jenkins picking himself up from the spot where he had fallen from his bicycle.

"Of course it's me," raged Flitcher, while trying to brush away the mud that now clung to his clothes with only the handkerchief he was carrying in his trouser pocket. "Who did you think it was? And what do you think you were doing scaring me like that? I thought you were the vampire."

"That's funny because we thought you were the vampire or the little vampire as we now call him," confided Bingo, who was feeling a little guilty that he had nearly staked his friend and classmate.

"What are you doing here, Flitcher?" demanded Trumper, somewhat irritated with Flitcher for getting in the way of their vampire hunt and even more so with Bingo for jumping the gun.

"Nothing, Trumper, I was on my way home after playing with Bertie," stuttered Flitcher, who looked rather nervous and was more than likely not telling the boys the truth.

"Really!" exclaimed Trumper, a little sarcastically because he didn't believe a word of Flitcher's explanation. "At this late hour?"

"I should be getting along home now," mumbled Flitcher, unwilling to answer Trumper's perfectly straightforward question.

"Is your bike damaged?" called out Bingo, as he walked over to where Flitcher's muddied bicycle lay.

"No, it looks just fine, but it could do with a good cleaning," confirmed Flitcher, who was now sitting on the seat of his bicycle and pointing it towards the narrow path that led to Dragonbutt pond, which, curiously, was the direction he had just come from.

"I'm sorry that I squirted you with holy water," conceded Bingo, while looking down at his holy water pistol that was now almost empty. "Before you go, do you want a garlic lolly?"

"Oh, is that what it was," replied Flitcher, now just noticing the wet patches on his coat and trousers where the holy water had hit him. "I'd love one, but I'm not supposed to eat garlic."

Without saying another word or even waving goodbye, Flitcher Jenkins set off on his bicycle to ride the short distance back to his home on Flamingo Crescent, leaving Trumper and Bingo in the darkness and alone once again on Pigswill Alley. Although Trumper was all too aware that Flitcher was not the brightest bulb in his class at Dragonbutt Primary School, his explanation for riding his bicycle alone on Pigswill Alley and so late at night, was in his opinion, rather peculiar.

If Flitcher had been going home as he claimed, then why was he riding his bicycle on Pigswill Alley and in the opposite direction to where he lived? And where was Bertie Bovington? The two of them were inseparable and lived only two streets apart, so if they had been playing together, then what had happened to Bertie? And one more thing was puzzling Trumper, why was Flitcher not supposed to eat garlic?

After discussing his concerns with Bingo, he then gave the younger boy a good telling-off and stressed that when he said 'be ready to squirt your holy water pistol on my command', it was meant for him to wait and then squirt the little vampire with holy water from the safety of the willow tree. It definitely did not mean run into Pigswill Alley with a holy water pistol and a wooden stake, yelling 'I'll get you, you bloodsucking vampire'.

Bingo just nodded his head and announced, "Well, you know me, Trumper, when my blood is up I just go crazy. Anyway, there was no harm done. So do you think we should go home now?"

"With all the noise that you've been making, I doubt any vampire will come within a mile of Pigswill Alley tonight," retorted Trumper, irritated that they may have missed their chance to capture the little vampire, or at the very least discover his true identity. "Let's give it another five minutes, after that, we'll head on home. Just return the wooden stakes to your backpack and then we can be on our way."

As Trumper and Bingo marched on, no more than a few minutes had passed before the boys could hear another loud and downright harrowing sound. This time they were quite sure that the noise they had just heard was of a person's terrifying scream. The scream sounded as though it had come from the direction of Dragonbutt Vicarage and not too far away by the sound of it. Before either of them could utter a word, they heard one more scream and then an eerie silence fell over Pigswill Alley yet again.

Remembering that his holy water pistol was desperately low on holy water and this meant he was probably down to his last squirt or two, Bingo dropped his Dr Who backpack on the ground and reached inside to retrieve two of the wooden stakes. Firmly holding one in each hand, he pulled the backpack over his shoulders once again and ran towards the scream. Trumper, naturally, was only a few steps behind, his holy water pistol in one hand and the torch in the other.

It took the boys barely any time at all before they came across an overturned bicycle that had been painted a familiar shade of Royal Mail red. Lying on the ground close by was what looked like a lifeless body of a rather tall person, face down in the mud with short red hair.

"Who is it?" asked Trumper, who shone the torch towards the ground to get a better look at the body. "Are they alive or dead?"

"I'll take a look," answered Bingo, as he walked up to the body and gave it a good hard kick.

"Ow!" howled the body, and then it uttered a crazy-sounding laugh that both of the boys immediately recognised.

"Dragonsbutts! It's Mad Tolly Butterworth," bellowed Bingo, unnecessarily calling her name out loud. "And it looks like she's been bitten on the butt, just like the others."

"I'll call for an ambulance," announced Trumper, reaching into his trouser pocket for the phone that Aunty J had insisted he always carry with him. Nine-Nine-Nine was the emergency number that Trumper knew he should dial. "Mad Tolly Butterworth has been attacked and bitten by a vampire. We're on Pigswill Alley, close to the rear entrance of Dragonbutt Vicarage and we need an ambulance and Dragonbutt police to come right away. Oh, and I'm Trumper Gallant, and Bingo Malloy is with me at the scene."

Although Dragonbutt Community Hospital was a good five minutes drive away, the ambulance, with its flashing lights and blaring siren, arrived in barely three. Because their local hospital was rather small and often short of funds, each of the two Dragonbutt and district ambulances was staffed by the hospital's own medical team. On this particular evening, it was the doctor on call, Hari Banjani, who was at the wheel and Staff Nurse Bone Cruncher Trudy Fanshaw sat resolutely by his side.

Hari Banjani had learnt to drive in a place that was far from the quiet streets of Dragonbutt and as such had never acquired much patience for the likes of speed signs and traffic lights. Once he received the call, and the staff nurse was securely fastened in her seat, he kept his pedal to the metal and drove like a madman down Dragonbutt High Street.

As the ambulance entered Pigswill Alley, it quickly became caked in mud and slid precariously from side to side, though that did not deter the doctor from continuing to drive at an unwise and wholly excessive speed. He would doubtlessly have kept on driving this way if it had not been for Trumper and Bingo waving frantically at him, and this, without question, was what finally made the ambulance grind to an abrupt and much-appreciated stop, only a few yards from where the boys were standing.

It was Bone Cruncher Trudy Fanshaw who jumped from the ambulance first, which Trumper thought was quite fortunate because if the little vampire was still nearby, then one look at the Bone Cruncher would soon scare him away, or so he hoped. Dr Banjani was next and immediately ran towards Mad Tolly Butterworth to check her vitals while the staff nurse placed a long stretcher beside her. Once the doctor saw that she was stable and in no immediate distress, he stepped back and allowed the Bone Cruncher to pick Mad Tolly up from the ground and place her onto the stretcher, which despite her considerable size, the staff nurse could do effortlessly and with ease. Both doctor and nurse then carried their patient to the ambulance and secured her for what would undoubtedly be a hair-raising ride with Dr Hari Banjani at the wheel.

"Boys, Dragonbutt police will arrive shortly, so please don't leave," called Dr Banjani, as he jumped into the driving seat again and looked around to see that the Bone Cruncher was already in the back of the ambulance caring for their patient.

With its ear-deafening siren and flashing lights, the ambulance suddenly reversed at a speed that was almost as fast as when it had arrived, only minutes before, and then it quickly disappeared down Pigswill Alley on its way to Dragonbutt Community Hospital. Luckily, Trumper and Bingo did not have to wait long before they could hear a very different type of siren and soon after that they saw the flashing blue lights of an unmarked Dragonbutt police car.

"Wow! It's a BMW M5," exclaimed Bingo, rather excitedly because he had always wanted to ride in a police car and a sporty high-performance M5 made it all the better.

Just like the ambulance driven by Dr Banjani, the police car also came to a screeching halt and out of the driver's side, stepped Heather Huntress, the young detective that Barry Beasley and their uncle had spoken about. At five-foot-ten she had large penetrating eyes that were dark brown in colour, an alluring smile and a set of flawless whiter than white teeth.

Heather Huntress had only been with Dragonbutt Police for about three months, and up until the attack on the Reverend Pinkerton she had considered her new job rather dull. After all, she had spent the previous five years as one of London's finest, a police constable with the Metropolitan Police. Still only twenty-six, the chief constable had offered her a promotion to the rank of detective, a position she had always aspired too. The only catch was that she would have to move from her beloved London, the city of her birth and where she had always lived, to Dragonbutt, a little village few had ever heard of. As police work had always been her passion, the detective position in Dragonbutt she dutifully accepted and brought to it her assertive big city ways.

"Boys, this is a crime scene, so please step back," she ordered, with her hand in the air.

"But we're the ones who called you," answered back Trumper, who did not like the detective's tone one little bit.

"Really! Then I will need to take a statement from the both of you right away, and afterwards, I will drive you home," informed Detective Huntress, while scrutinising the two boys as only a police detective could.

Thrilled that he and Trumper would soon get to ride in a police car, and a BMW M5 no less, Bingo suddenly blurted, "It was Mad Tolly

Butterworth, and she had been bitten by a vampire."

"Young man, vampires do not exist. They are entirely and unequivo-cally fictitious," began Detective Huntress, while taking out her official Dragonbutt police notepad and pen. "Now, let's start at the beginning. I need to know your names and what you were doing here this late at night? Then, in your own words, tell me how and where you discovered the victim? We'll make this quick because I am sure it must be long past your bedtime and your parents will be worried about you."

"I'm Trumper Gallant and this is Bingo Malloy," began Trumper, thinking that as the older of the two he should be the one to tell the police detective their story. "And we don't have parents as such; we live with our aunty and uncle, the Entwhistles of Counting House Lane."

"Would that be Perygrin Entwhistle, the editor-in-chief of the Dragonbutt Smoker?" asked the detective, as she scribbled something in her notepad.

"The very same," interjected Bingo, proud that his uncle had such a prominent position in the village.

Trumper went on to tell Detective Huntress that he and Bingo had been investigating the attacks on the Reverend Pinkerton and Roly Poly and this is why they were on Pigswill Alley. He then told her about the old legends, the Entwhistle journals and the Dragonbutt prophecy and how they believed a vampire was responsible for the attacks, none of which the stern-looking police detective had the inclination or the patience to listen too.

"I'm sure that these legends are fascinating and the journals must be an exciting read for boys of your age, but they are simply stories and old wives tales, and nothing more," insisted the detective, a little too sarcastically for Trumper's liking. "What I really need from you is an account of where you went and what you heard and saw, from the time you left your home until the moment you came across the victim."

It took another five minutes for Trumper to disclose almost everything about their adventurous evening to Detective Huntress, right up to where they found Mad Tolly Butterworth. The only part of the story Trumper left out, was the bit about bumping into Flitcher Jenkins, as he thought it was best not to get Flitcher into trouble as well. Besides, he really didn't think that Flitcher riding his bicycle on Pigswill Alley would be of any interest to a Dragonbutt police detective.

"So let me get this straight," declared Detective Huntress, believing that she had gained little from talking to the boys and wanted instead to finish the interview and drive them home as soon as she could. "You were walking along Pigswill Alley when you heard some screams and by the time you reached here all you saw was the victim laying on the ground but absolutely no sign of anyone else. You then dialled nine-nine-nine and waited for the ambulance and myself to arrive."

"That's right, detective," interrupted Bingo, yet again. "But I kicked her as well, just to make sure she wasn't dead."

"Um, I'm sure that helped," remarked Detective Huntress, using an impatient and somewhat sarcastic tone. "I'll be taking you home now before you get into any more trouble. Where did you say you live?"

"Twenty-Two Counting House Lane," uttered Trumper, rather sullenly.

Unlike Bingo, who was eagerly awaiting their ride home, Trumper was a little nervous about how their aunty and uncle would react to the two of them returning home in a police car so late at night, especially when they were supposed to be fast asleep in their beds. Before they left, he pulled the holy water pistol and garlic bulbs from his coat pocket and slipped them into the Dr Who backpack and then told Bingo to place the two wooden stakes he had been carrying into the bag as well.

"I'll sit in the front," yelled Bingo, as he ran to open the passenger door of the BMW M5.

"You'll both sit in the back," ordered the detective, her tone leaving no doubt in Bingo's mind that she really meant it.

Once the boys had fastened their seat belts, Bingo pleaded, "Detective Huntress, can you put the siren and lights on?"

Not surprisingly, the detective answered with an undeniably abrupt, "No!" After which, Bingo remained silent for the entirety of their short journey home.

It was just after midnight when Detective Huntress rang the doorbell of the bright red door at the little old house on Twenty-Two Counting House Lane. In no time at all the upstairs lights were turned on and the sound of someone rather heavy could be heard coming down the stairs. Within a matter of seconds, the front door abruptly opened with a creek, and standing before them was a rather dishevelled and surprised looking Uncle P wearing his pyjamas, a dressing gown and an old pair of slippers.

"Oh, Detective Huntress, what brings you here?" he asked, somewhat startled to see a police detective standing on his doorstep and at a time of night that was long past his usual waking hour.

"Good evening, Mr Entwhistle, or should I say good morning. I apologise for disturbing you so late, but I believe these two belong to you," replied the detective, as she glanced down to check the time on her stylish new smartwatch and then cordially stepped aside to reveal Trumper and Bingo looking decidedly sorry for themselves.

"Dragonsbutts! What are you two doing outside?" demanded Uncle P, shocked to see that instead of being upstairs, sleeping in their beds, both Trumper and Bingo were standing outside the front door, fully dressed in their outdoor clothes and accompanied by a Dragonbutt police detective. "Get inside at once, and would you like to come in too, Detective Huntress?"

111

"No, thank you, Mr Entwhistle. It's a little late, although I will pop by your office at the Dragonbutt Smoker in the morning so that we can have a talk," informed the detective, anxious to take one more look at the crime scene on Pigswill Alley before heading back to the police station. "Goodnight and Merry Christmas."

"Yes, of course, and thank you for bringing these two rascals home," replied Uncle P, who was eager to send Trumper and Bingo to bed so that he could go back to sleep and hopefully return to his exceptionally pleasant dream.

"Dragonsbutts! I thought you two were in bed," snapped an annoyed-looking Aunty J, who, after hearing all the commotion going on downstairs, had dragged herself out of her warm bed to find out what all the fuss was about.

"Mad Tolly Butterworth was attacked by the little vampire, and we were the ones who found her on Pigswill Alley," screeched Bingo, wrongly thinking his aunty and uncle would be pleased as he dropped his Dr Who backpack in the hallway. "We called Nine-Nine-Nine and probably saved her life. Do you think we'll get a reward?"

"The only reward you will be getting is my foot making contact with your butt as you run upstairs and jump into your bed," bellowed Uncle P, who at this time of the night did not have the patience to listen to one of Bingo's long explanations.

"What you boys were doing outside in the first place is quite beyond me," exclaimed Aunty J, with her arms crossed and a look on her face that meant she was definitely not amused. "You went to bed over two hours ago, and that is where I expect you to be within the next thirty seconds. That is after you take off your wellingtons and outdoor clothes and put your pyjamas back on."

"That's not a problem, we never took them off in the first place," uttered Bingo, with a weak smile on his face as he lifted up the pyjamas that were hidden beneath his trousers for his aunty and uncle to see.

112

Knowing that the most prudent course of action was to do as Aunty J had instructed, the boys silently slipped out of their wellingtons and carefully placed them on the now torn and very muddy copy of the Dragonbutt Smoker. After that, they hung their coats on the hooks in the hallway, removed their DPS woolly hats and warm woollen gloves and then ran upstairs before pulling off the rest of their outdoor clothes, which left the two of them wearing only their pyjamas as they climbed into bed.

"Are you still awake, Trumper?" whispered Bingo, who, because of the events of that night, was still too excited to sleep.

"Yes, but not for long," muttered Trumper, as he, unlike Bingo, had used up all his energy for that day. "What do you want?"

"Do you think that we did something good last night?" asked Bingo, now feeling the beginning of a yawn coming on.

"Yes, I think we did," acknowledged Trumper, as he quietly fell into a deep and long-overdue sleep.

"Good, that's what I think," yawned Bingo, who, just like Trumper, was now fast asleep.

Eleven

Buh! Buh! Buh!

❧

Breakfast that morning was a rather strained affair after Aunty J curtly woke Trumper and Bingo at eight. By the time they had made their way downstairs to the kitchen their uncle had already left for work, and the kitchen table that was usually overflowing with all kinds of yummy treats, to Bingo's displeasure, was ominously bare.

"Are we having sausages for breakfast?" asked a hungry Bingo, somewhat optimistically considering their aunty was still noticeably displeased with the two of them.

"Not this morning," answered Aunty J, quite brusquely. "After your antics last night you'll each have a bowl of porridge, a slice of toast and a glass of apple juice. And before you say anything, I don't want to hear any more stories about vampires from either of you. Your uncle will speak to Detective Huntress this morning, and after I finish work, he will let me know what both of you were really up to last night."

"Yes, Aunty J," nodded Bingo, who was glad that his aunty was not going to give them another scolding because of their little scrape with the law. "I hope the apple juice is Braithwaite's."

"Bingo, you know I always buy the best, and that's Braithwaite's," confirmed Aunty J, as she poured the boys two large glasses of their favourite beverage. "Eat your breakfast quickly because my first patient is arriving at nine, which means I have to leave soon. Coincidentally, it's Typsy Braithwaite, and he needs a tooth pulled."

"Alright, Aunty J," nodded Trumper, feeling refreshed after a good night's sleep and ready to hunt for the little vampire once again. "We're sorry for causing you so much trouble last night. Aren't we, Bingo?"

"Of course, and we'll make sure that we never get caught like that again," teased Bingo, with a sly look and a wink towards Trumper, that fortunately for him, his aunty, in her hurry to give the boys their breakfast and to leave the house for the dental surgery, completely missed.

Just then, the doorbell rang with one of those long ding-dong types of sounds that Bingo always thought of as quite tedious. For the simple fact that almost every house in Dragonbutt, the exception being Roly Poly's house, appeared to have a doorbell that sounded exactly the same.

"At last, that must be Old Mrs Dingle," exclaimed Aunty J, as she hurriedly walked out of the kitchen and along the hallway to open the front door.

Almost immediately, Trumper and Bingo heard something with four legs scampering towards them that they knew could not possibly have been Old Mrs Dingle, which meant, naturally, it had to be Baxter.

"Baxter, here boy," called Bingo, who was closest to the hallway and the first to see the old lady's funny-looking dog.

After darting into the kitchen and seeing the two boys at the kitchen table, he jumped up and started to lick their hands and faces. It was Trumper who finally calmed him down by scratching behind his ear, something that Baxter had enjoyed ever since he was a puppy.

"Woof-Woof-Woof," was all that Baxter could say, though the boys knew he was pleased to see them and they were happy to see him as well.

"Merry Christmas, boys, only another two days until Christmas," chuckled Old Mrs Dingle, as she walked into the kitchen with Aunty J close behind. "I heard from your aunty that you were up to a little mischief last night."

"It was a lot more than just mischief," rebuked the boys' stern-sounding aunty, who was looking up at the clock on the kitchen wall. "Anyway, I'm already late for Typsy Braithwaite's appointment so I will need to leave right now. Trumper, please call Wenna Loopey at the surgery to inform her I'm running about twenty minutes late."

"Oh, I do apologise for being late today, but I had to wait for Bucktooth Tom Blewitt to replace a pane of glass in my kitchen window that was broken over a week and a half ago," apologised Old Mrs Dingle, almost forgetting that she had promised to arrive by eight-thirty and it was now already nine. "Yesterday afternoon, he kindly drove all the way to Chelmsford to pick up the glass, although by the time he reached Dragonbutt it was already dark, so the earliest he could possibly install it was this morning."

Even though Aunty J was not exactly happy that Old Mrs Dingle had arrived more than a little late, she was in an awful hurry and so with a brisk goodbye and a Merry Christmas, their aunty was on her way to Dragonbutt dental surgery, which was located not too far away from Counting House Lane, close to the entrance of Old Privy Bottom.

"Boys, it's time for you to brush your teeth and get dressed, and then you can go and play with Baxter in the garden while I clear away these breakfast dishes," urged Old Mrs Dingle, who knew that her funny-looking dog was eager to play with Trumper and Bingo.

"Alright, Old Mrs Dingle," shrieked Bingo, as he raced upstairs with

Trumper just behind him. "Trumper, I'll brush my teeth first and then it's your turn."

"Very well, but once you're dressed don't forget to bring your backpack with you when we go into the garden," replied Trumper, in what sounded more like a command than a polite request.

"Yes, sir!" mocked Bingo, quite sarcastically as he gave Trumper a half-hearted bent hand salute. Although regrettably for Bingo, all that earned him was a not so gentle kick from Trumper that landed firmly on the cheeky younger boy's unprotected butt as he ran into the bathroom. "And Trumper, bring some money with you because we don't want to get caught out like last night."

Once Trumper and Bingo had brushed their teeth and were dressed in some clean warm clothing that their aunty had thoughtfully placed on Bingo's bed, the two of them ran back down the stairs and leapt from the third step into the hallway. Without delay, they pulled on their coats and DPS woolly hats, and then Bingo snatched his Dr Who backpack off the floor and slung it over one shoulder. Finally, the boys picked up their muddy wellingtons and carried them to the back door, where they placed them outside, just as their aunty had instructed.

Old Mrs Dingle came out of the kitchen to hand Baxter's lead to Bingo and his favourite ball to Trumper. The boys, happy to be going outside into the cold but thankfully fresh air, stepped out of the back door and slid their feet snugly into the wellingtons and then pulled on their warm woollen gloves. Bingo called to Baxter, who hurriedly came running from the kitchen, and then suddenly, just as if he had hit an invisible wall, the funny-looking dog stopped dead in his tracks about six feet from where the two boys were standing.

"Come along, Baxter, what's the matter?" called Bingo, who, like Trumper, had no idea why the funny-looking dog was acting so strange. "We're only going into the garden to play catch."

"That's odd," commented Trumper, as he stepped away from Bingo and started to walk down the long garden path. "I'll meet you at the red-brick shed, that's if you can manage to drag Baxter out of the house."

Before Bingo could move even an inch to grab hold of Baxter, he leapt right past the young boy and ran into the garden after Trumper. Bingo, carrying his Dr Who backpack and firmly holding onto Baxter's lead, followed the two of them while calling out to the funny-looking dog. All the time, he maintained his distance from Bingo, and instead, lingered close to Trumper.

"Put your backpack in the red-brick shed," called Trumper to Bingo, who was now running with the funny-looking dog. "I'm going to play ball with Baxter for a while, so come and join us."

Bingo shouted back his acknowledgement to Trumper and then retrieved the key from around his neck, unlocked the padlock and opened the door. He then dropped his Dr Who backpack on the floor, though not before pulling out the holy water pistol and the garlic bulbs from his coat pocket and placing them on top of the large chest of drawers. Once Bingo was outside again and had closed the door of the red-brick shed, Baxter ran up to him and gave the young boy a big slobbering lick across his face.

"Urgh! It looks like we're friends again," exclaimed a bemused Bingo, as he wiped his face and then picked up Baxter's ball and threw it towards Trumper.

After about twenty minutes of playing ball with the funny-looking dog, both of the boys needed a break and Baxter looked a little bit tired as well, what with all the running and catching, then running off and running all the way back, and then running and catching some more.

"Let's sit in the red-brick shed for five minutes," declared Trumper, who was definitely the more tired of the two boys.

"Good idea," agreed Bingo, while turning around to call for the funny-looking dog. "Come on, Baxter, we're going to have a break for a few minutes, so come and join us."

When the boys entered the red-brick shed, strangely, Baxter did not follow, and so Bingo went back outside to call for him again, "Baxter, come on boy." Despite this, he remained almost motionless, a good ten feet from where the young boy was standing. Bingo then walked over to Baxter and tried to pull him by his collar, yet the funny-looking dog, stubbornly, would not budge an inch.

"What's wrong with you today?" beseeched Bingo, who was somewhat irritated and definitely confused as to why Baxter was behaving like this.

Instead of yielding to Bingo, the funny-looking dog just looked at him with his sheep-like eyes and gave a rather distressed sounding whimper, before pulling away and running back up the long garden path towards the little old house.

"Oh well, I'm not running after you," shrugged Bingo, as he returned to the red-brick shed.

"Where's Baxter?" queried Trumper, who was sitting on one side of the brown leather sofa, thinking about the little vampire.

"He wouldn't come into the red-brick shed and instead ran back to the house," reported Bingo, as he closed the door and bolted it, before sitting down next to Trumper.

"That's not like Baxter," replied Trumper, although he did not spend more than a moment or two dwelling on what was wrong with the funny-looking dog as he knew there were more important things at hand, such as hunting for the elusive little vampire. "Anyway, never mind, we need to speak with Mad Tolly Butterworth, and come to think of it, I have a few questions that I would like to ask Bertie Bovington as well."

"She's probably still at Dragonbutt Community Hospital, and Bertie, I would guess, is playing with Flitcher as usual," disclosed Bingo, a little curious as to why Trumper wanted to question Bertie Bovington.

"Then let's head over to Dragonbutt Community Hospital right now," announced Trumper, as he jumped up from the brown leather sofa. "And this afternoon we will pay a visit to Bertie Bovington."

"Should I take my backpack?" yelped Bingo, excited that they were once again on the trail of the little vampire.

"No, we should be safe for now, until nightfall, that is," answered Trumper, while shaking his head. "But you can top up your holy water pistol because I get the feeling we are going to need it later."

After Bingo had filled the holy water pistol to the brim and put it in his Dr Who backpack, he placed a few garlic lollies in his coat pocket and then the two of them exited the red-brick shed and hastily marched back up the long garden path, only to see Baxter once again, standing next to the back door of the little old house.

"Hey, Baxter, do you want to come for a walk?" appealed Bingo, with his arms outstretched. Without hesitating, the funny-looking dog trotted right up to Bingo and obediently lowered his head so that the young boy could attach the lead to his collar. "You're an odd one. What was the matter with you earlier?"

With no response from Baxter, Bingo just shook his head and then opened the back door and shouted to Old Mrs Dingle, who was busy in the kitchen preparing a special lunchtime treat for the boys. "We're taking Baxter for a walk and will be home a little later."

Old Mrs Dingle yelled back, in what was a surprisingly loud voice for such an old lady, "Righty-ho, but make sure you're back by twelve. I'm making faggots for lunch today, and by the way, your aunty said that you are not to go anywhere near Pigswill Alley."

"Yummy, I love faggots," hollered Bingo, who was quite sure he would be especially hungry by lunchtime because of the meagre breakfast that Aunty J had served the two boys that morning.

Holding Baxter firmly by his lead, Bingo walked to the end of Counting House Lane, and naturally, Trumper was by his side.

Heeding the words of their aunty, the boys decided to take the longer route to avoid Pigswill Alley. This meant they had to turn right on Hunnickle Drive and walk along the grass-lined pavement until they reached Upper Dragonbutt High Street. It was then only a brief five-minute stroll before they saw the sign for Dragonbutt Community Hospital, which was located on one side of Old Dragonian Way, with Dragonbutt Police Station on the other.

Forgetting that he had Baxter with him, Bingo, while still holding onto the funny-looking dog's lead, confidently marched through the open glass sliding doors at the main entrance to Dragonbutt Community Hospital, and Trumper was no more than a few steps behind.

"There's the reception," pointed out Bingo, looking very sure of himself. "I'll ask for the directions to Mad Tolly Butterworth's room."

Before the three of them could take a step further, a large woman dressed in the spotless white uniform of a Dragonbutt Community Hospital staff nurse blocked their way. With folded arms she stood as still as an iceberg, a stern look chiselled into her face, that if it could speak would in all likelihood have said something like, 'You're most certainly not entering here!"

Staff Nurse Bone Cruncher Trudy Fanshaw was Dragonbutt born, and the niece of Wilimina Fanshaw, the owner of Fanshaw's the Baker's. She had been a nurse at Dragonbutt Community Hospital for ten years already and was certainly an unforgettable sight to see. At six-foot-tall and only a month shy of her thirty-fifth birthday, she was not only a fine staff nurse but also at the peak of her amateur arm wrestling career. With dark brown eyes and hair to match, that was regularly cut a little too short, the Bone Cruncher looked as strong as an ox, with a shot putters body and enormous hands that could famously bring tears to even the hardiest of her arm wrestling opponents.

"You two again! And where do you think you're going with that disease-ridden sheep?" boomed the thunderous voice of the Bone Cruncher, as she glared at Baxter while cracking the knuckles of her left and then her right hand.

"We're here to visit Mad Tolly Butterworth," squeaked Bingo, in what was quite a feeble voice for him. "And he is not a sheep; he's a Bedlington terrier, which is really a dog that only looks like a sheep."

"This is a hospital for people, and no filthy animals are allowed. And that includes a dog that looks like a sheep. So you can remove him now or I will!" snarled the angry staff nurse, who looked like she would have thoroughly enjoyed removing Baxter herself, and quite forcibly, of course.

"Don't worry, Nurse Fanshaw," interrupted Trumper, as he did not want to witness a brutal and potentially bloody scene. "We'll tie him up outside."

Trumper then hastily took Baxter's lead out of the younger boy's hand and walked the funny-looking dog back through the open glass sliding doors, followed by the somewhat rattled looking Bingo.

Once they were outside, Trumper laughed and said, "We should ask the Bone Cruncher to join us in hunting for the little vampire. I think having her around would be better protection than even garlic." And this made Bingo laugh too.

"Hey, Trumper, I'm getting hungry, and I don't think that I can last until lunchtime," proclaimed Bingo, while rubbing his tummy to emphasise his point and then telling Trumper that food was the best thing to calm his nerves after their run-in with the Bone Cruncher. "Let's tie Baxter's lead to a post and then we can get a snack to eat before we visit Mad Tolly Butterworth."

He wholeheartedly agreed, and once Baxter's lead was securely tied to the first post they could find, close to the entrance of the hospital, the boys walked back inside to see the Bone Cruncher eyeballing them from a good distance away, although thankfully, this time the staff nurse made no attempt to question either of them.

"Alright, Bingo, how much money do you have?" requested Trumper, as he took his woollen gloves off and pulled two shiny coins out of his trouser pocket. Bingo took his gloves off too and then rummaged around in his pockets to produce a single pound coin that he had taken out of his Hogswood piggy bank earlier that morning. "That's not much. I have two pounds, which means we only have a measly three pounds to spend on snacks."

"Dragonsbutts! I was hoping for a mug of hot chocolate and a warm mince pie in the cafeteria, but that's not going to be anywhere near enough money for the two of us," groaned Bingo, whose tummy rumbles were telling him that they would undoubtedly need more money if the demands of his sizeable appetite were to be met. "We'll just have to take a look at the vending machine on the other side of the reception and see what we can buy with three pounds."

The boys wasted no time at all and walked briskly over to the large vending machine to take a look at the price of each item. Crisps, which were not very filling in Bingo's opinion, were a whopping ninety pence and most of the other snacks were priced at a pound or over. Even though they could afford to buy one snack each and split a packet of crisps between the two of them, unfortunately, sharing was simply not an option for Bingo, who, not surprisingly, always liked to eat a whole packet of crisps by himself.

"Oh, look there!" cried out Bingo, as he pointed to the bottom row of snacks. "Choco Bombs are only seventy pence, so that means we can each have two."

"Here you go, Bingo, take my two pounds, and you'll have to use your pound coin as well," stated Trumper, who was pleased they had found one of their favourite treats to eat.

Bingo happily dropped his pound coin into the slot, followed by the two pound coins that Trumper had given him. He then selected two Choco Bombs for Trumper, which dropped noisily into the tray beneath and then did the same for himself. As for the twenty pence in change that fell into an opening underneath the slot, he immediately picked it up and quietly placed the coin into his now empty trouser pocket.

Choco Bombs had been a wonderfully decadent and surprisingly affordable creation of Bovington's Sweets and Chocolates that were first conceived some seventy-five years ago. They were not just cherished by Trumper and Bingo, as more or less the whole village of Dragonbutt had at some time or another considered Choco Bombs not only their favourite but also their most indulgent chocolate snack.

What made Choco Bombs so good was not simply the fact that they were made with Bovington's famous handmade and always exceedingly rich chocolate; instead, it was because at the heart of each one there was something very special. Once you bit through the outer shell of creamy sweet milk chocolate, anyone who had ever experienced a Choco Bomb knew, you were in for an unforgettable taste bud sensation. At first, your tongue would come into contact with its exquisite white chocolate filling, and if that was not enough, you would then be treated to the intense flavour of its heavenly fresh raspberry centre.

Trumper had yet to finish his second Choco Bomb, however, as usual; Bingo had already polished off both of his, leaving his hands and face smeared with milk and white chocolate and a bright red fresh raspberry stain.

"They were yummy," declared Bingo, while licking the chocolate and fresh raspberry from his hands. "It's a shame we don't have any more money because I could eat Choco Bombs all day."

"I think two was just what we needed and they should keep us going until lunchtime," acknowledged Trumper, as he finished the last bite of his second Choco Bomb. "Let's wash our hands before we visit Mad Tolly Butterworth, and you need to wash your face too."

Once Trumper and Bingo had washed the remains of the Choco Bombs from their hands and Bingo had washed his dirty face, they walked up to the reception to speak with one of the hospital staff on duty.

"Excuse me, but where can I find Mad Tolly Butterworth," inquired Trumper, to the nearest receptionist. "She was admitted late last night."

"Are you a relative?" demanded the young receptionist, somewhat abruptly.

Trumper was about to answer when Bingo chimed in, although not before giving the older boy a sly wink, "Yes, we're very close to her, and she comes to our house almost every day."

"Alright then, she's in room number thirteen on the Lady Eradorn Wyvern ward, which is straight down this corridor and you need to take the second turning on the left," directed the receptionist, sounding a great deal more polite than before. "It looks like she was admitted by Dr Banjani, and he is still on duty. I believe Staff Nurse Fanshaw is in charge of that ward today. Would you like me to inform her you are coming?"

"No thanks," answered Trumper, not wanting to have another confrontation with the Bone Cruncher. "We wouldn't want to take the staff nurse away from her important duties."

After a quick Merry Christmas to the receptionist, Trumper and Bingo hurriedly walked down the corridor she had pointed too, hoping to avoid the Bone Cruncher and any awkward questions regarding their connection to Mad Tolly Butterworth.

"What was that you said about being a relative?" questioned Trumper, as he kept an eye open for the Lady Eradorn Wyvern ward. "You lied to the receptionist."

"I didn't say that we were relatives, just that we are very close and see her almost every day," grinned Bingo, with a mischievous expression on his face. "It really wasn't a lie because she comes to our house nearly every day to deliver the post."

"Good thinking," responded Trumper, laughing out loud. And Bingo, naturally, joined in too.

The boys easily found the turning that led into the Lady Eradorn Wyvern ward and then they cautiously entered, wary that the Bone Cruncher could be close-by. Bingo was the one who spotted the number thirteen first, and because no one made any attempt to stop them, the two boys marched right into Mad Tolly Butterworth's room. What they saw was the village post lady lying on a bed and it appeared as though she was still sleeping. Standing next to her, with his back to the door and scribbling something in a chart, was a short dark-haired man in a long white coat holding a stethoscope, who could only have been Dr Hari Banjani.

"Hello, aunty," announced Bingo, who was by far the better of the two boys when it came to all forms of deception and that, of course, included lying.

Hearing the boys enter, the doctor quickly turned around to behold Trumper and Bingo standing just inside the doorway. "Oh, hello again, I'm Dr Banjani. You're the boys I met last night. I was told that Ms Butterworth's family were coming to visit this afternoon, but never mind, I've just finished my examination, so now is a good a time as any."

Hariyani Banjani, which the doctor had conveniently shortened to Hari Banjani, who, the boys had briefly met for the first time the previous evening, had come to work in Dragonbutt at the behest of his cousin, Raji Banjani, not more than two years ago. Raji, who was a culinary entrepreneur of some repute, owned two of Dragonbutt's four gastronomical establishments. An award-winning Indian takeaway named Chilli Dilli, and the popular pizza takeaway and delivery service, Dragonbutt Hut, or 'Butt Hut' as it was called by the locals.

As a business partner to his cousin, in his spare time, the forty-two-year-old doctor could often be seen delivering pizzas and Indian takeaway around Dragonbutt and the surrounding district. And with an astute business mind, every Monday evening he ran Bollywood night at Dragonbutt Victory Hall, which was billed as a cultural celebration of music and dance. However, it did not go unnoticed by some that it was also a rather clever way for the Banjani's to promote their Indian takeaway, Chilli Dilli.

"Hello, Dr Banjani. My name is Trumper, and this is Bingo. So how is Mad, I mean, how is our aunty doing?"

"Physically, your aunty is fine, although she is suffering from shock and the loss of some blood from two small puncture wounds on her buttocks," explained Dr Banjani, using the official medical term for someone's butt. "It's her mental state that I am more concerned about."

With a smirk on both of their faces, Trumper and Bingo looked at each other; thinking that Mad Tolly Butterworth's mental state had nothing to do with being attacked by the little vampire, though the doctor, of course, could not be expected to know that.

"It sounds like our aunty's injuries are pretty much the same as those sustained by the Reverend Pinkerton and Mr Poly," stated Trumper, who knew that Dr Banjani had unknowingly confirmed what the boys already suspected, that Mad Tolly Butterworth was the little vampire's third victim.

"You know I'm not supposed to discuss the medical details of my other patients, but unofficially, both of them were bitten and had lost about a pint of blood, just like your aunty," replied the doctor, as he was never one for adhering to hospital protocol. "What was strange about all three though, was not only the fact that their attacker must have had two exceptionally long upper canines, it was that I found no trace of blood on any part of their body or clothing. However, I did find a significant quantity of saliva in close proximity to their wounds."

"Saliva," repeated Trumper, unsure why that was so. "Do you know whether they were bitten by the same assailant?"

"I found no medical evidence that would lead me to believe there was more than one," confirmed Dr Banjani, without any hesitation. "My preliminary analysis of the saliva from Ms Butterworth's wound is that it points to a positive match with the saliva found on the Reverend Pinkerton and Mr Poly."

"Dragonsbutts! So that means there really is only one vampire, Trumper, just like you thought. Therefore the other pair of feet must belong to his sidekick," chimed in Bingo, happy he was able to get a word in, at long last.

"Vampire!" exclaimed the doctor, looking somewhat confused. "Boys, as a medical professional, I can assure you that vampires don't exist. Once I perform some more DNA tests, I am sure we will be able to identify their attacker and in due course the reason why, bizarrely, he bites his victims. And once your aunty is her normal self again, she may be able to shed some light on this as well. All she does now is wake up periodically and laugh, and rather idiotically I may add."

Just as if Dr Banjani had given her a sign, Mad Tolly Butterworth suddenly opened both eyes, raised her head a few inches and laughed hysterically. It lasted only a few seconds, though it certainly startled the boys and the doctor too. When the laughing subsided, her head fell back onto the pillow, and then she slowly closed her eyes to return to a deep and peaceful sleep once again.

The boys roared with laughter, and Bingo howled, "Don't worry, Dr Banjani, our aunty always laughs like that. She's not called Mad Tolly Butterworth for nothing."

"Oh, she's one of those Butterworth's," proclaimed the doctor, who joined in with the boys and laughed heartily as well.

At that moment, a rather imposing well-dressed woman silently entered through the open doorway and due to all the laughter going on, she had to loudly clear her throat to gain the attention of the doctor.

"Good morning, Dr Banjani," began Detective Huntress, who looked undeniably stylish in her black leather jacket and perfectly coordinated dark grey trousers. "And you too, Trumper and Bingo, although after last night, I thought that your aunty and uncle would have kept you locked up for the rest of the Christmas holiday."

"Dragonsbutts! It's you, Detective Huntress. We just came here to see how Mad Tolly Butterworth was doing after being attacked by the little vampire last night," jabbered Bingo, rather unwisely as it turned out.

"Vampires again! We haven't discovered the identity of Ms Butterworth's attacker as of yet, so I would appreciate that you did not spread these type of alarmist rumours, especially those concerning imaginary creatures that most of the village seems to be obsessed with lately," insisted the detective, somewhat harshly in the boys' opinion. "As I said last night, vampires do not exist and never have, and the last thing I need is for you two boys to convince the rest of Dragonbutt that they do."

Trumper and Bingo did not say another word, although they both knew that the young detective could not have been more wrong. Vampires certainly existed in the past, and the boys believed that whoever was behind the three recent attacks in the village was a regular person by day and a bloodsucking vampire by night, just like they had read in the Entwhistle journals.

"Dr Banjani, I have a few questions for you and would prefer we spoke in private," continued Detective Huntress, not wanting the boys to be present at an official Dragonbutt police interview. "I was under the impression that visitations were for members of the patient's family only, and to my knowledge, these two are not related to Ms Butterworth."

The doctor was about to say to the boys, "I thought that you told me she was your aunty," when all of a sudden, Mad Tolly Butterworth opened her eyes again and sat up in bed. With a vacant expression on her face, which was not at all unusual for the post lady, and oblivious to the other four in the room, she looked directly in front of her and pointed at the wall, as if she could see something, although, in reality, nothing was actually there.

"Buh! Buh! Buh!" she spluttered, in a croaky sounding voice. And then she gave her onlookers another burst of one of those hysterical laughs she was so well known for, before collapsing onto a pillow and falling asleep once again.

Before the boys had time to contemplate what they had just witnessed, the familiar sound of cracking knuckles could be heard from the direction of the doorway. Knowing that the ominous sound could only have originated from one person, and that of course was the Bone Cruncher, Trumper and Bingo slowly and rather apprehensively turned around. Without saying a word, both of them gave a rather uncharacteristic weak-looking smile as they beheld the stern face of Staff Nurse Bone Cruncher Trudy Fanshaw.

"Out, the both of you!" she bellowed, with an expression that would have turned an average person's legs to jelly. "And I mean now!"

With their heads down and moving as silently as a couple of mice that had nearly been caught in a trap, Trumper and Bingo quickly exited Mad Tolly Butterworth's room and then walked back through the Lady Eradorn Wyvern ward, with the forbidding staff nurse between them. As they were marched down the corridor, the Bone Cruncher firmly held onto one arm of each boy, until the three of them had passed by the reception and were standing on the other side of the glass sliding doors.

Unyielding, the Bone Cruncher simply raised her powerful right arm, that every arm wrestler in the village had come to fear, and pointed away from Dragonbutt Community Hospital, a gesture that needed no further explanation. Trumper and Bingo knew that it was time to leave, and swiftly, so Bingo hurriedly untied Baxter's lead from the post where they had left him. The boys and the funny-looking dog then ran back up Old Dragonian Way, not daring to slow down until they had reached Upper Dragonbutt High Street.

"I really don't like her," fumed Bingo, who was now quite out of breath. "Anyway, my tummy is rumbling, so it's got to be nearly lunchtime. Let's go home because Old Mrs Dingle must have finished cooking the faggots by now."

"Good idea," agreed Trumper, a little hungry himself. Although he was also thinking about the words that Mad Tolly Butterworth had called out from her sleep. Was 'Buh! Buh! Buh!' just some nonsense the village post lady had been babbling, or was it an important clue that could reveal the identity of the little vampire and help the boys solve this mystery?

It took about twenty minutes of running and walking, then running some more, before Baxter and the boys arrived back at Twenty-Two Counting House Lane. On entering the little old house, as Trumper and Bingo pulled off their wellingtons and outdoor clothes, they immediately knew by the strong smell of cooked meat and onions that permeated the air, their eagerly anticipated lunch was already waiting for them.

Faggots had been one of Trumper and Bingo's favourites ever since Old Mrs Dingle had first served the boys her popular and much sought after dish. She always made her faggots the traditional way, with a mixture of pork belly and a good-sized pig's heart and liver, which the old lady coarsely minced and then mixed with diced onion and a variety of dried herbs. The mixture was then shaped into plum-sized balls and wrapped in bacon and fresh white breadcrumbs, before being baked in a hot oven until each faggot was juicy and cooked all the way through.

"I'm hungry," screeched Bingo, as he ran into the kitchen with Baxter still attached to his lead.

"You need to wash your hands before you eat, boys," replied Old Mrs Dingle, who, with a pair of well-worn oven gloves, was taking a tray of the hot steaming faggots out of the oven. "I'm going to feed Baxter first, with some cold faggots that I made earlier. But no need to worry, your lunch will be on the kitchen table in a couple of minutes."

Knowing that there would be no lunch for them until they had washed their hands, Trumper and Bingo speedily raced upstairs and into the bathroom. Once their hands were washed clean and towel-dried, they ran back down the stairs and entered the kitchen just as Old Mrs Dingle placed two large plates onto the kitchen table. Each plate was filled with what looked like half a dozen faggots, a mountain of mashed potatoes and a generous serving of mushy peas, which happened to be the way her late husband liked to eat his faggots and so the old lady always served them this way.

All that Trumper and Bingo needed now was for Old Mrs Dingle to pour a bucketful of her tasty homemade gravy over each of their plates, which she had made using the juices drained from the meaty faggots and a rather copious amount of Butts Batch. Once the gravy was poured and because apple juice happened to be the perfect accompaniment to faggots, the old lady took two bottles of Braithwaite's out of the fridge and then without a word passing their lips, the boys hungrily dug right into their hearty lunch.

"Finished," declared Bingo, after devouring his plate of faggots in what could not have been more time than it would take to hard boil an egg. "What are we having for dessert?"

"I do believe that you both like mince pies, so I have warmed up half a dozen that your aunty baked yesterday," answered the old lady, with a pleasing smile. "And I have some fresh whipped cream that I'm sure you will appreciate as well."

"Goodie," bellowed Bingo, because even though he was happy to have eaten two Choco Bombs that morning, he still felt a little disappointed that he had missed out on eating another of his favourites, the always irresistible, warm mince pies.

"Old Mrs Dingle, I keep forgetting to ask you something," announced Trumper, who to Bingo's delight had just polished off his last faggot, which meant that the boys' dessert could now be served. "It's about the night you came across Mr Poly on Pigswill Alley. If he was attacked on a Thursday night and your bingo evening is always every Wednesday, then what were you doing on Pigswill Alley last Thursday, and so late at night?"

"Let me think about that for a moment because my memory is not what it used to be," replied the old lady, looking hesitant and somewhat uncomfortable. "Oh, I remember now, Baxter was a little restless that night, and he needed to go for the call of nature, so I thought it would be a good idea if I took him for a walk along Pigswill Alley. It was a little late, I admit, but Baxter was so desperate to get out of the house, and that's his favourite place for walks, you know. Now, enough of that, let me serve your dessert, and then the two of you should go and play with Baxter in the garden again."

As soon as the boys had eaten all the warm mince pies along with plenty of fresh whipped cream and drank the last of their bottles of Braithwaite's, they thanked Old Mrs Dingle for the wonderful lunch, and then, after dressing for the cold wintry afternoon, Bingo attached the lead to Baxter's collar and the three of them left by the back door.

"That was weird," remarked Bingo, as the boys and the funny-looking dog walked down the long garden path. "She went on a late-night walk along Pigswill Alley because Baxter needed to go for the call of nature!"

"I agree, Bingo, it is rather strange," nodded Trumper, and although he could not say for sure, it looked to him as if the old lady was hiding something.

"Do you think that Old Mrs Dingle is the little vampire?" exclaimed

Bingo, although only half believing what he had just said. "She's definitely short, and we know she was on Pigswill Alley when Roly Poly was bitten. And don't forget she was with the Reverend Pinkerton during bingo night, just before he was attacked."

"She may be small, but I doubt she can outrun and overpower two fully grown men, not at her age," responded Trumper, just as he started to laugh. "Old Mrs Dingle walks slower than Boosey Dooley, and besides, she has no teeth of her own and always wears dentures."

Bingo, of course, could hardly contain himself and burst out laughing too, and then he asked, "So are we going to visit Bertie this afternoon?"

"Yes, Bingo, we certainly are," confirmed Trumper, remembering that he had some questions for Bertie Bovington.

"You don't think that Bertie knows something about the little vampire, do you?" inquired Bingo, who was curious to know why Trumper wanted to meet with his good friend and classmate.

"I'm not sure just yet, but that's what I plan to find out," disclosed Trumper, as he checked the time on his phone. "And for that matter, I would be interested in speaking with Flitcher Jenkins as well."

"Dragonsbutts! Are you serious?" shrieked Bingo, who could not believe his friends were involved in the recent vampire attacks that had already hospitalised two upstanding residents of the village and Mad Tolly Butterworth. "Then let's not hang around here, we need to head over to Bertie's house right now."

Twelve

Investigating Bertie

~✦~

"We're going over to the Bovingtons' house, Old Mrs Dingle, and we'll take Baxter with us," yelled Bingo, after opening the back door of the little old house.

"That's alright, boys, but make sure you bring Baxter home by three at the latest. And your uncle called to say he is leaving work a little early today and would like to have a talk with you both," called back the old lady, who was still busy in the kitchen.

"I hope that doesn't mean we are in trouble again," groaned Bingo, thinking they could be in for another telling-off. "Come on, Trumper, let's get going."

With its imposing chocolate coloured front door, the Bovingtons owned the largest house on Counting House Lane. At the centre of the door was a shiny polished brass plate with the number eleven clearly displayed and a large cast-iron door knocker that had been crafted long ago in the shape of a horizontal letter B. Even though only four people lived at Eleven Counting House Lane, the house had six large bedrooms, an expansive playroom for the children and a large glass conservatory that overlooked a sizeable split-level garden.

Over the years, Bingo had visited the house more times than he could remember to play with Bertie and Flitcher. Trumper, on the other hand, tended to shy away from number eleven, not that he had anything against Bertie, or even Flitcher for that matter, rather it was Bertie's sister he preferred to avoid because as everyone at Dragonbutt Primary School knew all too well, she had a bit of a thing for him.

As Bingo was the frequent visitor to Bertie's home, it was he who had the privilege of using the old Bovington door knocker to announce their presence. With a little encouragement from Trumper, Bingo rapped the heavy cast-iron knocker on the door three times and then one more for good luck. Unfortunately, on the fourth rap, the door flew open to reveal, not Bertie, but his infuriating elder sister, Bunty Bovington.

Bunty, like Trumper, was in year four at Dragonbutt Primary School and akin to her brother, had the dull blue eyes and straight black hair that both their parents shared, although unlike Bertie, Bunty's was long and always immaculately groomed. She was much taller than her younger brother and was not chubby at all, in fact, she was rather skinny for a Bovington, which was probably because of her dislike for all things sweet, especially the chocolate that had made Bovington's Sweets and Chocolates such a celebrated name.

"Dragonsbutts! Not another one," squawked Bunty, who looked noticeably annoyed as she glared at Bingo, apparently unaware that Trumper was standing at the younger boy's side. "My mum and dad are working in the store today, and I've been stuck at home looking after Bertie and that annoying Jenkins boy. They've been playing video games since ten this morning, and all I can hear from them is bang-bang-bang, boom-boom-boom, kill-kill-kill. It's driving me positively mad!"

"Can Bertie and Flitcher come out to play?" spluttered Bingo, as he was always a little nervous of Bertie's scary and profoundly domineering sister.

"Please take them with you," implored Bunty, who looked happier now that she was going to rid herself of her little brother and his irritating friend. "And as far as I'm concerned, the longer you are away from here, the better."

"Merry Christmas, Bunty," announced Trumper, trying to force a smile as he stepped into the open doorway.

"Oh, Trumper, I didn't see you there," replied Bunty, while blushing, and patting her long black hair. "Merry Christmas to you too and please come in. Would you like some hot chocolate, and I'm sure we have some of my mum's homemade chocolate cake somewhere around here."

"No, thank you, Bunty," answered Trumper right away, as he knew that Bingo, given half a chance, would no doubt accept Bunty's tempting offer of hot chocolate and a slice of cake. "Once Bertie and Flitcher are ready, we'll be on our way."

Feeling somewhat dejected, Bunty asked the boys to wait and then she walked down the long hallway to the foot of the stairs and yelled, "Bertie! Trumper and Bingo are here and want to play with you outside."

After hearing no reply, she charged up the stairs and could be heard shouting at Bertie and Flitcher. In a matter of seconds, they appeared, running down the stairs while grabbing their coats off the hooks in the hallway and pulling on their woollen gloves and DPS woolly hats. Before leaving the house, they hurriedly slipped their feet into the wellingtons that were waiting by the doorway, and then, howling, they dashed out of the front door, to the obvious delight of Bunty.

Forgetting to say goodbye to Bertie's sister, who was gazing longingly at Trumper, Bingo ran after his friends while still holding onto Baxter's lead, and Trumper followed shortly after. At the entrance to Counting House Lane, the boys and the funny-looking dog finally caught up with Bertie and Flitcher, who were leaning against the old street sign and cracking up with laughter.

"I hear it's a little vampire you're looking for now. Have you captured him yet?" sneered Bertie, somewhat sarcastically as Flitcher fell on the ground in stitches.

"Not yet, but don't worry, Bertie, Bingo and I will find out who the little vampire is soon enough," confirmed Trumper, while staring at Bertie Bovington rather intensely.

"I'm not the little vampire if that is what you mean," spluttered an indignant looking Bertie, who then looked down at Flitcher for support.

"But Bertie, that's exactly what the little vampire would say," chuckled Bingo, and then Flitcher, to Bertie's displeasure, nodded his head and laughed too.

Once the laughter had subsided, Trumper led the other three boys along Hunnickle Drive to Dragonbutt pond, and Baxter happily trotted beside them. The moment they arrived, Bingo unhooked the lead from the funny-looking dog's collar, and then all four boys sat down on one of the vacant wooden benches that had been there for as long as anyone could remember.

"I guess you heard that Mad Tolly Butterworth was attacked on Pigswill Alley last night?" stated Trumper, as he looked directly at Bertie. "It was the little vampire again, which means three people have now been attacked and bitten in the space of a week and a half."

"Oh yes, my mum's sister works at Dragonbutt Community Hospital and was on duty when Mad Tolly Butterworth was admitted, and so my parents told me all about it at breakfast," interrupted Flitcher, whose smile quickly vanished after glancing at an annoyed-looking Trumper and realising that the question was not meant for him.

"And I first learnt of it from Flitcher, when he came over to my house this morning," revealed Bertie, a little defensibly. "What of it?"

"So where were you last night, Bertie?" probed Trumper, thinking that this was just the line of questioning that Sherlock Holmes would have pursued.

"I was playing video games with Flitcher until late in the evening, and after he left I went straight to bed," retorted Bertie, looking decidedly uncomfortable as he averted his eyes from Trumper's scrutinising stare.

Trumper was about to ask another question when Flitcher abruptly chimed in, "But Bertie, don't forget that after I arrived home, you texted me to meet you at..." Although before he had a chance to finish, Bertie suddenly jabbed his elbow into Flitcher's ribs, which resulted in his friend yelping out in pain.

"That was another night, Flitcher," hissed Bertie, whose face appeared more than a little bit flushed. "Don't you remember?"

"Oh yes, I remember now," gulped Flitcher, who, to Trumper, did not sound at all convincing.

"Flitcher, if you went directly home after leaving Bertie's house last night, then what were you doing riding your bike along Pigswill Alley?" demanded Trumper, as he was eager to get to the bottom of Bertie and Flitcher's conflicting stories.

"Well, I must have got lost or something," uttered Flitcher, while sporting a vacant look on his face and looking towards Bertie for help.

Bingo, sensing that things were getting a little tense, pulled from his coat pocket a handful of the garlic lollies that he had taken out of his Dr Who backpack earlier that day. He offered them to everyone and immediately Trumper accepted, while Bertie just backed away with a resounding, "No." And though Flitcher held his hand out to accept one of the pungent-smelling treats, Bertie, quite forcibly, just pushed him away.

"Dragonsbutts! I forgot again. You know Bertie hates the smell of garlic, and if I'm to play with him I had to promise to never eat any," explained Flitcher, who really would have loved to taste one of the garlic lollies that Bingo had just returned to his coat pocket.

While Trumper smiled and muttered to himself, "That's interesting," Bingo focused wholeheartedly on sucking his garlic lolly. After an uncomfortable silence that lasted only a minute or two, Bertie, who by now was sitting on another wooden bench far from the garlic lolly sucking boys, suddenly announced, "Hey, who's hungry?"

When it came to food, as always, it was Bingo who answered first, with a loud and decidedly affirmative, "Yes, I am." Quickly followed by Flitcher, because he knew that Bertie most likely meant the four of them were about to receive a wonderfully decadent chocolaty treat.

"Great, let's go to Bovington's Sweets and Chocolates right now. My mum is working in the store today and will be happy to give us a snack to eat," offered Bertie, who really wanted to get out of the cold and avoid any more of Trumper's awkward questions.

Everyone agreed this was a good idea and that included Trumper, who, while still eager to discover what Bertie was hiding, believed he would not learn anything by questioning Bingo's friends further. As the four boys walked to the other side of Dragonbutt pond, Baxter, for some unexplained reason, preferred to stay close to Bertie and Flitcher, and so it was Flitcher who held the funny-looking dog by his lead as they ran down the narrow path that led to Pigswill Alley.

Once the five of them had clambered through the opening between the two old willow trees, they marched up Bristletooth Lane and passed by Dragonbutt Victory Hall before reaching the bustling hub of the village, Dragonbutt High Street. From there, it took them only a few minutes of brisk walking before they arrived at Bovington's Sweets and Chocolates to see Mrs Bovington standing behind the counter. Just outside the store, Flitcher tied Baxter's lead to a lamp post and then followed the others inside to savour the tantalising smells of the sweets and chocolates within.

"Oh, it's you, Bertie. I thought you were staying at home with Bunty today," exclaimed Mrs Bovington, as she walked over to greet her son and the rest of the boys. "And Merry Christmas, Flitcher, and you too, Trumper and Bingo."

Hildy Bovington was a cheerful soul and one of those rare types of people that almost everyone liked. A little short and rather plump, she was Dragonbutt born and had a big broad smile and happy go lucky personality. And like the rest of the Bovington family, she had dull blue eyes and straight black hair, although nowadays, hers was showing a little grey here and there.

"Merry Christmas, Mrs Bovington," rang the voices of Flitcher, Trumper and Bingo, who were all hungrily awaiting one of her delicious chocolate creations.

"It's really chilly outside, but luckily I have the perfect remedy for cold winter days," declared Mrs Bovington, while smiling sweetly at each one of them. "How about hot chocolate all-round and let me see what I have for you to eat. I'll be back in a jiffy so take a seat at the table by the window, and you can hang your coats on the coat stand next to the door."

Bovington's Sweets and Chocolates was not a large store, yet it did have room for three small square tables, each with four chairs. Besides making the best chocolate in the county, or as many would say, the whole country, the charming old store did make and sell a number of other things. A variety of sweets, including Trumper and Bingo's favourite, spollies, were all handmade by Mr Bovington himself, and a small selection of scrumptious chocolate cakes and biscuits were baked daily by Mrs Bovington.

Christmas was always an exceptionally busy time for Dragonbutt's renowned chocolate and sweet shop. This meant that Bertie's father,

Henley Bovington, when not in the kitchen creating the chocolates he was so famous for and his mouthwatering sweets, was out making deliveries in his distinctive chocolate coloured van. This often left his wife to take care of the store and its customers and of course the all-important Christmas orders.

"Here you go, boys," announced Mrs Bovington, as she walked back into the store with a large tray. "Four large mugs of steaming hot chocolate with fresh whipped cream, and I also added some of my special caramel sauce. I hope you are all hungry because I have a chocolate lava cake for each of you. I've just taken them out of the oven, so please be careful, they're piping hot."

Each of the boys wasted no time in thanking Mrs Bovington at length, and all of them agreed that it was a marvellous idea of Bertie's to visit Bovington's Sweets and Chocolates on such a cold day. Bertie smiled, and simply said, "Thanks mum," and then Bingo eagerly stuck his spoon into the lava cake and watched the hot Bovington's chocolate ooze out of the steaming sponge.

"Wow, how do you get the melted chocolate inside the cake, Mrs Bovington?" asked Bingo, thinking it was such a clever thing to do.

"It's just magic, Bingo," chuckled Mrs Bovington, as she walked back to the kitchen. "And a good magician never reveals her tricks."

Although there was actually no magic involved, Hildy Bovington did use a little trick that she had never revealed to anyone, and that included her husband. To begin with, she baked the cakes in her oven and then let them cool before cutting a deep hole in the bottom of each. Then, she inserted a generous chunk of creamy Bovington's chocolate and sealed the hole with the piece of cake that had previously been removed. All it took after that was fifteen seconds in the microwave to create her delightful chocolate lava cakes, with their moreish hot melted chocolate centre, that all her customers loved so much.

By the time the boys had finished their hot chocolate and lava cake, their hands and faces were splattered with the luscious Bovington's chocolate. Bingo, as usual, looked the worst, after he insisted on picking up his plate and licking every last drop of the melted chocolate, most of which ended up on his face. Fortunately, Hildy Bovington was used to feeding messy young boys and had wisely placed a box of moist wipes in the centre of the boys' table.

"Please use the wipes to clean yourselves, and I have something for each of you before you leave. Just wait here, and I will be back in a few minutes," promised Mrs Bovington, as she helped Bingo wipe the remaining Bovington's chocolate from his face.

"Bertie, while we're waiting for your mum, I have another question for you," asked Trumper, who was looking directly at Bingo's short chubby friend once again. "Where were you on the night that Roly Poly was attacked?"

"Dragonsbutts! I can't remember that far back," exclaimed Bertie, shrugging his shoulders and looking ill at ease with Trumper's question.

"The attack on Roly Poly was only last Thursday," countered Trumper, trying his best to push Bertie for an answer. "Surely, you can remember where you were four nights ago?"

"Oh, I know where Bertie and I were on Thursday night," chimed in Flitcher, who had his hand raised as if Trumper had asked a question in a school quiz. Unfortunately for Flitcher, he did not have time to answer before Bertie savagely kicked one of his legs, which silenced him almost immediately after howling out, "Ah, that hurt!"

"I hope you like Choco Bombs, boys," beamed Mrs Bovington, while walking over to their table. "Mr Bovington had to whip up a fresh batch earlier today because the unsold Choco Bombs he made yesterday all mysteriously disappeared."

"What do you mean, Mrs Bovington?" questioned Trumper, thinking that although missing Choco Bombs were not the most pressing matter at the present time, he was still a little intrigued.

"Well, Mr Bovington is sure he had a tray of Choco Bombs leftover after he locked up on Sunday evening, but when he arrived at the store this morning they were nowhere to be found," explained Mrs Bovington, who was handing each of the boys a Choco Bomb and one extra for Bingo, on the condition that it was for Baxter and not him. "And you know, that's not the first time we've had Choco Bombs go missing lately."

Before Trumper had a chance to ask another question, Bertie, looking decidedly uncomfortable, abruptly stood up and said, "Thanks for the snacks, mum, but we have to go now. Come on, Flitcher." And with that, Bertie and Flitcher quickly pulled on their coats and DPS woolly hats, then without uttering another word; they hurriedly scurried out the store.

The boys just looked at each other in silence for a few moments, both thinking the same thing, that Bertie and Flitcher were surely hiding something. What it was, Trumper certainly suspected, although Bovington's Sweets and Chocolates was not the place to discuss such things, so they said goodbye and Merry Christmas to Mrs Bovington and thanked her again for the treats she had kindly given them. Once they were dressed in their coats, DPS woolly hats and warm woollen gloves, they marched out of the store to see Baxter sitting obediently by the lamp post where Flitcher had left him.

"Here you go, boy. We have a Choco Bomb for you," announced Bingo, while taking a bite out of his own. "Trumper, why didn't you ask Bertie and Flitcher about the night that the Reverend Pinkerton was attacked?"

"Because it is patently clear that Bertie was lying to us about where he was last night, and he obviously does not want to reveal where he was last Thursday night either. Flitcher evidently knows everything, but Bertie does not want him to tell," answered Trumper, thinking everything through carefully. "Therefore, pressing him to disclose his whereabouts on the night of the first attack won't get us any closer to discovering the truth."

"Maybe we should talk to Flitcher when he is alone because he's more likely to spill the beans when Bertie is not with him," suggested Bingo, after finishing his Choco Bomb and licking the remains of the chocolate and raspberry from his fingers.

"I don't think that will do us any good, Bingo," replied Trumper, while placing the Choco Bomb in his coat pocket, as a snack for later. "Bertie is undeniably the cleverer and more devious of the two and seems to have some sort of control over Flitcher. Don't forget, you know as well as I that Flitcher is a few chips short of a butty, and not only that, he's only a C-grade student at Dragonbutt Primary School."

"He got a B at sports," insisted Bingo, feeling somewhat obligated to defend his friend and classmate.

"Bingo, everyone gets at least a B at sports, and if you catch Puffer Hendrick vaping on school grounds and don't tell on him, then you can get an A," laughed Trumper, as he beckoned to Bingo to start their walk home.

"So that's how Chomper Baverstock Junior got his A. I thought it was odd because he barely moves at all during sports classes," chuckled Bingo, who had untied Baxter from the lamp post and was now walking along Dragonbutt High Street with Trumper.

"Exactly," acknowledged Trumper, eager to return to the little old house.

"What do you think this all means?" beseeched Bingo, as he was finding it difficult to comprehend that his two friends, who he had known for most of his life, had something to do with the three vampire attacks in Dragonbutt.

"It means that by day, Bertie and Flitcher may appear to be just two normal Dragonbutt boys, however, by night I believe that Bertie transforms into a little vampire and Flitcher accompanies him as his loyal sidekick," confirmed Trumper, feeling quite pleased with himself that he had ascertained the identity of the little vampire they had been searching for these past few days.

"Dragonsbutts! Are you sure, Trumper? I've never seen Bertie bite anyone, except the time Mad Maddox tried to give him a wedgie at school, and that was understandable," responded Bingo, as he slowly shook his head. "What makes you think Bertie is the little vampire and, of all people, Flitcher his sidekick?"

"Don't you see, Bingo, it's obvious," asserted Trumper, while grinning and thinking that this must be one of those Sherlock Holmes types of moments. "Firstly, Bertie is definitely short for his age, and as we both know the vampire has to be little because he never bites his victims on the neck, instead, he always bites their butt. Secondly, he is positively repulsed by the smell of garlic, just like most vampires, and that is the reason he will not allow Flitcher to eat any. Then, there are the first two victims who heard two pairs of feet, yet they only saw one pair of glowing red eyes before being bitten, so that means there must be an accomplice. Also, both of them live close to Pigswill Alley, and we even caught Flitcher there last night, just before Mad Tolly Butterworth was attacked. And don't forget that Bertie has not told us the truth about his whereabouts on the night of each attack. So Bertie has to be the little vampire, which means Flitcher must be his sidekick. Oh yes, and there's one more thing."

"And what's that, Trumper?" pleaded Bingo, who now believed that Trumper might just be right.

"There was a witness during the third attack that saw everything and knows the true identity of the little vampire," smiled Trumper, seeing that Bingo was quite taken aback.

"I don't remember anything about a witness; the only person at the scene of the attack was Mad Tolly Butterworth, and she was the victim," stressed Bingo, clueless to who Trumper was referring too.

"Precisely," stated Trumper, who was secretly pleased he had unravelled an important clue that Bingo had missed. "Mad Tolly Butterworth was the witness, and she gave us the identity of the little vampire this morning when we visited her at Dragonbutt Community Hospital. I didn't realise it at first, but it came to me a moment ago when I was thinking about something she uttered."

"What! When did she tell us anything?" roared Bingo, getting somewhat agitated. "The only thing I remember her doing was laughing like a crazy lady and mumbling something quite bizarre."

"She said 'Buh! Buh! Buh!'," responded Trumper looking triumphantly at Bingo. "I now believe she saw her attacker and although still in shock this morning, she attempted to reveal his name. You see what Mad Tolly Butterworth was really trying to say was Bertie! Bertie! Bertie! So now we know that the little vampire is without a shadow of a doubt, Bertie Bovington."

"Dragonsbutts! Good detective work, Trumper," declared Bingo, who was now convinced that the little vampire they had been hunting was Bertie after all and his sidekick was none other than Flitcher Jenkins. "What should we do now?"

"It's already a quarter past three so let's run the rest of the way home and then we can tell Uncle P all about what we have unearthed," replied Trumper, as he started to run as fast as he could towards Counting House Lane with Bingo and Baxter following close behind.

Thirteen

Back at Counting House Lane

"Old Mrs Dingle, we're home," yelled Bingo, as he unlocked and then opened the bright red front door with the shiny brass number twenty-two.

Before Trumper and Bingo had time to take their wellingtons off, the old lady rushed out of the kitchen and into the hallway. With an anxious expression on her face and a sense of urgency in the tone of her voice, she said, "Boys, you were supposed to be back by three, and it's already three-thirty. I need to take Baxter home right away because it's going to get dark soon. Oh, and your uncle is already here, and he has that young Barry Beasley with him in the living room."

Without saying anything more, Old Mrs Dingle took the lead from Bingo's outstretched hand and hastily led Baxter out of the little old house, to trudge the short distance back to her own home at the entrance to Counting House Lane.

"Dragonsbutts! She was in a hurry," grumbled Bingo, who was a little irritated with the old lady's disposition that afternoon. "And she didn't even say Merry Christmas to us."

Once Trumper had closed the front door, the boys placed their wellingtons on the now barely recognisable copy of the Dragonbutt Smoker and then took off their DPS woolly hats and warm woollen gloves before hanging their coats on the hooks in the hallway. As they walked towards the living room, Trumper and Bingo nervously looked at each other and then, hoping their uncle was no longer angry after their little escapade the previous evening, they warily opened the door before walking in.

"Ah, Trumper, at last, and I see that Bingo is with you." announced Uncle P, while greeting the boys with a smile as they entered the living room.

"We're sorry about last night, Uncle P," uttered Trumper, with Bingo repeating the same words only a second or two later.

"Forget about that, boys," continued Uncle P, as he waved his hand to one side as if to say it was no longer important. "I've invited Barry over to the house so that you can tell us everything you have learnt about the vampire attacks, and then hopefully we can have this whole mess cleared up in no time at all."

"Oh, that's great," answered Trumper, a little surprised yet definitely pleased that his uncle was not going to give them another telling-off.

"Hello again, boys," beamed Barry, in his usual friendly tone of voice. "I understand from your uncle that it was the two of you who came across Mad Tolly Butterworth, just after she was attacked last night on Pigswill Alley. I'd love to hear about what you saw and anything else you have uncovered since we last spoke."

After Trumper and Bingo had made themselves comfortable on the sofa, Trumper disclosed all that they had found out over the past couple of days. He spoke about the Entwhistle journals and their revealing meetings with the Reverend Pinkerton and Roly Poly. Then he went on to explain how they had surprised Flitcher Jenkins on Pigswill Alley just before coming across Mad Tolly Butterworth. And finally, he told them about their short but insightful visit to Dragonbutt Community Hospital that very morning.

"That's interesting," declared Barry, who was noticeably impressed with what the boys had discovered in such a short amount of time. "You reckon we're dealing with a little vampire then, and that's why all three victims were bitten on the butt. And you think that this little vampire is one of us, a resident of Dragonbutt by day and at night he transforms into a bloodsucker. Yes, it all makes perfect sense, and you believe he has a weak-minded accomplice as well, or sidekick, as you like to call him."

"That must be Boosey Dooley," sniggered Uncle P, making fun of the boastful landlord he loved to tease.

Barry smiled at Uncle P yet continued talking, "I tried to speak with Mad Tolly Butterworth this afternoon, but unfortunately I had another run-in with the Bone Cruncher, and so I didn't get the chance to interview her or Dr Banjani."

"Same here, we bumped into her this morning, although I managed to get us into Mad Tolly Butterworth's room, and we even got to speak with Dr Banjani," blurted out Bingo, who knew that this was quite an accomplishment.

"Well done, Bingo, it takes a fearless man to get past Staff Nurse Bone Cruncher Trudy Fanshaw when she is on duty at Dragonbutt Community Hospital," noted Uncle P, with an air of pride.

"Were you able to ascertain anything that may help us root out our little vampire?" probed Barry, as he was itching to hear more.

"Better than that," announced Trumper, looking pleased with himself. "We already know the identity of the little vampire and his sidekick."

"Dragonsbutts! You do. Who are they?" exclaimed Uncle P, who was clearly startled by Trumper's announcement.

"Bertie Bovington and Flitcher Jenkins," stated Trumper, with a corroboratory nod from Bingo.

"You mean Henley and Hildy Bovington's son, the small chubby one who is in the same class as Bingo at Dragonbutt Primary School?" asked Uncle P, in utter disbelief. "And if I'm not mistaken, Flitcher Jenkins is that curly-haired boy who lives on Flamingo Crescent, the one whose light always seems to be on but there is rarely anyone at home."

"Yes, the very same," replied Trumper, with confidence. "Mad Tolly Butterworth told us the little vampire's name this very morning, or at least she tried to by calling out 'Buh! Buh! Buh!', but we believe she was actually trying to say, Bertie! Bertie! Bertie! And we also know that Bertie and Flitcher have been hiding something and won't tell us where they were when each of the attacks took place. Oh, and to top it off, Bertie refused to accept a garlic lolly from Bingo, and he wouldn't let Flitcher have one either, even though, as everyone knows, no kid can ever resist a garlic lolly."

"Dragonsbutts! If you're right, Trumper, and I have every reason to believe that you are, then, what do you propose we do to capture this little vampire?" implored Barry, quite solemnly. "We can hardly force our way into the Bovingtons' house and accuse their young son of attacking three of Dragonbutt's residents, biting the butt of each and drinking their blood. If that ever happened, we would all be on the front page of the Dragonbutt Smoker after being arrested and locked up in the cells at Dragonbutt Police Station."

"I agree with Barry," added Uncle P, as he rose from his armchair. "What we really need to do is catch this little vampire in the act of attacking another of his victims. But the problem is we don't know where he will strike next and when."

Trumper had already thought about that very issue, and so he explained to Barry and his uncle that because all the previous attacks had taken place on Pigswill Alley, he did not believe the little vampire would move away from his favourite stomping ground to hunt in a different part of the village. Pigswill Alley was very dark, and only a few people ever walk there late at night, which meant it was the perfect place for a vampire to bite someone and drink their blood without getting caught. Besides, it was only a short walk from Bertie's home on Counting House Lane, and that made it not only the ideal location for the little vampire to hunt for his victims but also a very convenient one to go for a quick bite.

Having identified where the next attack was likely to take place, the only other question was when? Although Trumper could not be certain, the attacks were definitely increasing in frequency, and so he believed another attack could take place very soon. Tonight, he told the others, was therefore as good a night as any to set a trap and catch the little vampire. All they needed to do now was gather up a band of hardy vampire hunters to stake out Pigswill Alley that very evening. And of course, they would need a volunteer to act as the bait, to lure out the little vampire before he had a chance to bite another unwitting resident of Dragonbutt.

"Sounds good to me, although before we go, I have a couple of questions," chimed in Bingo, who was excited that they were about to embark on another vampire hunt. "Bertie is my classmate, so when we capture the little vampire, can I be the one who stakes him?"

"Bingo, apart from the fact that Bertie is supposed to be your friend, he has not seriously injured anyone and so nobody is going to be staked tonight, and that includes the little vampire," beseeched Uncle P, rather firmly so that the young boy understood.

"Alright," muttered Bingo, who was clearly disappointed by his uncle's reaction. "So, Trumper, where are we going to find someone gullible enough to be our vampire bait?"

With a furtive grin, Trumper said, "Bingo, the question you should really be asking yourself is where are we going to find a brave vampire hunter that wants to save the residents of Dragonbutt from the little vampire and in return would like to receive a whole lot of Choco Bombs as a reward?"

"Dragonsbutts! That sounds like me," confirmed Bingo, while greedily thinking more about the Choco Bombs than the danger involved in being the bait for the little vampire. "How many do I get?"

"You can have one Choco Bomb tonight, after we've eaten dinner, and Father Christmas will bring you a stocking full of them on Christmas Eve. As long as we capture the little vampire that is," promised Trumper, at the same time giving Uncle P a sly wink.

"Then you can count me in," smiled Bingo, as he thought about the number of Choco Bombs that Father Christmas could fit into his stocking.

"Trumper, who do you have in mind to join this band of vampire hunters?" queried Barry, who looked nearly as impatient as Bingo to start hunting for the little vampire.

Following a few moments of intense contemplation, Trumper named his band of courageous vampire hunters. All of them, he pointed out, needed to be believers in the old legends and the Dragonbutt prophecy, so they had to be Dragonbutt born. The others agreed, and then he explained that it was brains and brawn that was needed and not numbers because too many could scare the little vampire away.

In addition to the four that were seated in the living room, he named the strapping Angus Hogswood as one who would never doubt the existence of the little vampire and the muscle they most definitely needed. Everyone agreed that Angus was an outstanding choice and then Trumper revealed the sixth and last member of their plucky band. And to everyone's surprise, it was none other than Mad Maddox Butterworth.

"Dragonsbutts! Mad Maddox," wailed Bingo, in utter astonishment.

153

"Of all the people you could have chosen, why him?"

Trumper disclosed that he had not picked Mad Maddox willy-nilly or simply because he was Dragonbutt born, instead, he had a special task for the Dragonbutt Primary School student. What that was, Trumper did not reveal, although he did imply that it had something to do with the vampire trap he had only just then devised. Furthermore, being a Butterworth, Mad Maddox was renowned for being more than a little bit crazy, and for a dangerous vampire hunt that was not such a bad thing.

"How about I inform Dragonbutt police we intend to hunt for the little vampire tonight?" proposed Barry, who was concerned their band of vampire hunters were perhaps a little too few in number. "Because of the attacks, I understand that Detective Huntress is on duty every night this week."

"I think we should leave Dragonbutt police out of this for now," suggested Uncle P, believing Detective Huntress would be none too pleased. "We can call her after we capture the little vampire and not before, besides, a police siren would more than likely deter him from going anywhere near Pigswill Alley."

"That makes sense," acknowledged Barry, although he still wanted to ensure they took every precaution. "However, someone should really contact Dragonbutt Community Hospital because if we do manage to capture the little vampire tonight, we will probably need a tranquilliser to restrain him."

"Splendid idea, Barry," exclaimed Uncle P, with a grin aimed directly at the young reporter. "I'll contact the Bone Cruncher because she's Dragonbutt born and will understand, and I will let her know that tonight she needs to be prepared for our call."

"I'm glad it's you contacting her and not me," grimaced Barry, as he glanced at Uncle P. "She still scares me to death, but I think it's good to have her in reserve. The Bone Cruncher has the strongest right arm in all of Dragonbutt, so if she can't subdue this little vampire, then no one can."

"Good, then that's all settled," affirmed Trumper, wary that they had a number of things to do before setting the vampire trap, including, of course, their dinner. "Uncle P, you call the Bone Cruncher, and Barry, can you go to the Hogswood Piggery and pick up Angus Hogswood while I text Mad Maddox. It's four-thirty now, so all six of us should meet in the Dragonbutt Arms at eight sharp. Oh yes, and before I forget, everyone should bring a torch because it will be dark on Pigswill Alley, even with the moonlight."

Now that everyone understood what they had to do, Barry hauled himself out of the comfortable armchair he was sitting in and pulled on his black leather jacket and gloves before leaving the warmth of the little old house. He said his goodbyes and shouted, "See you all at eight." And then he jumped into his new Mini Cooper convertible with its racing green trim to drive to the Hogswood Piggery on the outskirts of the village.

"So what are we having for dinner tonight?" demanded Bingo, whose tummy had just started to rumble, which he knew was a tell-tale sign that dinnertime must be fast approaching.

"That's a good question, Bingo," answered Uncle P, who had only enough time to grab a cold sandwich for lunch and by now was getting a little hungry. "We have a long night ahead of us and are going to need all the strength we can muster, so let's order a takeaway from Chilli Dilli."

"Goodie," yelled Bingo, as he was always partial to a takeaway for the simple reason you can order as much food as you want. "I love Indian food, as long as it's not the spicy kind because I really don't like spicy!"

"You love all food," laughed Uncle P, and so did Trumper. "Don't worry, Bingo, the cooks at Chilli Dilli already know you don't like spicy."

155

At that moment, the creaky front door opened and then they all heard Aunty J's voice cry out, "Hello, anyone at home yet."

Uncle P called back, "In here, darling," and then their aunty walked into the living room after taking off her coat and leather zip-up knee-length boots.

"What a day," exclaimed Aunty J, as she sat down in the armchair recently vacated by Barry Beasley. "I can never understand why people wait so long to visit the dentist. And that reminds me, with the number of mince pies, cakes and sweets that you boys have been eating lately, I would like to give you a check-up and cleaning before you go back to school in the New Year."

"Do we have too?" sighed Bingo, since he was not what you would call a fan of visiting the dentist, even if it was his aunty.

"Yes, you do," barked Aunty J, who was all too accustomed to Bingo's protests regarding any type of dental treatment. "Don't forget I had to fill two of your teeth last summer due to all the sugary snacks that you and Trumper had eaten. Anyway, what have you boys been up to today? Your uncle has already filled me in regarding his meeting with Detective Huntress, and although you should have been in your beds last night, he said that you did the right thing by calling nine-nine-nine after coming across Mad Tolly Butterworth."

"Nothing much, Aunty J. We've just been playing with Baxter for most of the day," beamed Trumper, while crossing two of his fingers behind his back, the big one and the one he always used for pointing. Because he didn't think his aunty would appreciate hearing about what he and Bingo had really been up to.

Uncle P announced to his wife that he was just about to order a takeaway from Chilli Dilli, which she thought was a thoroughly excellent idea. Bingo was the first to make his request, a mild chicken tikka masala with two onion bhajees on the side, and Trumper said he would have the same. Aunty J wanted lamb madras, which was spicy, but not too much for her. And finally, their uncle ordered the spiciest dish on the menu, king prawn vindaloo, as it was known for its heat and therefore a good choice on a cold winter's day, or so he thought.

Hungry for his dinner, Uncle P picked up the phone and called Chilli Dilli to order the evening meal. In addition to everything he had written down, he requested four large garlic naans. Because everyone who has ever eaten Indian food knows all too well; naans are one of those essential accompaniments that you simply cannot do without. And before he had a chance to hang up the phone, Bingo enthusiastically reminded him they would also need plenty of crunchy poppadoms. The delicious snack he would have undoubtedly eaten by the dozen if only that decision had been his to make.

Chilli Dilli's busy owner, Raji Banjani, took their order and told Uncle P that he should expect the takeaway to arrive within the hour. This would allow the boys' time to prepare themselves for the vampire hunt later that evening. Meanwhile, their uncle would have to do the unenviable task of informing Aunty J of their plan, something that Trumper and Bingo were more than happy for him to do on his own.

As Uncle P spoke to their aunty, the boys quietly exited the living room and pulled on their coats and DPS woolly hats in the hallway. Once they were dressed again, they slipped into their wellingtons by the back door and then ran down the long garden path to the red-brick shed, whereupon Trumper unlocked the door, and the two of them stepped inside. Bingo switched on the light and immediately opened his Dr Who backpack to ensure everything they would need for the vampire hunt was there. He then took the remaining garlic lollies out of the backpack and placed them in his coat pocket, telling Trumper they would be safer with him.

"Make sure the holy water pistols are filled to their brim," stressed Trumper, who was unwilling to take any chances that evening. "And don't forget what Uncle P said about not harming the little vampire.

That means we won't need the wooden stakes and mallet, so you can leave them here."

Disappointed that he would not be allowed to run a stake through the little vampire, grudgingly, Bingo pulled the wooden stakes and mallet out of his Dr Who backpack and placed them on the floor. As a little of the holy water had already leaked out, he carefully topped up each holy water pistol while spilling only a little of the precious liquid that was so harmful to vampires. Once he was done, the young boy zipped up the backpack and slung it over his right shoulder. Both of the boys then made their way out of the red-brick shed, and Bingo, who was the last to leave, locked the door. They had not walked more than ten paces though, before Bingo exclaimed, "Sorry, Trumper, I forgot to turn the light off."

"You were the last to leave, so it was your responsibility to switch off the light," berated Trumper, annoyed that Bingo was not more responsible.

"Don't worry, I'll go back and turn it off," replied Bingo, who, in Trumper's opinion, looked a little too eager to correct his mistake. "You go up to the house, and I'll meet you there."

By the time Trumper had reached the little old house, Bingo had all but caught up with him. Along with his Dr Who backpack, which now looked decidedly heavier, he was also carrying the sturdy plastic container of holy water that the Reverend Pinkerton had given them the previous day. Before Trumper got the chance to ask him why he had brought the extra holy water and what else had he placed in his backpack, the boys heard their aunty calling to say that dinner was on the table. And with that, the thought of the holy water and Bingo's heavy backpack was all but forgotten in Trumper's overly preoccupied mind.

Two things were obvious to the boys when they sat down at the kitchen table. First of all, there was the wonderful smell of Indian food that filled the kitchen, which meant they were clearly in for an exotic and thoroughly yummy treat. And then there was an unusually quiet and solemn-looking Uncle P, sitting at the end of the table. This could mean only one thing, that he had been brave enough to speak to Aunty J about their pending vampire hunt and was now in the doghouse, a term they had often heard their aunty use. Bingo, not wanting to let the tense situation get in the way of his dinner, immediately placed a large poppadom in his mouth and bit into it. This resulted in a loud crunching sound that cut through the air and finally broke the uncomfortable silence in the little old house.

"I have already told your uncle that I don't approve of the two of you going on this ridiculous vampire hunt," snapped Aunty J, who looked extremely displeased with her husband. "Saying all that, he has convinced me that you will be safe and under his supervision at all times. Therefore, if allowing you to accompany your uncle will get this absurd notion out of your heads that a vampire is responsible for these horrendous attacks then I will permit you to go, but only this once."

"Hurrah!" shrieked Bingo, jubilant that his aunty had come to her senses. Although in return he just received one of those 'don't you dare go there' kinds of glares.

With that all settled, Trumper reached across the table and helped himself to one of the poppadoms, just as Bingo was polishing off his second and would have eaten another but for the fact that his aunty had said he could only eat two and no more. While the younger boy liked to gobble them plain in half a dozen enormous bites, Trumper preferred to place a large dollop of mango chutney on each piece before popping the scrumptious savoury snack into his mouth.

As the others were eating their poppadoms, Bingo wasted no time by starting on his first onion bhajee, which was crunchy on the outside and soft on the inside, and although it was a little bit spicy, the young boy did not hesitate to eat another. "They were yummy," he wailed, after swallowing the last mouthful of his second onion bhajee. "Do we have anything to drink?"

"Oh, silly me, I completely forgot about the drinks," confessed Aunty J, who immediately leapt from her chair, walked across the kitchen to the fridge, and returned with four bottles of Braithwaite's and a glass for each of them.

Once the poppadoms and the boys' onion bhajees were all gone, their main course followed with Bingo being the lucky one because he was served first. Aunty J piled the steaming chicken tikka masala onto his plate along with two large spoonfuls of fragrant basmati rice, which always accompanied one of Chilli Dilli's mouthwateringly delectable curries. Uncle P then handed him one of the large garlic naans that he yearned for so much and choosing not to wait for the others, he tucked right in.

Not surprisingly, it was their uncle with his king prawn vindaloo that was the last to finish. To the amusement of everyone, he had a flushed face and beads of sweat were rolling down his forehead and into his eyes, so many, in fact, that he had to use his large white handkerchief to wipe them away.

"A tad too spicy for you, dear?" smiled Aunty J, thinking that her husband deserved to suffer a little for encouraging the boys with all his talk of monsters from those made-up stories in the old Entwhistle journals.

"Not at all," winced Uncle P, as he poured the last of the Braithwaite's into his glass and then drank it all in one titanic gulp. "Although another bottle of Braithwaite's would be very much appreciated."

Aunty J and the boys all laughed because everyone in Dragonbutt knew Chilli Dilli used a four-star scale to rank the spiciness of their dishes. One to three indicated; mild, medium and hot, but four, which was reserved for only the bravest to order, was dragonfire hot, and their uncle's vindaloo was as spicy as dragonfire hot can possibly get.

As soon as their dinner was over, the boys and Uncle P waited patiently for their dessert. With no time to bake another batch of mince pies, their aunty had popped into Fanshaw's after work to pick up another of Trumper and Bingo's favourites. So without much ado, she placed one of Wilimina Fanshaw's adored and extremely sought after Battenberg cakes onto the kitchen table.

After clearing away the dishes, Aunty J gave each of them a large slice of the colourful Battenberg cake and another bottle of Braithwaite's, which was certainly a welcome sight for Uncle P as he was still glowing from the aftermath of eating one of Chilli Dilli's extra spicy vindaloos. With its distinctive pink and yellow squares, wrapped in a thick layer of yummy sweet marzipan, Fanshaw's Battenberg cake was a delightful treat that when offered a second slice, Trumper and Bingo could never refuse. So when their aunty handed them another piece of the exquisite cake, they were both overjoyed and accepted without the slightest hesitation.

"Thanks for the cake, Aunty J. It's time for me to change my clothes before we head out," announced Bingo, as he slapped his tummy and abruptly walked out of the kitchen and into the hallway, whereby he picked up the container of holy water and loudly climbed the stairs.

That was odd, thought Trumper to himself, as Bingo was never one to change into clean clothes without first being nagged by their aunty. And then, about ten minutes later, the young boy trudged back down the stairs, somewhat slowly for him, and walked into the living room where Trumper and Uncle P were now sitting.

"Dragonsbutts!" cried out Trumper, while staring at Bingo. "What on earth are you wearing?"

Bingo gave a smirk that broadened into an expansive smile before answering, "I'm not stupid, you know. Everybody that has been attacked by the little vampire was bitten on the butt. But that won't happen to me. I'm not going to have my butt bitten by anyone!"

"But what have you done to yourself?" asked Trumper, just as Aunty J entered the living room to see the prodigious bulge around Bingo's butt. "It looks like you're about to explode."

The young boy smiled once again and said, "Can't you see that I am wearing my running bottoms, the ones that are elasticated and expand the more I eat. And underneath, there are two of my old pull-up nappies that I never used, which have been sitting in my underwear drawer for years."

"I'm glad they have never been used, but how will two pull-up nappies prevent the little vampire from biting your butt?" inquired Trumper, thinking Bingo was sounding as crazy as Mad Maddox.

"Ah, that's the clever bit," revealed Bingo, as he grinned from ear to ear. "I soaked the nappies in holy water then placed them in a plastic bag and taped the bag to my butt. So if the little vampire tries to bite me tonight, he's going to have the surprise of his life when he gets a mouthful of holy water instead."

Everyone laughed, including Aunty J, and Trumper could not help but agree that Bingo's idea was certainly an original one. Although it did make him look quite funny as he waddled around with a butt that would have been more suited to Boosey Dooley than a young boy of six.

"Alright, boys, it's time for us to go," declared their uncle, after checking the time on his wristwatch. "Wrap up warm, and that means coats, woolly hats and woollen gloves. And I have a torch for each of us, which you should keep with you at all times."

"Bingo. Trumper and your uncle already have phones, and you should have one as well, so take mine," insisted Aunty J, as she pulled a phone from her bag and handed it to him. "Now, don't forget to keep them turned on as I may want to call you."

"Of course, dear," nodded Uncle P, while checking his own phone.

"Oh, dragonsbutts! My battery is getting low. Anyhow, it will have to do. Trumper, how's the battery on yours?"

"Mine is nearly full," replied Trumper, after quickly glancing at his phone. "Shall we take the short-cut to the Dragonbutt Arms?"

"No, let's avoid Pigswill Alley for now and, instead, walk along Hunnickle Drive. Although it's still early, we don't want to take a chance and bump into the little vampire without Barry and the others," responded Uncle P, as he entered the hallway to retrieve his coat and gloves.

"Hey, I haven't had my Choco Bomb yet," pleaded Bingo, who was clearly not going to take another step without the Choco Bomb he had been promised.

"Sorry, Bingo, here you go," answered Trumper, while taking the Choco Bomb from his coat pocket and handing it to the smiling Bingo, just as the young boy pulled the rather heavy looking Dr Who backpack over his shoulders.

Now that the three of them were ready to depart, they said their goodbyes to Aunty J and then patiently listened to her lecture about being safe or something like that. Once that was over, Trumper, Bingo and Uncle P confidently strode out of the little old house to meet the other brave fellows that would make up their audacious band of vampire hunters.

Fourteen

A Band of Vampire Hunters

I t was a cloudless sky with plenty of moonlight on the wintry December evening that the boys and Uncle P set out on their perilous venture. Not wishing to be late, they hurriedly marched towards the Dragonbutt Arms, and when they arrived at their destination, without any hesitation all three of them walked straight in.

On such a cold night, the roaring fire in the hearth made a welcoming sight and so did the hulking figure of Angus Hogswood standing at his usual place by the bar. Barry Beasley stood beside him and had just finished eating one of Flanna Dooley's wholesome and always delicious steak and kidney pies, and was now washing it down with his second pint of Dragonstone Fire. Reluctant to see the young reporter drink alone, Angus had been considerate enough to quaff several pints of the local favourite as well, which Barry had kindly paid for. This meant that the Dragonbutt Arms regular was now in quite a jolly mood. That is for someone who later that evening was likely to encounter a bloodthirsty vampire.

"Ah, Perygrin," cried Barry, after he saw the three of them enter and make their way towards the bar. "Perfect timing, as usual, I've just finished my dinner, and as you can see, Angus is with me. I have already brought him up to date regarding the identity of the little vampire and how we hope to catch the blighter this evening."

"Merry Christmas, Perygrin, and you too, Trumper and Bingo," bellowed Angus, whose huge right hand was firmly holding onto his partly drained pint of Dragonstone Fire. "You can count on me to capture this little vampire; however, I'm not sure that it's necessary to involve the Bone Cruncher when all you really need is Angus Hogswood." Then he flexed the powerful muscles in his tree trunk-like arms and smiled, though not particularly convincingly as he still had a very vivid recollection of the Bone Cruncher crushing his hand at the Dragonbutt Arm wrestling tournament. And, not surprisingly, he was in no hurry to reminisce with her anytime soon.

"Good evening, Perygrin, and what will it be?" called a rather merry-looking Boosey Dooley from behind the bar.

"A pint of Dragonstone Fire for me and the boys will each have a bottle of Braithwaite's, please Boosey," answered Uncle P, who then looked at his two friends standing by the bar. "Better make it three pints, as I see Angus and Barry could do with a top-up. Oh, and don't forget to pour one for yourself."

"Coming right up," boomed a chirpy Boosey Dooley, as he had already accepted several pints of Dragonstone Fire from happy customers that evening. "And this round will be on the house."

"Dragonsbutts!" exclaimed Angus in astonishment, while staring at the smiling landlord. "In all my years of patronising your establishment, I have never witnessed you giving away free drinks."

"Well, there is one small condition," pointed out Boosey Dooley, with a broad grin across his face. "All three victims of this vampire were customers of mine, and I'm not having any more of them attacked and bitten, not on my watch. So if you five are going on a vampire hunt this evening, then you're going to need to bring a Dooley along for protection."

Everyone at the bar laughed and agreed that Boosey Dooley could join their band of vampire hunters, especially Angus, who, though still in disbelief at what he had just heard, wholeheartedly nodded his approval to a free round of drinks. This, due to the nature of the notoriously tight-fisted landlord, was one of the three things that the big man thought he would never witness during his lifetime. The other two, he chuckled to himself, were for him to drink a bad pint of Dragonstone Fire and see a Hogswood pig fly over the Dragonbutt Arms.

With the addition of Boosey Dooley, the band of vampire hunters had grown to seven. Six were present, and only Mad Maddox had yet to arrive, which was not at all unusual as most of the crazy Butterworth family were notoriously unreliable. Trumper texted him once again, and a reply came back almost immediately that he was riding in a tractor driven by his father, Mad Farmer Butterworth, and would arrive soon.

"I'll stick you all in the backroom so that you can have some privacy," announced Boosey Dooley, as he brought everyone their drinks and then went back behind the bar to pull himself another pint of Dragonstone Fire.

The backroom of the Dragonbutt Arms was not a place that Boosey and Flanna Dooley typically opened to the general public. It was much smaller than the front bar and with no dartboard or even a fruit machine, the backroom had very little to offer most of the residents of Dragonbutt. As a matter of fact, the only time it was really used was by Boosey Dooley himself. Not for his personal use, but for the Dragonbutt Arm's infamous lock-ins or special occasions as he liked to call them, which tended to take place a little too frequently in his wife's opinion.

Special occasions at the Dragonbutt Arms were only ever held after Boosey Dooley had drunk one too many during the evening opening hours. As was his custom on those nights, just after calling time he would ask a few of his loyal regulars to walk through to the backroom while he locked the front door after the rest of his customers had left. There, undisturbed, they could have a drink or two with the merry landlord and chat into the wee hours of the morning. Not strictly legal, a lock-in was always on a need to know basis by the residents of Dragonbutt. Of course, it should be assumed that Dragonbutt police, who really did not need to know, were all too aware of the landlord's little transgressions. But considering Dragonbutt police's own chief inspector was often rumoured to attend, the Dragonbutt Arms special occasions went on without interruption, year after year.

Once they were in the backroom, all but one of the vampire hunters sat down at the largest of its three tables. Bingo, because of the holy water sodden nappies that were taped around his butt, had wisely chosen to stand, though he did place his heavy Dr Who backpack on the floor. Within a minute or two, Boosey Dooley entered the room carrying his pint of Dragonstone Fire, and Trumper, not wanting to wait any longer for Mad Maddox, announced it was time for him to reveal the details of his plan.

Just as Trumper was about to start, unfortunately, Boosey Dooley spotted Bingo's oversized butt and roared, "Dragonsbutts! It looks like you've put on a few pounds, young fellow, and it's all on your butt." He then burst out laughing and once Angus saw what all the commotion was about, he joined in as well, which almost drowned out the landlord's already tumultuous laughter.

As Bingo fumed and turned the brightest shade of red, Trumper quickly intervened to explain why the young boy's butt had expanded so much since the last time they met. After the laughter had died down, both Boosey Dooley and Angus agreed that Bingo's idea was a truly inspired one, and this, fortuitously, made him feel much better.

"That calls for another round of drinks on the house," proclaimed an overly exuberant Boosey Dooley, while slamming his fist on the table. "Will it be the same again for everyone, or would you like to try something different?"

Each of the vampire hunters, except one, declined the landlord's unusually generous offer. This was because Uncle P and Barry knew they should stay level-headed, and Trumper had barely drunk half of his bottle of Braithwaite's. As for Bingo, he simply wanted to avoid the need to go for the call of nature, which would have been rather awkward with two holy water-soaked nappies strapped to his butt. Angus, on the other hand, who was quite speechless after witnessing two miracles that evening, eagerly raised his glass to request another pint of Dragonstone Fire.

While they were waiting for the landlord to return, Bingo pulled out a dozen garlic bulbs from his Dr Who backpack and distributed them amongst the other four sitting around the table. He then offered each of his fellow vampire hunters a garlic lolly, yet to his surprise and obvious delight, all but Trumper declined, and Barry helped himself to a spolly instead.

Once Boosey Dooley had returned to the backroom with another two pints of Dragonstone Fire, Trumper began to disclose the details of his plan to capture the little vampire. Not only would the band of vampire hunters be staking out Pigswill Alley that evening and using Bingo as the bait, but they were also going to construct an artfully conceived vampire trap. And due to the location of Bertie Bovington's home on Counting House Lane, the trap he had in mind would be set at the place on Pigswill Alley where the narrow path leads to Dragonbutt pond.

"Very good, Trumper, but what sort of trap do you have in mind?" chimed in Barry, who had just finished his third and final pint of Dragonstone Fire and was ready for the vampire hunt to commence.

Before Trumper had time to answer, he heard the distinctive beeping sound of a text message and then his phone began to vibrate. Guessing who it must be, he picked up the phone to see that Mad Maddox had at last arrived and was waiting in the Dragonbutt Arms front bar. Immediately, Trumper replied to the text and told him to come through to the backroom, as he was anxious to ensure the Butterworth boy had brought everything he had requested.

Mad Maddox was wearing one of those crazy looking Butterworth smiles when he entered the backroom carrying a large vermillion coloured backpack. And although it was not the colour that Trumper would have chosen when hunting a dangerous vampire during the dead of night, he thought it was far too late to make changes to his plan now.

As was common in his family, he had bright red wavy hair, and just like Bingo, it was rarely combed and nearly always looked thoroughly messy. And while most residents of Dragonbutt would describe him as somewhat characterless, he was a rather tall and stocky boy with emerald green eyes, about a year older than Bingo and therefore one year younger than Trumper.

When Bingo first joined Dragonbutt Primary School, Mad Maddox, who was well-known for giving the younger boys wedgies at that time, was the scourge of the school and had often been described as a rascal, a mischief-maker and on some occasions, that little monkey. It was therefore left up to Bingo and his gang, comprised of Bertie Bovington and Flitcher Jenkins, to put an end to his loutish behaviour. After a particularly unpleasant day in which three boys from year one had received wedgies, including the unfortunate Flitcher; Bingo thought enough-is-enough and decided to take the matter into his own hands.

On cornering Mad Maddox in the playground, Bertie and Flitcher pushed the older boy to the ground, while Bingo gave him the rather tricky to achieve, yet definitely very humbling, full wedgie.

With his underpants completely removed, Bingo hung them from the flag pole at the entrance to Dragonbutt Primary School, which was a cringeworthy sight to see and one that was witnessed by not only the students and their teachers, but many astounded and rather shocked parents as well. After the four of them were brought before their headteacher, Dr Wimbish, there were two repercussions to this alarming incident. Firstly, Bingo's gang was forced to part ways, and secondly but more importantly, Mad Maddox never tried to give another boy a wedgie during school hours again.

Just like the rest of the Butterworth family, Mad Maddox was not much of a talker, and so he simply nodded his head before plonking himself down next to Trumper, although not before sniggering and smiling in an out-there kind of way at Bingo's expansive butt.

"Mad Maddox, did you bring everything?" inquired Trumper, who was looking awfully impatient to see what was in the backpack.

The Butterworth boy was never annoyed or even a little bit offended by the residents of Dragonbutt calling his family 'mad', because, as even he knew all too well, they were. Instead of acknowledging Trumper though, he just opened his backpack and deposited its bizarre contents on the table.

"Is that a goalpost net?" exclaimed Uncle P, while peering at one of the items Mad Maddox had taken out of his backpack.

"That's right, Uncle P. It's from Dragonbutt Primary School's football pitch, the one that the Dragonbutt Flamers always use," confirmed Trumper, who was secretly relieved Mad Maddox had done something right for a change. "We're borrowing it for the vampire trap."

"I hope you can return it before Puffer Hendrick finds out it's gone," stressed Angus, as he finished his pint of Dragonstone Fire and pondered whether he should have just one more for the road.

"No need to worry about that, Angus, we'll make sure the net is back in its proper place before he knows it was ever missing," responded Trumper, while taking a gander at the second item Mad Maddox had brought, his mother's brand new and up till now unused washing line.

Fortunately for the band of vampire hunters, the trap that Trumper had in mind was quite straightforward, and not only that, Pigswill Alley at night was the perfect place to set it into motion. All they needed to do, he told the others, was to tie the corners of the heavy goalpost net to four stout willow trees using the washing line appropriated from Mad Maddox's mother, Mad Ma Butterworth. The net, he went on, should be hung at least ten feet off the ground, so that in the darkness neither the little vampire nor his sidekick would know of its existence until it was too late.

It was now a quarter to nine and time to leave, so Trumper asked everyone to exchange phone numbers and ensure their torches were in perfect working order. Mad Maddox then returned the goalpost net and washing line to his all too conspicuous vermillion backpack and slung it over his shoulders. Bingo did the same with his Dr Who backpack, which meant everyone was now ready to head over to Pigswill Alley in the hope of capturing the little vampire.

While the adults excused themselves to go for the call of nature, Trumper was reminded that he had not yet revealed to Mad Maddox the identity of the little vampire and his sidekick. Although he showed no sign of surprise after Trumper disclosed their names, the Butterworth boy did have a wicked looking grin across his face, as the thought of getting his revenge on Bertie Bovington and Flitcher Jenkins had not only made him feel that Christmas had come a little early this year, but it had also given him a depraved kind of delight. With the memory of his full wedgie vividly etched into his crazy mind, his only disappointment was that Bingo had not turned out to be one of the little vampire's sidekicks as well.

Once the adults had returned, the seven fearless vampire hunters marched out of the backroom and into the Dragonbutt Arms front bar. As they passed the kitchen door, they witnessed what could only be described as Flanna Dooley's much-practised psychic ability to sense when her husband was up to no good. "Tad! Tad Dooley! Get in here right now!" she shrieked, at a decibel level that shattered the pint glasses of several startled and now open-mouthed customers.

Boosey Dooley, with his usual bravado vanishing before their very eyes, smiled weakly and uttered, "Dragonsbutts! This won't take a moment." Then he guardedly opened the kitchen door before entering.

From inside the kitchen, the others could hear the occasional scream and an awful lot of shouting, originating almost entirely from the ear-splitting voice of Flanna Dooley, which made even Angus Hogswood's often deafening roar sound more like a church mouse. Although in truth, the only words they could clearly make out, were, "No, you're not!" and something like, "Over your dead body!" Which everyone presumed referred to the landlord's dead body and not his wife's. It was therefore not a surprise to see Boosey Dooley looking quite pale and sheepish as he opened the kitchen door to return to the front bar.

"Well, everyone, I've decided that for the safety of my customers I should remain here, at the Dragonbutt Arms," announced Boosey Dooley, while keeping one eye on the kitchen door. "I'll be in the reserve team, shall we say. Just in case the little vampire escapes and comes this way."

"Good idea, Boosey," chuckled Uncle P, with a wry smile creeping across his face. "We will do just fine on our own. Unlike you Dooleys, hunting for vampires is what we Entwhistles are bred for."

The band of vampire hunters now numbered six once again, and so knowing they must be on their way, each of them said their goodbyes and a Merry Christmas to Boosey Dooley. With a reddened face and an angry scowl that was clearly aimed at Uncle P, the landlord discreetly handed Angus Hogswood a hipflask of Dragonsbreath before bidding them all good luck and farewell. After an appreciative nod and a wink from the big fellow, they stepped out of the Dragonbutt Arms into the cold night air to walk the short distance to Pigswill Alley, where they intended to set their trap and lay in wait for the dastardly little vampire to appear.

Fifteen

Setting the Trap

⁓◦◦◦⁓

It was Trumper who led the way, with Bingo to his left and Mad Maddox to his right, and Uncle P, Barry and Angus followed close behind. While Bingo silently offered Mad Maddox a garlic lolly, which he brusquely accepted, to Trumper's annoyance, the adults noisily chatted about all sorts of nonsensical things, something he had noted was a common occurrence when grown-ups frequented the Dragonbutt Arms. Therefore, once they turned the corner into Bristletooth Lane, it was forced upon Trumper to give the three of them a rather loud and unmistakably firm, "Shush!" And to his satisfaction, their voices instantly quietened to a barely audible whisper.

With their torches turned on, they stepped through the opening between the two old willow trees and entered Pigswill Alley. Walking quickly but vigilantly, it wasn't long before the band of vampire hunters had reached their destination, the place where the narrow path leading from Dragonbutt pond met Pigswill Alley. Trumper then instructed Mad Maddox to take the goalpost net from his backpack and spread it out across the nigh-on frozen ground, which he accomplished without uttering a single word.

The washing line came next, and Mad Maddox also handed Trumper his trusty pocket knife that packed a whopping fourteen tools. While the others stood guard to ensure they would not be surprised by the little vampire, Trumper began to cut Mad Ma Butterworth's new washing line into several smaller pieces. He then attached a six-foot length to each of the four corners of the goalpost net using a 'loose butt'. This was a special quick-release knot that he had learnt to tie during his time as a Dragonbutt Dragoneer. The club run by Puffer Hendrick to teach outdoor and adventure skills to Dragonbutt Primary School students.

Once Trumper had completed this task, it was time for Angus and Barry to do their part in setting the trap. Trumper selected four willow trees, two on one side of Pigswill Alley and two on the other, located directly across from one another so that they formed a square. He then directed the two of them to climb the willow trees, and just beneath their canopy, Trumper told Angus and Barry to tie one piece of the washing line to each tree trunk using a secure knot. However, he cautioned, they had to be careful not to pull on any of the quick-release knots he had just tied as no one wanted to see movement in a loose-butt, at least not until the time came when he would release the heavy net on top of the little vampire.

In no time at all, Angus and Barry secured each corner of the goalpost net to the four willow trees that Trumper had carefully chosen. As he had hoped, in the darkness it was barely visible and anyone coming from the direction of Dragonbutt pond, or for that matter, Pucclechurch Crescent or Dragonbutt Vicarage, would have to pass under Trumper's first-rate vampire trap. All that remained, for now, was for Angus to attach a twelve-foot length of washing line to the corner of the net that was tied to the largest willow tree, which conveniently faced the narrow path on the far side of Pigswill Alley.

"Perfect," declared Trumper, while looking at the trap and admiring his fellow vampire hunters' handiwork. "When I pull hard on the washing line, the loose-butts should release the goalpost net, thereby trapping the little vampire beneath."

A little breathless from all his climbing, Angus pulled out the hipflask that Boosey Dooley had given him and took a hefty swig of Dragonsbreath. Looking like his head was about to explode while gulping down a copious amount of air, he passed the hipflask to Barry, who in turn gave it to Uncle P, and then the potent tipple was handed back to Angus. Although not before the two Dragonbutt Smoker colleagues were gasping for air themselves.

After Barry had recovered from the effects of Boosey Dooley's powerful homemade potato and acorn vodka that was rumoured to put hair on your chest, whether you want to or not, he remarked, "Trumper, what happens if the little vampire enters Pigswill Alley from either Brimstone Close or Pucclechurch Crescent? I know it's unlikely, but if he does and attacks someone there, then he may not even pass this way."

"Good point, Barry," croaked Uncle P, whose voice had yet to recover from the Dragonsbreath he had just drunk. "Two of us should walk there and stay hidden behind the willow trees, one to Brimstone Close and the other to Pucclechurch Crescent. And if anyone sees or hears the little vampire, they should call the others for help right away."

"Agreed. You go to Brimstone Close, Barry, and Uncle P, why don't you head over to Pucclechurch Crescent," stated Trumper, in a decisive tone of voice.

"But I promised your aunty I would not let you boys out of my sight," protested Uncle P, who really did not want to walk all the way to Pucclechurch Crescent on a cold winters evening. "Maybe Angus should go, and I stay here?"

"I still believe the little vampire is most likely going to come from the direction of Dragonbutt pond, and so Angus being the biggest and strongest of us would be most useful if he was stationed here, ready to jump into action if we catch the little vampire in the trap," explained Trumper, as he wanted to be firm with his long-faced uncle.

Unable to refute Trumper's sound logic, reluctantly, Uncle P agreed to be the one to go to Pucclechurch Crescent, and without making a fuss like his editor-in-chief, Barry just smiled and nodded his head before telling Trumper he would hide in the willow trees close to Dragonbutt Vicarage. The two vampire hunters then hurriedly yet silently went their separate ways, although not before accepting another nip of Dragonsbreath from Angus, for Dutch courage, of course.

During the time it had taken them to set the trap, both Bingo and Mad Maddox had remained unusually quiet. For that reason, Trumper looked around and saw that the Butterworth boy was mischievously carving his name into the trunk of an old willow tree. Ordinarily, he would have reprimanded him for such a transgression, but on this occasion, he chose to let it slide as the unruly boy was misbehaving very quietly for a change. Bingo, on the other hand, was standing on the other side of Pigswill Alley and appeared to be shining his torch into the darkness in the hope of catching a glimpse of the little vampire. To Trumper's surprise, Bingo was still carrying his Dr Who backpack, and to the older boy's disapproval, he was sucking another garlic lolly.

"Hey, Bingo," called Trumper, a little louder than he would have liked. "We should save the remainder of the garlic lollies for later, and why don't you take your backpack off and place it behind the big willow tree, next to Mad Maddox."

"I prefer to keep my backpack with me, just in case," answered Bingo, as he pulled what was left of the garlic lolly from his mouth. "And this is the last garlic lolly, but there is no need to worry because we still have plenty of garlic bulbs."

"Dragonsbutts! I thought we had two or three left?" continued Trumper, while trying to remember how many garlic lollies they had already polished off.

"We had two, but you took too long setting the trap, so I had both of them while I was waiting," responded Bingo, who was looking a little bit guilty he had not offered Trumper one of the two remaining garlic lollies.

Looking somewhat exasperated with Bingo, Trumper decided he would not make a fuss as there were more pressing matters at hand. He then pulled out his phone and called Barry and Uncle P, to ensure they were both at their assigned locations. The young reporter was already standing outside Dragonbutt Vicarage and had found himself a good hiding place behind an exceptionally large willow tree. From there, he could not only see Pigswill Alley but also the entrance to Brimstone Close. His uncle, being somewhat slower, had not quite reached Pucclechurch Crescent, though he assured Trumper he would be there before you could shout, Dragonsbutts!

After finishing his garlic lolly, Bingo, curious to take a look at what Mad Maddox had been up to, walked to the other side of Pigswill Alley. Trumper strolled over too and shone his torch at the willow tree the Butterworth boy was now leaning against. "MAD M WOZ ERE," announced Trumper, pronouncing each syllable slowly while rolling his eyes. "Well done, Mad Maddox, you must really excel at English. Old Cat Litter would be proud of you."

Trumper and Bingo both laughed, though Mad Maddox remained silent until he gruffly exclaimed, "I'm looking forward to this. Can I stake the little vampire and his sidekick after we catch them in the trap?"

"No, you can't," scolded Trumper, knowing that he had to be firm with Mad Maddox. "We've left the wooden stakes at home because the idea is to capture the little vampire unharmed, and that goes for his sidekick as well. Don't forget who they are, it's Bertie Bovington and Flitcher Jenkins we're trying to catch. If anything goes wrong, then we have garlic and holy water for protection, and then there is always Angus. Is that clear? Now, Mad Maddox, you go and sit with Angus behind the big willow tree and don't forget the both of you need to be as quiet as mice. Bingo, I want you to take out your holy water pistol and walk around making plenty of noise, but stay close to the trap. And if you're attacked by the little vampire then make sure you are not standing under the goalpost net when I release it."

"Should I shout to get his attention?" asked Bingo, who immediately pulled the holy water pistol out of his coat pocket with his right hand while holding the torch in his left.

"No, only if you are attacked," stressed Trumper, as he retrieved his own holy water pistol. "Just stamp a lot and whistle so that he can hear you."

As Bingo was never much of a whistler, he tried the best he could by blowing through the gap between his two front teeth, which really made more of a blowing sound than a whistle. Although this was somewhat disappointing, Trumper concluded it was better than nothing and therefore would just have to do. The younger boy then marched noisily up and down Pigswill Alley with his torch shining brightly and his holy water pistol ready for action, first in one direction and then the other, yet always being careful to remain close to the trap. Puzzlingly, he was still carrying his Dr Who backpack, and this reminded Trumper he had forgotten to ask Bingo what was in the backpack to make it appear so heavy, but that he thought, would have to wait until later.

Now the vampire trap was set with its live and extremely noisy bait, Trumper sauntered over to the far side of the big willow tree to see that Angus and Mad Maddox were thankfully sitting in silence. He then checked that the twelve-foot length of washing line, which would release the goalpost net when pulled, was adequately concealed before vigilantly listening for the two pairs of feet that undoubtedly belonged to the little vampire and his sidekick.

"This is taking far too long," complained Mad Maddox, who was looking bored already. "So, what happens now?"

"We wait, and with a bit of luck the little vampire will be along in no time at all," whispered Trumper, while crossing his fingers in the hope that he was right.

"If we must, but can I hold your holy water pistol?" pleaded Mad Maddox, who thought that if he wasn't going to be allowed to stake the little vampire, then at least he could squirt him with holy water.

"Alright, as long as you're careful and only shoot him if it's absolutely necessary. Holy water won't have any effect on his sidekick, but it burns vampires, and we want to capture the little vampire unhurt if at all possible," cautioned Trumper, as he handed his holy water pistol to Mad Maddox, who, without any hesitation, gave the trigger a squeeze. A stream of holy water shot out hitting Trumper squarely in the face, although before he could retaliate, the Butterworth boy gave a loud chuckle and then hastily walked back to where Angus was sitting.

At least Angus is behaving himself, Trumper muttered to himself, as he looked at the big man who was sitting on a tree stump, motionless and uncharacteristically silent. He then heard the low resonance of a snore and realised that their muscle and protector was now, and had been for quite some time, fast asleep. After deliberating whether to wake him, Trumper decided it was better to let him snooze as he really wasn't making too much noise, and besides, he could always be roused once they had the little vampire within their grasp.

"How much longer?" whined Bingo, who was still making the blowing sound through the gap between his two front teeth and laboriously stomping up and down Pigswill Alley.

"How would I know, and keep your voice down," hissed Trumper, as he didn't want the little vampire to get wind that there bait was not alone.

Unfortunately for Bingo, forty minutes passed by and there was still no sign of the little vampire or his sidekick. Meanwhile, Trumper sent texts to Barry and Uncle P, and they returned their own saying everything was quiet at both ends of Pigswill Alley. Somewhat disheartened, he called over to Bingo and told him they should hang around for another twenty minutes before calling it a night. The younger boy agreed by sticking his thumb into the air and then continued pacing up and down Pigswill Alley.

While Bingo was preoccupied with strengthening his woefully inadequate whistle, he missed the characteristic clomping sound of two pairs of feet trudging across the cold hard ground from the direction of Dragonbutt pond. Thankfully, Trumper heard the footsteps and instantly alerted Mad Maddox, who happened to be standing next to him and was kicking the trunk of a willow tree at the time. Without hesitating, he instructed the Butterworth boy to quietly wake Angus and then tried his earnest to signal Bingo, who regrettably had his back to the big willow tree that the other vampire hunters were hiding behind.

Just then, Trumper saw that Bingo had stopped pacing and was peering into the darkness of the narrow path that led to Dragonbutt pond. It was not the footsteps that had alerted him though; instead, it was the sound of two noisily chattering boys. And as the familiar voices got louder and therefore closer, he knew Trumper had been right all along, that the little vampire and his sidekick were unmistakeably Bertie Bovington and Flitcher Jenkins.

Although it was certainly an inopportune moment, rather than following Trumper's plan of drawing the little vampire into the trap, Bingo found he was now bursting for a pee. This was not an uncommon occurrence for anyone who drank more than one bottle of Braithwaite's, and sadly the young boy had drunk three. After stamping his feet and trying his best to think of something else, he realised that it was simply too late for all that and hurriedly dobbed behind the nearest willow tree.

As the other three vampire hunters looked on in disbelief, Trumper, knowing he was probably going to regret this, whispered, "Mad Maddox, they're nearly here, so you're going to have to be the bait. Once you lure them over to the trap, I'll release the goalpost net."

"No problem," responded a gleeful-looking Mad Maddox, with the crazy looking Butterworth grin on his face once again.

At the same time Mad Maddox emerged from behind the big willow tree, two dark figures that were loudly shooting the breeze entered Pigswill Alley. What sounded like the voice of Bertie Bovington, yelled, "Who's there?" and then a bright torchlight shone in the direction of the startled Butterworth boy.

Flitcher Jenkins was then heard shrieking, "It's Mad Maddox, let's get him!" And the next thing Trumper and Angus saw were the two dark figures running towards their adversary, the holy water pistol-toting Mad Maddox.

By this time, Bingo had finished his urgent call of nature and was running towards what he believed to be the little vampire and his sidekick. In the same breath, the young boy was firing his holy water pistol into the darkness for all he was worth and screaming at the top of his voice, "Vampire." Then, just as Trumper had planned, in all the confusion and because of their eagerness to attack Mad Maddox, the little vampire and his sidekick ran into the cleverly concealed vampire trap.

Seeing that their opportunity to capture the pair of them was now or never, Trumper tugged as hard as he could on Mad Ma Butterworth's washing line. As he intended, the heavy net fell crashing to the ground, right on top of an astonished Bertie Bovington and the equally shocked Flitcher Jenkins.

"Gotcha!" cried out Bingo, as he triumphantly pointed his holy water pistol at the two boys, who were now firmly ensnared under the Dragonbutt Primary School goalpost net.

Cackling as he moved closer to the vampire trap, Mad Maddox shone his torch at the little vampire and his sidekick, and against Trumper's express wishes he gave both of them a couple of squirts of holy water.

"Dragonsbutts! What are you doing?" raged the two trapped boys, who were doing their damnedest to free themselves from the sturdy net.

Fearing that they might be able to escape, Trumper asked Angus to secure each side of the goalpost net with a large willow tree branch, which could be found in abundance on either side of Pigswill Alley. He then made the call to Detective Huntress, to inform her they had captured the two responsible for the recent attacks, and then went on to say she would need to bring the Dragonbutt police van and the Bone Cruncher to Pigswill Alley right away.

Once Trumper had finished with the phone call, he asked Bingo to keep an eye out for the police van, as he knew it would not take long to arrive. He then turned around to see that Angus had already secured each side of the goalpost net with the heaviest willow tree branches he could find. To Trumper's dismay though, Mad Maddox was now kicking their two captives as they struggled beneath the heavy net, and if that was not bad enough, he then proceeded to squirt what was left of his holy water, as they whined incessantly to be released.

"Hey, I told you to only use the holy water if absolutely necessary. And stop kicking them!" fumed Trumper, whose patience with Mad Maddox was wearing a little thin by now.

"If I must, but this is the most fun I've had in a long time," groaned Mad Maddox, as he pointed the holy water pistol at the little vampire one more time and squeezed the trigger. "Anyhow, it doesn't work."

"What do you mean?" implored Trumper, who was now shining his torch at the two boys.

"Your holy water doesn't burn Bertie," shrugged Mad Maddox, as he gave the little vampire another kick. "And I thought vampires were supposed to have glowing red eyes."

"That's strange," admitted Trumper, yet before he could say another word, he was interrupted by the sound of a police siren.

And then Bingo shouted, "They're here!"

A few seconds later, the flashing blue lights of a Dragonbutt police van could be seen tearing along Pigswill Alley towards them. Bingo frantically waved his arms, and the gleaming white vehicle with its yellow and blue checks came to a screeching halt about ten yards from where Trumper was standing. Detective Huntress, Barry Beasley and the Bone Cruncher, with her black medical bag containing the tranquilliser, jumped from the van and walked over to take a look at who Trumper and the other vampire hunters had caught in their trap.

"Did I miss anything?" asked Barry, who had hitched a ride after flagging down the police van as it entered Pigswill Alley. "You didn't call me, but when I heard the police siren, I guessed you must have been successful and caught at least one of them."

"We caught both of them," rejoiced Bingo, while pointing at the two squirming figures underneath the goalpost net.

"Sorry, Barry, in all the excitement I completely forgot about you and Uncle P," admitted Trumper, as he retrieved the phone from his pocket and called his uncle. However, all he got was an automated recording asking him to leave a message. "Dragonsbutts! His battery must be dead."

"I'll go and get him," volunteered Bingo, who was looking forward to telling his uncle the story of how they had caught the little vampire and his sidekick. "It will only take me fifteen minutes to walk to

Pucclechurch Crescent, and it's perfectly safe now that the little vampire is in the trap."

Without thinking twice, Trumper agreed, and so Bingo noisily stomped off into the darkness with his torch shining brightly and Dr Who backpack still strapped to his shoulders.

"Let me take a look at these so-called vampires of yours," announced Detective Huntress, as she shone her torch at the goalpost net.

"It's only one vampire, and the other is his sidekick," corrected Trumper, who was now taking a closer look at their two captives as well.

"Dragonsbutts! We're not vampires," bawled the two boys, as they desperately wanted to be released from the trap.

"Get us out of here, or I'm telling my mum," wailed Bertie Bovington, all too loudly.

"Um, so you believe one of these two boys is a vampire?" probed the detective, who sounded more than a little sarcastic as she directed her question at Trumper.

"Yes of course," hesitated Trumper, because as Mad Maddox had just pointed out, Bertie's eyes were not glowing red, and as Trumper looked closer, nor did he have any long sharp vampire fangs.

"I'll interrogate these two," chimed in Mad Maddox, as he chuckled to himself while once again kicking each of the unhappy boys. "How about I waterboard the both of them?"

"No one is going to be waterboarded," ordered Detective Huntress, thinking this Butterworth boy must be as mad as everyone claimed. "Don't forget you are living in Dragonbutt and we don't get up to that sort of thing here."

"I told you I'm not a vampire and neither is Flitcher," screamed Bertie Bovington once again, as he opened his mouth so wide, everyone present could clearly see his unsightly fillings and numerous tooth extractions, which meant this little boy was without a doubt incapable of biting anyone.

"But, Bertie refused a garlic lolly, and he wouldn't let Flitcher have one either," pleaded Trumper, out of desperation.

"Dragonsbutts! Not liking garlic doesn't mean I'm a vampire," snarled Bertie, who was still thrashing about under the heavy goalpost net.

"That's true," added Angus, while shaking Boosey Dooley's hipflask and unhappily finding it empty. "I was never fond of garlic either, and I'm not a vampire."

"So where were the two of you when the previous attacks took place?" argued Trumper, who was feeling somewhat frustrated that Bertie and Flitcher were now looking decidedly less guilty by the second. "And what were you doing on Pigswill Alley this evening?"

"We were stealing Choco Bombs," bawled Flitcher, just as Bertie Bovington punched his friend's arm and told him to keep quiet.

Wanting to be released from the vampire trap sooner rather than later, Flitcher ignored his best friend and hastily told them the whole story. It was Bertie's idea, he blurted, to take the Choco Bombs after he had inadvertently discovered where his parents hid the spare key to their store. Late at night, once the Bovington household had fallen asleep, Bertie had been sneaking out of the house to meet Flitcher at Dragonbutt pond. And from there they would always walk to Bovington's Sweets and Chocolates by taking the short-cut, through the opening between the two old willow trees on Pigswill Alley.

Like almost all the residents of Dragonbutt, Bertie and Flitcher loved eating Choco Bombs, and if they only took a few each night, then his parents would never miss them, or so Bertie had claimed. The boys had been going out every evening for the past two weeks, and admittedly, they had taken more than the handful that Bertie originally intended. In fact, the two of them had amassed such a large stash of Choco Bombs they would undoubtedly be eating their ill-gotten gains for weeks to come.

"So what about last night?" asked Trumper, who was looking decidedly downcast by now. "Why were you riding your bike along Pigswill Alley, just before Mad Tolly Butterworth was attacked by the little vampire?"

"That was because I fell asleep at home and Bertie had to walk to Bovington's Sweets and Chocolates on his own. He was really angry when he texted me, but he still insisted that I meet him at the store. So I jumped on my bike and rode as fast as I could because it would be quicker than walking," responded Flitcher, rather angrily. "And then you and Bingo attacked me as I was riding down Pigswill Alley, so instead of meeting Bertie I decided to return home, which annoyed him even more."

"Right, I've heard all I need to," declared Detective Huntress, whose patience with Trumper and the rest of the vampire hunters had reached its limit. "These boys may be responsible for the petty theft of Choco Bombs, which I will be talking to their parents about, but they obviously have nothing to do with the recent attacks in the village. As I have stated on several occasions, vampires don't exist, and these attacks were perpetrated by something that does not come out of the realm of fantasy stories. Angus, I need you to release these two boys at once, and then I want everyone to stop this nonsense and go home."

"Trumper, that means the little vampire must still be out there somewhere," warned Barry, who had remained quite speechless up till then.

"Dragonsbutts!" exclaimed Trumper, as he reached inside his coat pocket for his phone. "I have to warn Bingo!"

Sixteen

Don't Worry; I'm Not Going to Kill Him!

〜୧Ⴧ୨〜

During the time the band of vampire hunters, Detective Huntress and not forgetting the Bone Cruncher were standing by the vampire trap and scrutinising the two captive boys, no one noticed the stealthy and almost noiseless arrival of a little visitor to Pigswill Alley. Hidden in the darkness between the branches of the willow trees was a menacing creature with glowing red eyes and long sharp fangs that had an insatiable thirst for blood. After looking at the crowd gathered around the trap, he sniffed the cold night air and immediately caught the scent of his next unwitting victim. So without delay, he set off once again, although this time it was in the direction of Pucclechurch Crescent.

"Bingo, are you alright?" screeched Trumper, who was now hoping the little vampire was not hunting for his latest victim on Pigswill Alley that evening. "You need to come back here, right now!"

"Someone is following me," uttered Bingo, rather quietly. "I can hear footsteps, and they're getting closer."

"Dragonsbutts! Are you sure?" replied Trumper, with a worried tone in his voice. "No one has passed this way."

"Of course, I'm sure. It sounds like two pairs of feet approaching, and they're coming from your direction," hissed Bingo, as he was a little irritated that Trumper was questioning him.

"What you need to do is run as fast as you can towards Pucclechurch Crescent and don't stop until you see Uncle P," urged Trumper, who had now turned on his speaker so that everyone could hear.

Trumper anxiously looked at the others who were listening intently to the conversation between the two boys. For what seemed like an eternity, yet in reality was only about ten seconds, his phone lay silent. Just as he was about to speak again, Bingo, in a shaky voice, said, "Too late for that, something with glowing red eyes is coming towards me, and it's breathing heavily. Luckily I brought..." Unfortunately, the young boy was unable to finish his sentence, and the only thing anyone could hear before Trumper's phone finally went silent was a long ear piercing, "Aaah!"

"Come on, we need to help Bingo," screamed Trumper, who was frantic to get to him as quickly as possible.

Detective Huntress wasted no time at all in taking control of the situation by ordering everyone into the Dragonbutt police van. She jumped into the driver's seat and started the engine while Trumper sat beside her, his holy water pistol in one hand and a torch in the other. Barry, Angus and the Bone Cruncher all squeezed onto the backseat, which was a difficult task to achieve on account of the formidable size of Angus Hogswood, although they managed it all the same. With no room anywhere else, Bertie and Flitcher had to sit with Mad Maddox in the cage at the rear of the van. And though this sounded like a marked improvement on the vampire trap, regrettably, the Butterworth boy had already reverted back to his old ways and was now in the process of giving Flitcher a very uncomfortable wedgie.

189

"When are you going to let us out of this cage?" protested an irate Flitcher Jenkins, while trying his best to push the exposed pair of underpants down under his trousers.

"That will have to wait," shouted back the detective, while driving the police van as fast as she dared along the pothole-ridden Pigswill Alley.

Steadfast, she drove with the deafening police siren blaring and its blue lights flashing, in the hope that Bingo's attacker would be scared away before it could hurt the defenceless young boy. Thankfully, within no time at all, they arrived at the spot where he had been attacked. Imagining the worse, Detective Huntress applied the brakes heavily, and the police van came to an abrupt halt around twenty yards from what looked like the silhouette of Bingo. And then, turning on the headlight's main beam, she purposely lit up Pigswill Alley so that everyone could clearly see the spine-chilling scene.

It was Trumper who bravely jumped out first, closely followed by Detective Huntress holding her Dragonbutt police issue baton, the extendable sort she could enlarge with a much-practised flick of the wrist. Everyone else, except the boys who remained locked in the cage, quickly exited the police van in the hope of aiding Trumper and the detective. Although to their surprise and horror, what they saw stopped them dead in their tracks.

Expecting to see Bingo lying injured on the ground, every one of them was astonished to discover he was not only standing but appeared to be unharmed. With a smile on his face, it was now plain to see that one of his wellington clad feet was pinning down what looked suspiciously like a little black sheep. And not only that, high above his head he was wielding a dangerous looking two-headed battleaxe, which Trumper knew all too well had the letters 'M' and 'O' carved into its short but solid wooden handle.

"No, Bingo!" yelled Trumper, knowing right away the young boy was brandishing Little MO, the nickname he had given to his Monster Obliterator.

"Don't worry; I'm not going to kill him!" chuckled Bingo, who, after seeing the others had arrived, was now lowering the fearful looking weapon.

Cautiously, Trumper and the others inched closer to take a look at what Bingo had actually captured. Whimpering on the ground was indeed a little vampire with glowing red eyes and long sharp fangs. And out of his mouth came little wisps of smoke and an unpleasant burning smell, doubtless the result of the creature coming into contact with some of the Reverend Pinkerton's noxious but highly effective holy water.

"Is that a sheep?" inquired Detective Huntress, who was surprised to see what at first sight appeared to be such a funny-looking thing. Yet on closer inspection was rather grotesque and decidedly fearsome.

"Dragonsbutts! It's not a sheep," retorted Bingo, while dangerously swinging Little MO to and fro as he spoke. "By day he is a Bedlington terrier, and his name is Baxter, but obviously at night he turns into a vampire."

"Nurse Fanshaw, can you sedate Baxter right away. And Bingo, drop Little MO at once before you hurt someone," appealed Trumper, knowing he had to act quickly to ensure the little vampire was not given the opportunity to escape.

Bingo, who was still breathing rather heavily due to all the excitement, did as Trumper had requested and placed his Monster Obliterator on the ground. Meanwhile, the Bone Cruncher gave Baxter an extra-large dose of the tranquilliser she had brought with her. Within a matter of seconds, he was snoring as peacefully as a sheep, and then at that very moment, a breathless and red-faced Uncle P came into view.

"Did he hurt you, Bingo?" implored Uncle P, as he was afraid the young boy may have been bitten.

"No, but he came close," smiled Bingo, who was looking pleased with himself. "When I turned to run, he tried to bite my butt, although all he got was a mouthful of nappy soaked in holy water. That really gave him a shock, and then I squirted him with my holy water pistol. After that, I managed to hold him down with my foot, which allowed me enough time to pull Little MO out of my backpack and then I waited for the others to arrive."

"It was lucky we got here so quickly," pointed out Trumper, thinking the outcome of this night could have been much worse.

"There was no need to worry about me, I had everything under control," grinned Bingo, as he glanced at his two-headed battleaxe lying on the ground.

"Yes, I can see that. I was actually referring to Baxter. He would probably have been the late Baxter if we had arrived any later," teased Trumper, while pointing at Little MO.

"I already told you, I wasn't going to kill him!" grumbled Bingo, who was somewhat offended by Trumper's inference that he would have dispatched Baxter with his Monster Obliterator. "All I was going to do was give him a close shave, and that was only if he tried to bite me again."

"Baxter!" exclaimed Uncle P, as he was still under the mistaken belief the little vampire was Bertie Bovington. And it was only now he could see the unconscious body on the ground was really Old Mrs Dingle's funny-looking dog.

"I'll explain everything to you, Perygrin," chimed in Barry, who then took Uncle P to one side to apprise him of all that had come to pass.

Although Trumper had been noticeably open-mouthed to find out that Baxter was the little vampire they were looking for, it did not take long for his sharp mind to swiftly piece everything together. What was obvious to him now, was that the Reverend Pinkerton and Roly

Poly had not heard two pairs of feet before they were attacked; instead, it was the four-legged Baxter all along.

He now understood that when Mad Tolly Butterworth had cried out 'Buh! Buh! Buh!', it was not 'Bertie! Bertie! Bertie!' she was struggling to say, it was 'Baxter! Baxter! Baxter!'. This made perfect sense because dogs are a postal worker's greatest adversary. Therefore, Mad Tolly Butterworth would have known every dog in Dragonbutt by sight.

And of course, there was one more thing that had been staring him in the face all this time. The reason why Baxter had been behaving so strangely when the boys were sucking their garlic lollies at Dragonbutt pond and his odd behaviour in the garden of the little old house. It was the garlic he was afraid of, and the wooden stakes and holy water in Bingo's Dr Who backpack and the red-brick shed.

"Well, I think if I leave now, I can just about make last orders at the Dragonbutt Arms," announced Angus, as he looked at his wristwatch. "Someone's got to let Boosey Dooley know what has happened and so it might as well be me."

"Yes, you should all be on your way," remarked Detective Huntress, who was still not sure what to make of all this. "Barry, you go with him, and Perygrin, please take your two boys home right now. Nurse Fanshaw and I can handle Baxter on our own."

"Hey, what about us!" came the shrill voices of Bertie Bovington, Flitcher Jenkins and Mad Maddox, all of whom were still locked in the cage at the back of the police van.

"Oh yes, here's the key to the lock. Nurse Fanshaw, can you let those three out and then place Baxter in the cage, and make sure you lock the door so that he can't do any more harm," instructed the detective, as she tossed the Bone Cruncher her key. "I will return the three boys to their homes and drop Nurse Fanshaw off at Dragonbutt Community Hospital before taking this strange little fellow to the police cells."

Without uttering a sound, the Bone Cruncher unlocked the cage, and with two of them still complaining about their groundless and very uncomfortable imprisonment, the boys promptly jumped out. She then lifted Baxter off the ground and rather harshly threw him into the empty cage. And although Trumper and Bingo thought this was no way to treat the funny-looking dog, they wisely chose to remain silent.

After Trumper had thanked Angus and Barry for their help in capturing the little vampire, everyone watched as the two thirsty men trudged back down Pigswill Alley at a remarkably brisk pace. Uncle P then walked over to the police van to take a closer look at Baxter, and although he was sleeping with both eyes tightly shut, his telltale long sharp vampire fangs were still clearly visible.

"Dragonsbutts!" mused Uncle P, while scratching his head. "Who would have guessed the little vampire was Baxter. He's always been such a funny-looking dog, but I never dreamt he had a dark side to him. What I don't understand is that he has been with Old Mrs Dingle for years, yet the attacks in the village only started a couple of weeks ago. Anyway, boys, let's head home because your aunty will be wondering what has happened to us. Trumper, can you call her to say we are on our way and will be back shortly."

"Detective Huntress, can we visit Dragonbutt Police Station tomorrow?" pleaded Trumper, as he believed this mystery was far from solved.

"Yes, you might as well," confirmed the detective, who was thinking about how she was ever going to write-up this baffling case. "I would like you two boys to help me complete my police report, so make sure you are at the station by ten in the morning because tomorrow is Christmas Eve."

Just as Detective Huntress was about to return to the police van to drive Bertie, Flitcher and Mad Maddox to their homes, the Bone Cruncher to Dragonbutt Community Hospital and Baxter to a cell at Dragonbutt Police Station, a little further down Pigswill Alley a torchlight was now clearly visible.

"Don't tell me that's Angus and Barry coming this way?" remarked Uncle P, who thought it unlikely Angus Hogswood had chosen to return and miss out on the opportunity of drinking a pint or two of Dragonstone Fire.

"No, it can't be," affirmed Trumper, while looking at the message he had just received on his phone. "I have a text from Barry saying they arrived at the Dragonbutt Arms a minute or two ago. And to celebrate, Boosey Dooley has announced he will hold one of his special occasions, and drinks are on the house for Angus and Barry."

"Dragonsbutts! Maybe it's another vampire," screeched Bingo, as he raced over to the spot where he had left his Monster Obliterator and picked up the two-headed battleaxe in both hands.

"Vampires don't use torches, stupid," scoffed Trumper, while slowly shaking his head. "You won't need Little MO again tonight, so return it to your backpack before you hurt anyone."

Everyone peered into the darkness to see the light from the torch grow brighter as whoever was holding it was slowly but surely getting closer by the second. Then all of a sudden, a whistle could be heard, followed by a cry from a fragile agonised voice, "Baxter! Baxter! Come here, boy."

"It's Old Mrs Dingle," shouted out Trumper, as he could recognise the old lady's voice practically anywhere.

"Ah, the owner of this dangerous dog," stated Detective Huntress, who immediately pulled out her baton once again, just in case the old lady gave her any trouble. "I have quite a few questions and a nice cosy cell for her at Dragonbutt Police Station."

"Surely there is no need for that," beseeched Uncle P, as he was all too aware London trained police officers were often a little too eager to use their batons. "Old Mrs Dingle is not a threat to anyone, and I

195

am sure she has a perfectly rational explanation for all of this, although as of this moment, I really can't think what it is."

"Waterboard her! Waterboard her!" chanted Mad Maddox, because he was itching to try the waterboarding techniques he had recently seen on a website called 'Interrogation for Beginners'. From a country that had found it worthwhile to get their unfortunate detainees to say exactly what the interrogator wanted to here.

Thankfully, it only took an inhospitable scowl from the detective to silence the Butterworth boy, and then she secured her baton before reassuring Uncle P, "Yes of course, but I will still need to take Old Mrs Dingle into custody and detain her at Dragonbutt Police Station for questioning in the morning."

Not long after that, the old lady slowly walked into view, and everyone could clearly see the troubled expression on her face. Seeing Detective Huntress and the others standing before her, she trembled and said, "Oh dear, I've lost my Baxter. He's such a sweet dog, but he managed to get out of the house again, and I'm so worried something bad has happened to him."

"Baxter is in the police van," asserted Detective Huntress, with her arms folded. "He is sedated and is now secured in a cage."

"Oh no, has he been a naughty boy again?" responded Old Mrs Dingle, who had a sombre but unsurprised expression on her face.

"If you mean, has he tried to attack and bite another resident of Dragonbutt, thanks to Trumper and Bingo the answer is not this night," barked Detective Huntress, while staring down at the old lady with one of those stern police-type looks.

Old Mrs Dingle just hung her head and rather shakily confessed, "Oh dear, I was afraid of that. He's a good boy really, although lately he has been acting very odd and changes into something quite different. You see, when the sun goes down his eyes start to glow a ghastly red and he grows long sharp fangs. And that's not all detective; he also gets a dreadful craving for blood. I tried feeding him a bowl of Hogswood's black pudding at first, but it was fresh blood he wanted. My blend number twelve seemed to work, though it's so difficult to find a good supply of kangaroo blood in Dragonbutt. I'm at my wit's end and just don't know how to control him any more; he was never like this before."

While Detective Huntress gave the old lady a steely glare, the others just looked at each other and wondered what she had been babbling about. What was blend number twelve? And why did she need kangaroo blood? Trumper was not alone in thinking Old Mrs Dingle had gone a little doolally, though he was polite enough to keep it to himself, as were all the others bar one.

The exception, not surprisingly, was Mad Maddox, who, with a grin on his face, howled, "Cuckoo! Cuckoo!" It took a grimace from Detective Huntress to silence him again, and then the weary detective informed the old lady she would be spending the night in a Dragonbutt police cell next to Baxter.

"Oh, that's alright, Detective Huntress," confirmed Old Mrs Dingle, who was now smiling and looking a little more like her old self again. "Banged to rights he was, and so I really can't complain. Besides, it's like going to a hotel, isn't it? Do you provide a full Dragonbutt breakfast, or is it one of those continental affairs? Because I always believe it's nice to have a hot breakfast when you go away."

Shaking her head in bemusement, the detective brusquely led the old lady to the police van and helped her onto the back seat. It was a tight fit by the time Bertie and Flitcher squeezed in beside her as Mad Maddox had already appropriated a sizeable chunk of the seat for himself. And then with a quick wave and a Merry Christmas, Detective Huntress reversed at breakneck speed with the Bone Cruncher sitting silently in the passenger seat.

"Right, it's too cold to hang around here any longer, and it's very late for you boys, so let's go home," declared Uncle P, as he was all too wary Aunty J was waiting for them.

The boys couldn't agree more, and so Bingo tossed his Dr Who backpack over his shoulders, and then the three of them hastily made their way along Pigswill Alley before turning onto the narrow path that led to Dragonbutt pond. Needless to say, by the time they reached Counting House Lane, they were all exceedingly tired. Although Bingo still had enough energy to run to the bright red door of number twenty-two and enter the little old house yelling, "Aunty J, I captured the little vampire all by myself."

"Take your wellingtons off, young man, and that applies to all of you!" cried Aunty J, as she glanced down at Bingo's muddy boots and those of her husband and Trumper who followed him. "Warm yourself by the fire in the living room while I make you each a mug of hot chocolate, and I have some freshly baked mince pies that have just come out of the oven."

To everyone's delight, it was not long before Aunty J walked into the living room with a tray containing four mugs of steaming hot chocolate, along with a large plate of warm mince pies. Trumper and Bingo immediately ate their marshmallows and then spooned out the fresh whipped cream before drinking their deliciously rich and wonderfully warming hot chocolate, which left the two adults to slowly savour theirs.

Aunty J refrained from eating even a single mince pie, which the boys knew meant more for them, so Trumper and Uncle P both ate three and the always hungry Bingo managed to eat a rather greedy four. Once everyone had finished, their aunty announced it was bedtime for the boys and because it was now past midnight, she reminded them Christmas Eve had already arrived. Not that they really needed reminding, especially Bingo, who was already thinking about the multitude of presents he would receive from Father Christmas.

"Goodnight, Aunty J, and you too, Uncle P," yawned Trumper and Bingo, as they walked out of the living room and wearily climbed the stairs to their bedroom.

After brushing their teeth and changing into pyjamas, the boys jumped into bed and quickly fell asleep after the hectic day that had just come to a close. Bingo slept soundly and dreamt of fighting the little vampire with Little MO and counting the presents he would be able to open on Christmas Day. Trumper, on the other hand, was somewhat restless, tossing and turning and thinking about what could have happened to Baxter to transform him from a funny-looking and usually harmless dog into a ferocious little vampire.

Seventeen

Behind Bars

"Breakfast is ready," called Aunty J, from the bottom of the stairs. So Trumper immediately threw back his duvet and climbed down the ladder of the bunk bed, impatient to start the day. Unusually, Bingo was still in a deep sleep, and so Trumper gave him a firm shake in the hope he would wake-up.

"Vampire!" he spluttered, and then half-dazed the younger boy asked, "Where's Little MO?"

"The little vampire is safely locked up in a cell at Dragonbutt Police Station," Trumper reminded Bingo, "And you won't need Little MO today. Let's go downstairs and eat breakfast."

Although only seconds had passed since Trumper had woken him, Bingo's tummy was already starting to rumble, and so he chose not to complain about being disturbed in the middle of an exciting dream. One in which he had defeated the Little vampire by chopping off the contemptible creature's head with Little MO. Instead, he eagerly followed Trumper down the stairs and into the lovely warm kitchen that smelled of something quite yummy once again.

"What are we having?" demanded Bingo, who already thought he knew the answer to his question.

"It's Christmas Eve today, and you have a big day ahead of you. So I've made your favourite," replied Aunty J, with a smile. "There's a large stack of pancakes ready for you in the oven, and there is an unopened jar of Botters honey on the table. Your uncle has already left for work, which means all these pancakes are for the two of you."

Both Trumper and Bingo thanked their aunty and hungrily attacked the mountain of mouthwatering pancakes that she placed on the kitchen table, before smothering each one in lots of Botters heavenly sweet and always delectably gratifying honey. Then, to their delight, she gave them both a mug of her steaming hot chocolate topped with fresh whipped cream and a wonderfully gooey marshmallow.

"Your uncle told me about your exciting evening last night," imparted Aunty J, as she watched Bingo eat his fifth pancake. "Who would have thought that Baxter was behind these terrible attacks on Pigswill Alley. I always thought he was such a nice dog, but you can never tell, can you. Anyway, I'm glad you both got this nonsense about vampires and monsters out of your system. And let's hope Old Mrs Dingle is released soon because owning a mad dog is not really her fault."

Before Bingo could correct his aunty, Trumper kicked the younger boy to garner his attention and then made an unmistakable sign that meant he should not say a word. Bingo just shrugged yet wisely said nothing, and instead focused his energy on devouring another five pancakes. Once they had finished eating their breakfast, the boys thanked Aunty J for the lovely and much-appreciated meal and then climbed back up the stairs.

"So Trumper, what now?" asked Bingo, as the two boys descended the stairs after washing their faces, brushing their teeth and changing into some clean warm clothing.

"I want you to take everything out of your Dr Who backpack, and that includes Little MO," informed Trumper, who was wary of the time and knew Detective Huntress was expecting them to arrive at Dragonbutt Police Station by ten. "Then bring the empty backpack with you because the two of us are going to retrieve the goalpost net we left behind on Pigswill Alley. And hopefully, Mad Maddox will keep his promise to return it, preferably before Puffer Hendrick discovers it missing."

"Do I have to leave Little MO behind?" groaned Bingo, looking disappointed. "What if I'm attacked again?"

"Yes, you do, and you won't be attacked, at least not by a vampire," promised Trumper, as he stared at the Monster Obliterator the younger boy was now wielding.

Bingo reluctantly agreed and stomped back upstairs before emptying the backpack in his bedroom. Just in case Aunty J was to enter the room, he placed Little MO under his mattress and the remaining bulbs of garlic and the empty holy water pistols in his underwear drawer. In the meantime, their aunty had already prepared herself for work and left the little old house to walk to Dragonbutt Dental Surgery, where she intended to remain until the middle of the afternoon. Although not before telling Trumper that while she would allow the two boys to visit Dragonbutt Police Station, they were to stay well away from Baxter.

Upon discovering Aunty J had already departed and would not be home until after their lunchtime, Bingo exclaimed, in somewhat of a concerned tone, "But what are we going to eat for lunch?"

"Don't worry about that, she told me we can have anything we like from the freezer," reassured Trumper, who was smiling because he knew their freezer was always well stocked with plenty of their aunty's delicious homemade food.

"Dragonsbutts! Everything from the freezer," grinned Bingo, naughtily.

"Not everything, greedy, she said 'anything'," restated Trumper, with a laugh.

Once the boys were wearing their coats, along with their DPS woolly hats and warm woollen gloves, and had pulled on their muddy wellington boots by the back door, they were ready for the brisk walk to Dragonbutt Police Station. With Bingo carrying his Dr Who backpack, they walked down the long garden path to the muddy footpath behind the little old house and then marched resolutely towards Dragonbutt pond.

As it was already nine-thirty, the boys hastily made their way to Pigswill Alley and immediately saw what they were looking for. The Dragonbutt Primary School goalpost net was right where they had left it, along with what remained of the new but now ruined washing line that belonged to Mad Ma Butterworth. Without squandering any of their precious time, they placed the washing line, albeit in several pieces, into the backpack. Then they carefully folded the goalpost net that had most definitely proven its worth, if only to capture Bertie Bovington and Flitcher Jenkins, and placed it into the backpack as well.

"Good job, Bingo," confirmed Trumper, as he was happy their first task that morning could now be ticked off his to-do list. "I'll text Mad Maddox to let him know he can pick up the goalpost net from Counting House Lane and return it to Dragonbutt Primary School before the New Year. As for his mother's new washing line, I'll leave it to him to explain why it's a whole lot shorter now. She's Dragonbutt born and should understand, besides, as a Butterworth, she knows crazy things always happen to members of her family."

Because it was located close to Dragonbutt Community Hospital on Old Dragonian Way, it took no more than another quarter of an hour of brisk walking and then running like the clappers before the boys reached Dragonbutt Police Station. As they entered, it appeared to be unusually quiet and bereft of people. In fact, they could only see one person, and that was the office administrator, Doris Clutterbuck, who appeared to be nattering on the phone to her cousin, Barry Beasley.

According to many, Doris Clutterbuck was the prettiest girl in the village, at least those Dragonbutt born that is. At twenty-four she was still very young and had what used to be rather long medium brown hair, but was now what her hairdresser liked to call, burnt orange with just a hint of a highlight here and there. Her eyes were exceptionally dark in colour, and she stood a very respectable five-foot-seven. And although she was known to have quite a fondness for Bovington's chocolates in her youth, she had remained extraordinarily slender all the same.

"Oh, Merry Christmas, Trumper, and you too, Bingo," Doris warmly announced, after promptly ending her call. "Barry was just telling me how you caught the vampire we've all been hearing about. It's been such a long time since Dragonbutt was last plagued by monsters that even the people born here, including myself, found it difficult at first to believe we had a vampire amongst us. As you know, we were all raised on the old legends and the Dragonbutt prophecy. But who could ever have thought it would come true with the discovery that Old Mrs Dingle's dog was really a bloodthirsty little vampire."

The boys both nodded their heads at the talkative Doris Clutterbuck and greeted her with a smile and a hearty, "Merry Christmas to you too, Doris."

"I know Detective Huntress never really believed a vampire was responsible for the attacks, but that's understandable because she's not Dragonbutt born," continued Doris, who had the uncanny ability to be able to talk rapidly without ever seeming to take a breath. "You know these big city people don't know the history of Dragonbutt, especially the predicament we had during the dark days with all those monsters on the loose. Between you and me, I don't think the detective knows what to make of all this because last night she made a bed for herself in one of the cells, to keep an eye on Baxter. And how do you think Old Mrs Dingle is involved in all this? I've known her all my life, and I never imagined she could be mixed up with anything as gruesome as vampires. Dragonsbutts! This whole thing just makes my head want to explode."

Knowing Doris Clutterbuck was a renowned gossip and had a reputation in the village for incessant chattering, the boys simply nodded every now and again in the hope she would soon run out of things to say.

"Oh, I nearly forgot, Detective Huntress told me to send you over to the cells once you were here," giggled Doris, who was also well-known for being rather forgetful. "But let's have a mince pie first as it is Christmas Eve."

"Goodie," howled Bingo, as he was getting a little peckish by now and could feel his tummy start to rumble. "Is there any hot chocolate as well?"

"Yes of course," nodded Doris, as she walked over to the kitchen. "It's store-bought I'm afraid, but it will only take me a minute or two to whisk up a couple of mugs for you. And please take your coats and woolly hats off as it's far too warm in here to be wearing all those outdoor clothes. Just throw them over the back of the empty chair next to my desk, and Bingo, you can leave your backpack there as well."

Dragonbutt had never been a hotbed of crime, so its police station had always been on the small side, which is just how the residents of Dragonbutt preferred it. Although the station was typically quite austere during most of the year, Doris was a great believer in celebrating the Christmas season. Consequently, with an abundance of Christmas spirit, she had spruced up the place with her homemade decorations and a small but rather elegant silver Christmas tree. The tree was covered from top to bottom in an assortment of flashing coloured fairy lights and shiny ornaments. And to Bingo's delight, there were bundles of chocolate gold coins hanging from its branches.

The boys hurriedly ate their mince pies, two for Trumper and three for Bingo, and drank every last drop of their hot chocolate. They then thanked Doris and walked over to the door that was clearly marked 'POLICE CELLS' and waited for the office administrator to buzz them in.

"You can enter now," called Doris from behind her desk, as the automatic door swung open.

Trumper and Bingo walked through the open doorway and into a sparsely furnished plain white room. One side of the room accommodated a comfortable looking black leather swivel chair, along with three simple metal-framed chairs and a large desk containing a telephone and a laptop. On the other were four steel doors with a different number painted on each. And every one of them had a small hatch located about five feet off the ground, two of which remained closed, while the other two were wide open.

Sitting on the black leather swivel chair behind the large desk was Detective Huntress. She was obviously engrossed in whatever she was typing on her laptop because when the boys entered the room, she made no attempt to raise her head. For that reason, Trumper decided to clear his throat to get the detective's attention, something he had often seen adults do in situations like this.

"Ah, Trumper and Bingo," acknowledged Detective Huntress, as she looked up to see the boys standing at the far end of the room. "Just give me a minute while I finish my initial police report into the capture of this strange dog. Oh, and I hope you didn't bring that crazy Butterworth boy with you. He called this morning to say the only way to make Old Mrs Dingle talk was to waterboard her, and he was the only person in Dragonbutt with the expertise to do it."

"No, it's just the two of us, but that's typical of Mad Maddox. Knowing him, he will probably try waterboarding several of the students at Dragonbutt Primary School in the new school year," responded Trumper, while he and Bingo walked over to the cells to take a look through the open hatch of cell number one.

Bingo could see the hatch was too high for either of the boys to peer in, so he dragged one of the chairs over to the door of the cell to enable the both of them to take a quick look inside. Standing on the chair, they could clearly see that the little vampire Bingo had caught the previous night, with his glowing red eyes and long sharp fangs, was nowhere to be seen. What they saw instead, sleeping on a rather narrow bed and breathing very heavily, was Baxter, the funny-looking dog that looked very much like a sheep.

"The tranquilliser that Staff Nurse Fanshaw gave him last night has not worn off yet," explained the detective, who for the past two hours had been struggling to write her police report. This was because the facts of the case, frustratingly, still made little sense to her. "Old Mrs Dingle is awake though, and she's already finished her breakfast so I will question her now."

Detective Huntress eased herself out of her comfy chair and walked over to cell number two, whereby she unlocked the door. Old Mrs Dingle looked a little tired as she was escorted out of the small room, although after seeing Trumper and Bingo standing close by, the old lady smiled and said, "Hello boys, how are you this morning?"

"We're good, Old Mrs Dingle," replied Trumper and Bingo, in unison.

Picking up the chair the boys had previously been standing on, the detective placed it in front of the large desk. She then arranged the other two chairs next to her own so that there were three chairs on one side of the desk and only one solitary chair on the other.

"Please take a seat, everyone," beckoned Detective Huntress, as she sat down on the well-worn swivel chair. "Trumper and Bingo, you sit with me, and Old Mrs Dingle, I would like you to sit opposite the three of us." Once everyone was seated, the detective started a voice recorder she had just then placed on the large desk and stated, "This is Detective Heather Huntress of Dragonbutt police interviewing Old Mrs Dingle regarding the attacks on the Reverend Pinkerton, Shadwick Poly and Tolly Butterworth. I also have Trumper Gallant and Bingo Malloy in attendance."

She went on to say a number of other official police-type things that Bingo found to be quite boring. The most important being that the interview was to be recorded and the old lady had not been charged with any crime as of yet.

"Old Mrs Dingle, I would like you to tell us in your own words, how long have you owned Baxter? Where did he come from? And when did you first notice he was, shall we say, abnormal?" asked the detective, who was deliberately avoiding the term 'vampire' in her line of questioning.

"Abnormal! He's a vampire," pointed out Bingo, as he had no qualms about calling a dog a dog, or in this case a funny-looking dog a little vampire. Although after receiving a stern glare from Detective Huntress, he decided it would be more prudent to remain silent and listen to what the old lady had to say.

After a short pause, she explained that Baxter had been given to her around five years ago, as a gift from the late Old Mr Dingle. Though she never knew where he came from and her husband sadly passed away a few weeks later. Baxter had always been a sweet loving dog and had never hurt anybody before, she told the detective. In fact, he was often chased by the other dogs and even some of the naughtier children in Dragonbutt.

Bingo raised his eyebrows and looked at Trumper, then muttered, "Mad Maddox."

The old lady went on to say that everything changed just over two weeks ago when Baxter started to get very agitated around sunset and became uncommonly restless during the night. For hours he stared out of the kitchen window and clawed at the pane of glass as if something inside him was telling the funny-looking dog to get out of the house.

"So was that around the time you found out Baxter was a vampire?" challenged Trumper, who was finding it difficult to resist asking the old lady a question. "And did his eyes glow red and his long sharp fangs start to appear?"

"Oh no, dear, that wasn't until a couple of days later," she responded, while shaking her head. "He was still very much the same playful and always adorable Baxter at that time."

It was the Wednesday before last, she told them all, that the situation with her precious dog worsened. Wednesday night, of course, was bingo night. This was one of only two nights of the week that Old Mrs Dingle was able to get out, socialise and really let her hair down. Although Bingo, who was looking at the old lady somewhat suspiciously, believed this was highly unlikely considering her hair could not have been more than three or four inches in length. And what's more, it was usually hidden beneath one of the colourful silk headscarves she was so fond of wearing.

She had never missed one of the Reverend Pinkerton's bingo nights, except during the week that Old Mr Dingle had passed away. And she had no intention of missing another, not even for her beloved Baxter. After sunset that night, the old lady tried feeding him a couple of uncooked Hogswood pork chops, which she had taken out of the freezer and de-thawed earlier that day. To her surprise, instead of wolfing them down as soon as he saw his favourite raw meat, the funny-looking dog merely licked the blood from the chops. He then discarded the meat, and to her utter dismay, he started clawing at the pane of glass in the kitchen window once more.

Unfortunately, pets were not welcome at bingo night, a rule the

Reverend Pinkerton always strictly enforced. Not wishing to be late, Old Mrs Dingle secured all the windows and doors of her home so that Baxter could not get out and then gave him a new rubber bone to gnaw on before leaving. As she said goodbye to the edgy and rather perturbed looking dog, the old lady thought to herself what possible harm could befall her treasured companion. In any case, it wasn't as if she would be gone for long, a couple of hours or so and she would be home again.

As it turned out, those two hours were more like four, and by the time Old Mrs Dingle had returned home, to her alarm, Baxter was nowhere to be seen. After noticing a pane of glass in the kitchen window had been shattered, she immediately realised the worst had happened, and her cherished but troubled dog had escaped. At once, the old lady picked up Baxter's lead and holding onto her torch, she ran out of the house and headed towards the place he would most likely be, Pigswill Alley.

With a torch in one hand to light her way, Old Mrs Dingle did not have to wait long to track down the wayward Baxter. As she made her way up the narrow path that connected Dragonbutt pond with Pigswill Alley, her funny-looking dog was thankfully walking slowly towards her. Although to her horror, he now had glowing red eyes and long sharp fangs. Yet in her heart, the old lady knew he was still the amicable dog she had always known him to be.

"When you saw Baxter coming out of Pigswill Alley with 'glowing red eyes and long sharp fangs', I assume you realised something was very different about him?" queried the sceptical detective, thinking the old lady must be hiding something.

"Dragonsbutts! I think it's pretty obvious to everyone that Baxter had turned into a vampire," chimed in Bingo, who was leaning forward on his chair to emphasise what he believed was a very pertinent point.

After another less than appreciative frown from Detective Huntress and a brief silence, she added, "And, at that time were you aware he had just attacked the Reverend Pinkerton?"

"Oh no, detective, it was not until we returned home that I could see blood around his mouth and in his fur. Baxter was always a messy eater, you know, but the bloodstains made him look like a hideous monster. I knew right away he had been a naughty boy, although I thought the blood had come from a small animal he had killed. So I gave him a nice warm soapy bath and cleaned him from head to toe," replied Old Mrs Dingle, while shaking her head. "I had absolutely no idea he had attacked poor Reverend Pinkerton, not until the next day when everyone was talking about it. And, naturally, I read young Barry Beasley's article in the Dragonbutt Smoker the following Saturday. It was only then I knew Baxter was really a vampire."

"Why didn't Baxter attack you?" challenged Detective Huntress, as she stared at the old lady with her inquisitive police officer's eyes.

"Oh, he would never harm me, detective, I can assure you of that," asserted Old Mrs Dingle, smiling confidently.

"After you discovered Baxter had acquired a taste for human blood and was now a vampire, why didn't you tell anyone?" appealed Trumper, rather firmly.

"I was hoping his little indiscretion on that Wednesday night was just a one-off. Because by the time I had walked him home, he looked like his old self again, that is with the exception of the bloodstains," revealed Old Mrs Dingle, who was trying to force another smile. "What I've noticed about him is that once he has had his fill of blood, soon after he always returns to normal. What's more, he's not a greedy boy, one pint is all he needs, and it's not just human blood Baxter craves, he likes other kinds of blood as well, though human appears to be his favourite."

"As we all know by now, it obviously wasn't a 'one-off' as you mistakenly and may I add irresponsibly thought," stated the detective, thinking she was still no closer to getting to the bottom of this case. "And how do you know Baxter likes other kinds of blood? What on earth have you been feeding him?"

Believing it was best to tell Detective Huntress the whole of her extraordinary tale, the old lady gathered her thoughts and straightened the headscarf she was wearing before commencing. She told them that the very next day she cleared away the shards of glass from the broken window pane in the kitchen and then Bucktooth Tom Blewitt kindly came over to mend it. He fastened a good strong piece of wooden panelling over the gaping hole and told her that he would make a full repair as soon as he could get his hands on a new pane of glass. Frustratingly for Old Mrs Dingle, it not only took a good week and a half to arrive but it had to be picked up from Chelmsford. And as she reminded the boys, it was not until yesterday that he was finally able to finish the job.

Just like the previous day, once the sun began to set, Baxter became increasingly frustrated and started to scratch and claw at the wooden panel that covered the broken window pane. Fortunately, just like Bucktooth Tom Blewitt, the panel was far too strong for him to break. Not wishing to take a chance though, the old lady prudently locked the kitchen door so that there was no way for him to escape. And that is when, right before her very eyes, to her veritable consternation the funny-looking dog transformed into a vampire once more.

Seeing him angrily parade up and down the long but rather narrow kitchen, Old Mrs Dingle knew that Baxter must be hungry again. Although she suspected it was not food he wanted, instead it had to be blood. Opening the door of the fridge, the old lady grabbed the first bloody thing that came to hand, a full pound of Hogswood's black pudding. Yet alas, to her disappointment, the funny-looking dog would not even take a single bite. Panic-stricken by this time and out of desperation, she drained the blood from a chicken that had been defrosting in the fridge and gave it to him in his favourite drinking bowl.

"So did he like the chicken blood?" interrupted Bingo, who had been uncommonly quiet while listening to the old lady's astounding story.

"Not really, but he liked it more than the black pudding because during the night he drank the whole bowl," disclosed Old Mrs Dingle, while nodding her head.

Now the old lady was aware that animal blood could help with Baxter's vampire induced blood cravings, she became a regular visitor to Baverstock's the Butcher's, Dragonbutt's acclaimed meat emporium. Its current proprietor, Chomper Baverstock Senior, was the father of Bingo's classmate, Chomper Baverstock Junior. Initially, the head of the Baverstock family business found it a little odd that Old Mrs Dingle had suddenly taken a liking to a diverse assortment of various types of animal blood. Nonetheless, he was never one to turn away good business and therefore always accommodated her peculiar requests with a welcoming smile.

At first, she requested the regular and most common types of animal blood; cow, sheep, goat, and of course, pig. And not only that, "The fresher the better," she always told the unfailingly cooperative butcher. The old lady fed each one to Baxter with varying and very limited degrees of success and then moved on to the more exotic; ostrich, alligator, camel (with one hump and never two), and finally kangaroo.

On one occasion, she even tried to order koala blood but was all too brusquely told by an irate Tasmanian customer, who by chance had been waiting in the queue behind her, "koala. You can't eat bloody koala!"

It was a blend of the pig and kangaroo blood that seemed to work the best, or to be precise, three parts pig to one part kangaroo with just a dash of Butts Batch for taste. Calling her bloody concoction blend number twelve, for no other reason than it was the twelfth blend she had tried on Baxter, Old Mrs Dingle was justifiably pleased with herself. As long as he drank it before sunset, the funny-looking dog never turned into a vampire and would remain his normal loveable doggy self.

"If this blend number twelve of yours was so successful then why did Baxter attack and bite Shadwick Poly last Thursday night and Tolly Butterworth on Sunday night. And not forgetting last night, when young Bingo was attacked and very nearly bitten on Pigswill Alley?" beseeched Detective Huntress, while impatiently waiting with her arms folded for the old lady to answer.

To the bemusement of the detective and the boys, Old Mrs Dingle remained silent at first and then asked for a pencil and a sheet of paper. She then started to draw what looked suspiciously like a line graph with both a vertical and horizontal axis. Once she had finished drawing, the old lady explained in her own carefully chosen words a whole lot about the law of supply and demand. Which even Bingo understood to mean she had a demand for blood that exceeded the current supply.

"Surely Baverstock's can supply you with all the animal blood you could ever need," remarked Trumper, as he studied the old lady's well-drawn graph.

Old Mrs Dingle reminded everyone that the two key ingredients of blend number twelve were a precise mix of pig and kangaroo blood. While Baverstock's always had plenty of pig's blood, as they could purchase all the pigs they wanted from the Hogswood Piggery, regrettably, there were absolutely no kangaroos living in Dragonbutt. For that reason, her supply problem did not allude to the commonplace pig, but rather the far rarer and altogether more exotic kangaroo.

"So where do kangaroos come from?" chimed in Bingo, who would have known the answer to that question if only he had paid more attention in his geography class.

"Down under, of course," answered Old Mrs Dingle, with a confident tone in her voice. "Chomper Baverstock Senior has them shipped all the way to Dragonbutt from a place called Gunduhwindy. However, they are not just for anyone, he only sells them to his special customers that have a more refined taste in their meat, or so he told me. The problem is the shipments are not regular enough to meet the demand. So when I asked him for more kangaroo blood last Thursday he simply had none to offer and told me his next shipment would not arrive until after Christmas. And with no kangaroo blood to make my blend number twelve, I had no way to stop Baxter turning into a vampire when the sun started to set that evening."

Refusing to take anything but the old lady's blend number twelve, the utterly vexed and altogether discontented little vampire paced up and down the kitchen and clawed at the boarded-up broken window pane. Later that night, Old Mrs Dingle rather foolishly thought that with nothing to satisfy his bloody urges, maybe a good long walk would calm Baxter down. So even though his eyes were glowing red and his fangs were long and sharp, she fastened the lead to his collar and led him out of the back door to the muddy and little-used footpath behind her house.

Once they had arrived at Pigswill Alley and were walking towards Dragonbutt Vicarage, the old lady noticed the little vampire looked remarkably passive and more like her Baxter of old. Due to the lateness of the hour and the fact that it was the dead of winter, she thought it unlikely they would bump into another living soul. So forgetting for a moment that her funny-looking dog was now a vampire with a yearning for human blood, Old Mrs Dingle unwisely unhooked the lead from his collar. Instead of obediently walking beside her as he typically would have done, the wily little vampire immediately lifted his head into the air, sniffed a few times and then bolted in the direction of Pucclechurch Crescent.

Beside herself, the old lady called out Baxter's name over and over again, but troublingly he did not return. Worried he was up to no good yet again, she followed him as speedily as she could, though due to her advanced years this was frustratingly slow. Then, after hearing an awful scream, Old Mrs Dingle came across a terrible and literally horrifying scene. Lying face down on the ground was a middle-aged man with the long sharp fangs of the little vampire apparently sunk deep into his plump and irrefutably fleshy butt.

Whistling as loud as she could and shouting, "Here boy, come along, Baxter," Old Mrs Dingle was not sure what the little vampire would do next. Turning around and seeing that it was the old lady, he slowly walked towards her, and by the time he stood by her side, his glowing red eyes had dimmed, and his long sharp fangs were barely visible. Within a matter of minutes, to her unmitigated joy, Baxter was his old self once again.

"Dragonsbutts!" shrieked Bingo, who couldn't resist using the all too common Dragonbutt term that seemed so appropriate at that moment. "What about Roly Poly?"

The old lady revealed that she cautiously made her way over to the spot where the man was outstretched on the ground, hoping he was still alive yet fearing he may be dead. With a considerable amount of effort, she managed to turn him onto his back, whereby she immediately recognised the chubby face of Shadwick Poly. He was still breathing, and so Old Mrs Dingle promptly called nine-nine-nine and requested an ambulance and Dragonbutt police. To conceal Baxter's guilt, she quickly cleaned the blood from his mouth and fur with a handkerchief and then apprehensively waited for the emergency services to arrive.

"That was when I first met you, Detective Huntress," recalled Old Mrs Dingle, while smiling sweetly at the detective.

"Yes, I remember, and I also recall asking that night whether you witnessed the attack on Shadwick Poly and your answer was 'No, I saw absolutely nothing'. When, in fact, you not only knew the identity of the attacker but at that very moment he was actually standing right next to you," accused Detective Huntress, as she frowned at the old lady. "As an officer of the law, we typically call that, lying to the police."

"That's quite true, detective, but I didn't see the attack myself, and the last thing I wanted was for you to take Baxter away from me," sobbed Old Mrs Dingle, who accepted a tissue from the stern-looking police officer to wipe the tears from her eyes. "Do you also want me to tell you about the night Mad Tolly Butterworth was attacked?"

"Does it involve Baxter turning into a vampire, yet again?" replied Detective Huntress, somewhat sarcastically.

"As a matter of fact, it does, but you know without my blend number twelve it's just so difficult to control him," admitted Old Mrs Dingle, looking disconcerted with the police officer.

"Then no!" retorted the indifferent detective, who intentionally used a decidedly blunt tone in her reply to the old lady.

"Old Mrs Dingle, let me recap the situation that you claim you found yourself in," asserted Detective Huntress, as she took a long hard look at her lengthy notes. "It was around two weeks ago that Baxter started to behave strangely and a few days after that he attacked and bit the Reverend Pinkerton. You then discovered he was literally turning into a vampire after sunset and now had a craving for human blood. In your attempts to control him, you fed Baxter various types of animal blood and eventually came across a bizarre concoction that you believe actually worked as good as human blood, which you subsequently named 'blend number twelve'. After finding you were unable to obtain a reliable supply of kangaroo blood for this blend number twelve, you were no longer able to control Baxter. This resulted in the attacks and hospitalisation of Shadwick Poly and Tolly Butterworth, and of course, the attack on Bingo last night. Is that a fair and accurate summation of the events over the past couple of weeks?"

"Yes, detective, I don't think I could have said it better myself," answered the old lady, while slowly nodding her head. "I was so happy after my success with blend number twelve and truly believed I could manage his little urges. It was only after my supply issue with the kangaroo blood arose that I realised I would need to ask for help."

"I have already checked with Doris, and there is no record of you contacting Dragonbutt police for help," disclosed Detective Huntress, as she impatiently tapped her fingers on the large desk.

"Oh no, detective, I didn't mean ask Dragonbutt police for help," stated the old lady, sounding quite emphatic yet chuckling all the same.

"And so if you didn't believe Dragonbutt police could help with your so-called vampire dog problem, then who?" inquired Detective Huntress, who was looking somewhat perplexed by the old lady's answers.

"Why, the DWI of course," proclaimed Old Mrs Dingle, with a smile.

Eighteen

The DWI

N ow quite convinced the old lady was more than a little loopy, Detective Huntress repeated what she had just heard, "The DWI! But what has the Dragonbutt Women's Institute got to do with all of this?"

"The DWI is not the Dragonbutt Women's Institute, detective. It's the Dragonbutt Witch's Institute," revealed Old Mrs Dingle, whose turn had come to stare at the open-mouthed and astonished looking police officer.

"So we have witches as well as vampires now," exclaimed Detective Huntress, after she had recovered from her initial surprise. "Old Mrs Dingle, do you really expect any of us to believe all this? The next thing you'll be telling me is that we have fire-breathing dragons and countless other monsters roaming around Dragonbutt."

"Of course not, detective. It's not the dark days," responded Old Mrs Dingle, as she shook her head. "As far as I am aware we only have one little vampire and about a dozen or so witches in Dragonbutt, although

I'm not sure about the rest of the district. But don't worry Detective Huntress, we're not bad witches, the DWI is a society of good witches."

The old lady told them the Dragonbutt Witch's Institute had been meeting every Sunday evening for almost three years, under the leadership of their Grand Witch, Elvira Wyvern. The DWI had started out as just a bit of fun, where a small group of ladies from the village could get together at Dragonbutt Victory Hall, share the local gossip and cast a few spells before popping over to the Dragonbutt Arms for a round or two of drinks. Though over the past six months, the Grand Witch had become far more serious about her witchcraft and had even taken on a young apprentice.

"And what do you mean by 'more serious'?" implored Trumper, who was impatient to find out as much as he could about this enigmatic Dragonbutt Witch's Institute.

Old Mrs Dingle disclosed that the Wyverns were an ancient family and the current household was widely considered to be 'old money'. This, she explained, meant their ancestors had acquired lots of land and wealth by dubious means. And so their descendants never had to lift a finger and work like most ordinary people. Elvira Wyvern was therefore what you would call a lady of leisure, and had plenty of time on her hands to pursue a variety of interests. Although since establishing the DWI, for the most part, she had become consumed with all things magic.

The Wyverns had lived in Dragonbutt since the day it had been founded, and their family library at Wyvern Manor was famed for its collection of old books that dated back to the early days of the village. One day, some six months or so ago, while cataloguing the titles in her collection, Elvira Wyvern had come across a very old set of dusty and slightly moth-eaten books. To her jubilation, they turned out to be the lost volumes of 'The Dragonbutt Witch's Guide to Witchcraft and Spells from beginner to the more advanced'. These were authored by none other than the Lady Eradorn Wyvern, the legendary Grand Witch who had lived many centuries ago during the dark days.

Elvira Wyvern became so enthralled with Lady Eradorn's books on witchcraft and spells that she read all of them from cover to cover. The more she read, the more Elvira became obsessed, and she even started to believe that with the aid of these books the Dragonbutt Witch's Institute could finally begin to cast spells that would actually work. None of the other witches really believed this, yet Elvira was a Wyvern, and the Wyvern name stood for quite a bit in Dragonbutt. So the witches all agreed that their Grand Witch should teach them the art of witchcraft and spell making as practised by Eradorn Wyvern so long ago.

"Dragonsbutts! So you mean to say that for the last six months the Dragonbutt Witch's Institute has been casting real spells?" questioned Trumper, who was still somewhat surprised the old lady had confessed to being a witch.

"Well, not in the beginning," admitted Old Mrs Dingle, looking noticeably thrilled to be talking about the DWI. "Every week we tried a new spell from one of the earlier volumes of Eradorn's books, which she had specifically written for beginners. However, we really didn't have much success and this frustrated Elvira immensely. Although that all changed about a month ago when something magical started to happen."

"And what was that?" asked Detective Huntress, who was finding all this talk of witches and witchcraft increasingly hard to believe.

Paying no attention to the interruption from the detective, the old lady continued with her story and said that none of the other witches really minded their spells did not work because they were having such a wonderful time. All of them enjoyed reading about witchcraft and collecting the ingredients to cast their spells, then practising the words and joking about how this spell or that spell would turn out. On the other hand, the opinion of the Grand Witch was that spell making should be taken far more seriously. As such, Elvira started to spend much of her time reading the more advanced books on witchcraft and spells, especially the last book that focused on dark magic. She tirelessly worked on these spells with her new but very enthusiastic apprentice, and it was then, to the other witches astonishment, some of their spells began to work.

Hearing a rather loud rumble come from Bingo's tummy, Trumper guessed it had to be nearly lunchtime and knew the younger boy would never willingly miss his lunch for anything. And of course, that included a bunch of Dragonbutt witches. Fortunately, it was not just Trumper who could hear the rumblings of Bingo's tummy as Detective Huntress had perked up her ears too.

"Oh, I nearly forgot about lunch," she announced, still listening with disbelief to Old Mrs Dingle's rather fanciful yarn regarding the Dragonbutt Witch's Institute. "I took the liberty of asking Doris to order pizza for everyone, and it should be here very soon."

"That's perfect," called out Trumper, as he was pleased they would not have to trudge all the way back to Counting House Lane and miss out on the remainder of the old lady's eye-opening story.

"Is it from Butt Hut?" yelped Bingo, expecting the answer would be yes, considering it was the only pizza delivery service in Dragonbutt.

"And what is Butt Hut?" inquired the detective, looking confused once again.

"I mean is the pizza from Dragonbutt Hut," corrected Bingo, forgetting that Detective Huntress was not Dragonbutt born. And having only recently moved to the village would not have known the residents of Dragonbutt nearly always called their local pizza takeaway, Butt Hut.

"Oh yes, I understand it's coming from Dragonbutt Hut, and Doris said that if Trumper and Bingo are eating as well, then she would need to order 'The Beast'. Whatever that is," disclosed the clueless detective, who was still examining her notes.

Bingo was in seventh heaven that Doris had ordered his favourite pizza, what Raji Banjani had fittingly named The Beast. It was definitely not a pizza for the faint of heart, with no less than twelve toppings and measuring a whopping three feet by two. More than sufficient for half a dozen or more hungry adults, and hopefully enough for the four sitting in the Dragonbutt police cells. Nonetheless, considering one of them was Bingo, no one could really know for sure.

At that moment, the phone's intercom rang. So Detective Huntress turned on the speaker to hear Doris Clutterbuck's voice announcing the arrival of The Beast. Knowing that Bingo's hungry-looking eyes were staring at her, she asked Doris to bring the pizza through to the cells right away. Less than a minute later, the trusty office administrator entered the room and placed an enormous box onto the detective's thankfully large desk.

"One moment and I will bring paper plates and a bottle of Braithwaite's for each of you," announced Doris, as she hurriedly ran back through to the main office of the police station and into the kitchen.

As he was too hungry to wait for the plates to arrive, Bingo greedily grabbed at the huge slice of pizza that was closest to him. And as she knew his bad habits all too well, Old Mrs Dingle gently slapped the young boy's hand away and firmly said, "Manners, Bingo, you need to wait for your plate." Fortunately for the ravenous boy, Doris returned in no time at all with the four bottles of Braithwaite's, a stack of paper plates and a pile of Dragonbutt police embossed serviettes.

"Thank you, Doris. And please help yourself to some of this gargantuan pizza," beckoned the detective, as she now realised why it had been named The Beast. "There's enough here to feed at least ten starving people."

"Maybe in the big city, Detective Huntress, but this is Dragonbutt, and we take our lunch far more seriously here," declared Bingo, who was not really trying to be funny yet everyone laughed all the same.

"I think one slice is more than enough for me," confirmed Doris, which was a relief for Bingo. Because he believed ordering only one pizza may have been an awful miscalculation on Doris Clutterbuck's part, even if it was The Beast.

Volunteering to be mum, the old lady placed a slice of The Beast onto each of their paper plates. With everyone munching on the tasty pizza and drinking from a bottle of Braithwaite's, Old Mrs Dingle could again return to her perplexing and frightfully bewitching story.

"Now, where was I?" hesitated the old lady, as it was not uncommon for her to forget what she had just been talking about.

"You were saying that around a month ago Elvira Wyvern started to practise dark magic with her new apprentice and it was at that time some of your spells began to work," prompted Trumper, who was barely half-way through his first slice of pizza, while Bingo was helping himself to a second.

In truth, Old Mrs Dingle was not at all sure what the Grand Witch and her apprentice had actually done. Although after so many months of practising their newfound spells with little to show for it, the witches of the DWI were overjoyed they had finally achieved some success. This had come as a big surprise to almost everyone, except Elvira Wyvern and her loyal apprentice. Both of whom never seemed to lose faith in Eradorn Wyvern's ancient texts.

"So, Old Mrs Dingle, which of your spells actually worked?" asked Bingo quite nonchalantly, as he finished the last bite of his second slice of pizza and was now greedily eyeing a third.

She revealed their first success came with Flanna Dooley's 'Transmutation' spell. This, according to Eradorn Wyvern's detailed notes, allows a witch to turn an ordinary lump of coal into pure gold, thereby bringing riches and wealth to her whole family.

"Old Mrs Dingle, are you telling me Flanna Dooley was able to turn coal into gold?" questioned Detective Huntress, looking more than a little stupefied.

"Well, not exactly, detective," answered the old lady, while shrugging her shoulders. "No one uses coal any more, not with global warming and all, so Flanna used her national lottery ticket instead. And can you believe it, after the spell was cast, she won, and not just a small amount but a whopping 500 pounds. Then there was Emblyn Gribble, who had almost lost hope of finding a husband. She was asked out by Dr Banjani only the day after she cast the 'Find yourself a lover' spell."

The detective looked at the old lady, and with a bewildered expression on her face, she inquired, "How often does Flanna Dooley buy a lottery ticket?"

"Twice a week without fail for nigh on twenty years and she has never won. That is until she cast that spell of hers," replied Old Mrs Dingle, while nodding enthusiastically to emphasise her point.

"Um," gestured Detective Huntress, who was shaking her head again. "And had Emblyn Gribble met Dr Banjani before she cast this miraculous spell that you believe resulted in him 'asking her out'?"

"I think from time to time she had seen him around Dragonbutt, as we all had, and Emblyn is rather fond of the food at Chilli Dilli. So he probably delivered a curry to her home every now and then," explained the old lady, while answering what the detective thought to be a straightforward yes or no with one of her long-winded and entirely unabridged accounts. "But socially she only met him once, during the previous week when the two of them attended Boosey Dooley's speed dating evening at the Dragonbutt Arms."

"Out of interest, is speed dating a regular occurrence at the Dragonbutt Arms?" queried the detective, who was all too single herself.

"Not at all, as a matter of fact, it was Boosey Dooley's first venture into speed dating. Apparently, he was trying to attract more customers into the Dragonbutt Arms on one of his few slow nights," expounded Old Mrs Dingle, while trying to suppress a giggle. "He only managed to attract four people though, and one of those was Angus Hogswood who is usually seen propped up against the bar on most nights anyway. Dr Banjani was the only other man, and the other woman was Hildy Bovington. But of course, Boosey had to bar her from participating."

"Why was that?" probed Detective Huntress, knowing she was probably going to regret asking that particular question.

"She's already married," chuckled the old lady, who had to take a deep breath to compose herself.

"Old Mrs Dingle, let me propose a very different explanation for these two incredulous occurrences that you believe were the result of your fellow witches practising some kind of bygone magic," began the detective, sounding a little impatient with the old lady. "Is it not more plausible that Flanna Dooley, after religiously buying lottery tickets for more years than she can possibly remember, simply won by chance? And is it not more likely that after attending Boosey Dooley's failed attempt at speed dating, Dr Banjani chose to ask out Emblyn Gribble purely because he happened to like her?"

"Oh no, detective," replied Old Mrs Dingle, vigorously shaking her head. "All the witches of the DWI knew it had to be our spells that made the magic work."

"And what possessed you and your fellow witches to think that?" appealed Detective Huntress, while rolling her eyes.

A little disappointed that the detective did not appear to believe her story, the old lady asserted, "It was because the dark magic spells cast by Elvira and her apprentice started to work as well."

These were the ones found in the last of Eradorn Wyvern's books on witchcraft and spell making, and strangely, this was the only book that none of the other witches of the DWI was ever allowed to read. Although this did not unduly concern most of the witches, there were mutterings and some words of caution amongst just a few that no good would ever come of this!

"I bet the Grand Witch was the one who turned Baxter into a vampire," called out Bingo, who, while contemplating whether he should help himself to a fourth slice of pizza, was getting a little impatient with the pace of the old lady's story.

"Not quite, dear. Elvira's first breakthrough with her dark magic was the 'Bring back the dead' spell," shuddered Old Mrs Dingle, because she thought things that were dead should probably stay that way.

"Wow, who did she bring back from the dead?" shrieked Trumper, a little too enthusiastically.

"Well, at first, Flanna Dooley nominated her husband, who she said was half-dead most of the time but that's how she preferred him," disclosed the old lady, laughing so much she nearly fell off her chair. "But in the end, it was Emblyn Gribble who implored the Grand Witch to bring her beloved cat, Mr Pibs, back to life. He had died the previous day, and that very morning she had buried him in her garden. Elvira agreed and asked Emblyn to bring two of Mr Pibs hairs, a recent photo and a large box of Bovington's assorted chocolates to the next meeting of the DWI."

"And then she tossed them all into her witches cauldron to cast the dark spell," interrupted Bingo, whose mouth and most of his face by now had become encrusted with tomato sauce and the other eleven toppings of The Beast.

"Only two of them," laughed Old Mrs Dingle, while using a serviette to clean Bingo's dirty face. "Mr Pibs hairs and his photo were to be used to cast the spell. The box of Bovington's assorted chocolates had nothing to do with reincarnating Mr Pibs. They were for Elvira because she always had a weakness for chocolates and Bovington's happened to be her favourite."

"Ah, good idea," exclaimed Bingo, who couldn't agree more when it came to Bovington's chocolates.

At the next meeting of the Dragonbutt Witch's Institute, the Grand Witch and her apprentice placed an old iron cauldron, which had been in the Wyvern family for generations, onto one of the gas burners in the kitchen at Dragonbutt Victory Hall. They added an assortment of special witches' ingredients and then poured two pint-size bottles of Butts Batch into the cauldron as well. Once the ingredients were bubbling, the apprentice added the two hairs and then Mr Pibs photo while reading aloud the dark magic words from Eradorn Wyvern's ancient book. Elvira proceeded to wave her wand to cast the spell and then confidently announced to the other witches that it was all done.

"Dragonsbutts! You mean Mr Pibs jumped out of the cauldron," blurted out Bingo, thinking if ever he accidentally dispatched anyone with Little MO, a spell that could bring them back to life could prove most useful.

"No, of course not," chortled the old lady, as that would have made even the Grand Witch jump. "Once the witches brew was ready, Elvira refilled one of the empty bottles with her dark magic concoction and told Emblyn to dig up Mr Pibs. She then instructed her to pour a few drops from the bottle into his mouth and then rebury him and drink the remainder herself."

Aside from drinking a further three pints of Butts Batch at the Dragonbutt Arms with her fellow witches, later that evening she did exactly as the Grand Witch had told her to do. And to her surprise but obvious delight, the very next day, something quite magical happened. By the time Emblyn had walked downstairs, she could hear the distinct flip-flap of the cat door that led into the garden at the back of her house. Entering the kitchen, she was literally at a loss for words, as standing before her and meowing noisily, was Mr Pibs. And astonishingly, he was no longer dead; instead, her much-cherished cat looked almost as good as new.

"That's quite a story, Old Mrs Dingle, and a rather imaginative one at that. How do you know this cat was not just a stray that looked like Mr Pibs? It could have simply been wandering around the neighbourhood and entered the cat door in Emblyn Gribble's kitchen to forage for food," asserted Detective Huntress, thinking she had just thrown a proverbial spanner into the old lady's far-fetched tale.

"Oh no, detective, that's impossible," retorted Old Mrs Dingle, as firmly as she could. "Emblyn assured me that it was the same old Mr Pibs, black all over with a white tip on his long tail."

"Um, that sounds like half the cats in Dragonbutt," countered the detective, who did not believe a word of what the old lady had been saying.

"Yes, that's perfectly true. But this cat only had three legs, just like Mr Pibs," revealed Old Mrs Dingle, looking triumphant as though she had just scored the winning goal for the Dragonbutt Flamers.

"Three legs!" repeated Bingo, all too loudly.

"That's right, although he wasn't born with three legs, you know," pointed out the old lady, shaking her head again. "It was all Angus Hogswood's fault. A couple of years ago he was shooting rabbits up at the Hogswood Piggery, and the halfwit mistook Mr Pibs for a rabbit. He shot off the poor cat's left hind leg, and the Bone Cruncher had to be called to sew up the stump. Angus was very upset about the whole incident and swore he would never shoot another rabbit again. Though I still believe he eats one of Flanna's rabbit pies every once in a while; but who can really blame him for that."

"If the Grand Witch could cast a spell to bring Mr Pibs back to life, you'd have thought she would have brought him back with four legs and not three," uttered Bingo, who had found that after eating three slices of The Beast, even his famously bottomless tummy could take no more.

"I'm sure Elvira could have easily grown another leg for Mr Pibs, but

Emblyn never thought of asking her for that, only to bring him back to life again," speculated Old Mrs Dingle, being somewhat defensive of the DWI's revered founder.

"So how did Baxter become a vampire?" probed Trumper, wanting to get the old lady to focus on the matter at hand, and that was the little vampire locked away in cell number one.

"Oh, that was more a terrible mishap than anything else," lamented Old Mrs Dingle, as she sadly hung her head.

The old lady began to tell the story of how Baxter, her beloved dog and dearest companion, had been transformed into the vampire that was terrorising the residents of Dragonbutt. It all happened by accident, she told them all, on the night of the DWI meeting that took place the week after Mr Pibs had been resurrected from the dead, which, out of interest, was three days before the attack on the Reverend Pinkerton.

As usual, the witches were to meet at Dragonbutt Victory Hall. And because pets were not just welcome but positively encouraged at the Dragonbutt Witch's Institute, Old Mrs Dingle had brought Baxter along as well. The two of them were the first to arrive at a little after seven-thirty, on account of the old lady's enthusiasm after the exciting events of the previous week. Unbeknownst to all the witches though, except the Grand Witch and her apprentice, sitting in the kitchen at the back of the hall was the Wyvern family old iron cauldron containing the remainder of Elvira's witches brew.

Baxter, being awfully thirsty after their brisk walk, immediately ran into the kitchen as he knew the old lady would surely follow to give him a bowl of his favourite drink, which happened to be tap water with just a drop of Butts Batch. To his delight, someone had already left him a very large bowl with some rather colourful liquid inside. Although it was not water and the taste was a little strange, he could definitely smell the Butts Batch, and so the funny-looking dog started to drink to his heart's content.

Finding Baxter with his sheep-like head in the old iron cauldron, Old Mrs Dingle gave a good firm yank on his collar to pull him out. Though to her horror, the greedy dog had lapped up every last drop. Not knowing the effect the mysterious witches brew would have on the living, she immediately attached the lead to his collar. And then forgoing the DWI meeting, the distraught old lady walked him home without delay.

"Before we go any further, I have an important question," chimed in Bingo, once again. "What's for dessert?"

While Trumper just rolled his eyes, Detective Huntress smiled and called Doris Clutterbuck on the intercom to check if there was any dessert in the kitchen for the sweet-toothed Bingo. Barely a couple of minutes later, the office administrator entered the cells carrying two bags of the chocolate coins that the boys had seen hanging from the Christmas tree earlier that morning.

"I'm afraid we're all out of dessert, but you can help yourselves to these chocolate coins," announced Doris, as she placed the coins on the large desk, closest to Bingo. "Naturally, they're from Bovington's."

Although Bingo considered chocolate something you eat as a snack between meals rather than a proper dessert, they were made from Bovington's chocolate, and so he eagerly peeled away the gold wrapping of the largest coin he could find and popped it into his mouth. Trumper and Old Mrs Dingle did the same with the smaller coins, but the detective simply raised the palm of her hand as if to say, "Not for me."

Returning to her remarkable story, the old lady told them that once they were safely home, Baxter became a little restless. Although at first, she put that down to the abundance of Butts Batch in the witches brew. It was not until the next evening that things started to get worse and everyone now knows what happened two nights after that on bingo night.

"But couldn't the other witches at the DWI help?" beseeched Trumper, while watching Bingo devour the first bag of chocolate coins and then start on the second.

Old Mrs Dingle sadly shook her head and said that because she had discovered how to control Baxter's blood cravings with her blend number twelve, she was able to take him to the next meeting of the DWI to do just that. However, the old lady knew that because her dear Baxter had been changed by some kind of insidious dark magic, only the two witches who practised this type of sorcery could possibly help. And that of course was the Grand Witch and her young apprentice.

After she heard what had happened, Elvira Wyvern reminded her fellow witches they had all sworn a solemn oath not to reveal anything about the Dragonbutt Witch's Institute to any outsider. And naturally, that included turning a funny-looking dog into a vampire. Understanding the urgency of the old lady's dilemma, that very evening, she began to scour Eradorn's ancient books on witchcraft and spells to learn how to reverse Baxter's terrible dark magic curse.

Unexpectedly, it was the Grand Witch's apprentice who eventually discovered the cause of Baxter's gruesome nightly transformation. Magic, she told the other witches, especially the dark kind, is a very precise kind of science. And so when Baxter drank the witches brew intended to bring Mr Pibs back from the dead, he inadvertently brought back the spirit of something that had long been dead itself.

This time it was Trumper's turn to cry out, "Dragonsbutts! Can the Grand Witch reverse her dark spell or will you have to find a reliable supply of kangaroo blood to stop Baxter turning into a vampire?"

"She doesn't know, so I guess my only hope is for Baverstock's to secure more kangaroo blood from Gunduhwindy," disclosed the old lady, looking somewhat downcast. "I was hoping her apprentice would have better luck, but she seems to be more interested in replicating the spell than helping Baxter."

At that very moment and without a word of warning, the distinctive Woof-Woof-Woof sound of a barking dog could be heard coming from cell number one. Detective Huntress instantly leapt to her feet and whipped out her police baton as she walked over to the cell, with the boys and Old Mrs Dingle only a few steps behind her.

"I knew that I should have brought Little MO with me," grumbled Bingo, just as the detective peered through the open hatch of the cell door.

Seeing that Baxter appeared to be his normal doggy self once again, with a smirk on her face, Detective Huntress opened the door of cell number one to reveal his butt awkwardly staring back at them. To the old lady's annoyance, her funny-looking dog had climbed onto the toilet seat, and with his head obscured in the toilet bowl, he was thirstily and quite noisily lapping up the water.

"Dragonsbutts! You dirty little boy," snapped Old Mrs Dingle, as she walked into the open cell and grabbed his collar. "Detective Huntress, could Baxter have something to eat because he must be quite hungry by now."

As soon as the old lady had led him out of the cell, the detective placed the box that held The Beast onto the concrete floor so that Baxter could eat the two remaining slices of pizza. To the dismay of Bingo, who had intended to take the leftover pizza home for a late afternoon snack, he wolfed down both of them right there and then. Except for some scorched fur caused by a few well-aimed squirts from Bingo's holy water pistol, along with a minor burn around his mouth after biting into the young boy's holy water-soaked nappy, the funny-looking dog seemed much the same as he had always been.

"He looks fairly harmless right now, nonetheless, until I decide what to do with him, he must remain locked in his cell," declared Detective Huntress, who had just turned off the recording device and was now dragging the reluctant Baxter back to cell number one. "I think a five-minute break is in order while I make an important phone call in the main office."

The instant the detective had left the police cells, Trumper inquisitively asked the old lady, "So how did Baxter escape last night?"

"I got the distinct feeling Detective Huntress was not interested in hearing about Baxter's other follies. She certainly did not want to hear about the night he escaped and attacked Mad Tolly Butterworth," remarked Old Mrs Dingle, as she sat back down on the chair and folded her arms.

"We just want to know how Baxter was able to get out last night and attack Bingo. You've got a few minutes to tell us, and we won't say a word to Detective Huntress," assured Trumper, who had returned to his seat along with Bingo. "She's not Dragonbutt born and is having a hard time believing in all of this anyway."

Old Mrs Dingle agreed and told the boys that after going through the anguish of knowing Baxter had already attacked three of Dragonbutt's residents, she was determined to keep him from slipping out of the house again and getting into any more trouble. For that reason, just as the sun began to set on Monday afternoon, the old lady locked him in her kitchen with a large bowl of fresh pig's blood she had procured over the weekend. Although it was better than nothing, she was acutely aware it was not her blend number twelve and so as the evening wore on it was hardly a surprise when the funny-looking dog transformed into a vampire yet again.

It must have been some time past ten, the old lady recalled, that she was disturbed by a loud knock on her front door, followed by another and then one more. After three knocks, she could hear the sound of a group of people singing the familiar seasonal words, "God rest ye merry, gentlemen…" Unfortunately for her, it was the Dragonbutt Christmas Carol Society. And regrettably, Old Mrs Dingle knew they would not be leaving without a boisterous rendition of at least three Christmas carols, a warm mince pie and a nip of something strong to keep out the cold.

With Baxter safely locked away in the kitchen, the old lady grabbed a small bottle of Dragonsbreath from her well-stocked cocktail cabinet and then opened the front door just a little. Seeing the tall gangly figure of Bucktooth Tom Blewitt, she handed him the bottle and wished the carol singers a very Merry Christmas before returning to the kitchen to warm-up a plate of Fanshaw's mince pies. After passing the bottle of Dragonsbreath around and bellowing a raucous, "Cheers," the congenial group then resumed singing their festive carols.

Once the mince pies had been warmed in the oven, Old Mrs Dingle carefully placed them onto a large round plate. While wisely ensuring Baxter was sitting at the far end of the kitchen, she cautiously unlocked the door and opened it just enough for her to barely squeeze through. Seeing that his opportunity had at last arrived, the little vampire leapt to his feet and burst out of the kitchen, knocking the old lady to the floor. And this sent the plate of mince pies flying unceremoniously through the air before landing with a thud on her impeccably clean but decidedly unfashionable lime green shag pile carpet.

Slipping through the gap left by the partially open front door, the little vampire made his escape by toppling the elderly Bucktooth Tom Blewitt before dashing out of Counting House Lane. Although not before careering into some of the other startled carol singers who failed to notice that it was not the ordinarily affable Baxter they had just encountered but something altogether more dangerous. This was hardly a surprise because, after four hours of walking the streets of Dragonbutt and singing carols to every house that opened their door, they had all quaffed more Christmas tipples than any of them could count. And this meant by that late hour the members of the Dragonbutt Christmas Carol Society were wholly incapable of telling the difference between a funny-looking dog that looks very much like a sheep and a bloodthirsty vampire.

"Dragonsbutts! So that's how he got out and bit my butt," exclaimed Bingo, who stood up and gave his butt a firm pat.

"He didn't really bite your butt," corrected Trumper, while grinning from ear to ear. "It was the holy water-soaked nappies that you taped to your butt. Those nappies and the holy water were the only things that saved you from being bitten."

Before Bingo had a chance to reply, Detective Huntress returned to the police cells with a serious look on her face. She reported that after a lengthy discussion on the phone with her chief inspector, they had come to the decision that Old Mrs Dingle would not be charged with any crime and was free to leave. In truth, the decision had really been made by the chief inspector, who had told the detective that no court in the land would ever believe an upstanding resident of Dragonbutt, particularly an old lady of seventy-two, would willingly harbour such an obviously crazed animal.

"Oh, thank you, Detective Huntress," squealed the old lady, as she clasped her hands together and smiled with glee. "Baxter and I can't wait to get home before the Christmas celebrations start tomorrow."

"I said that you can leave, Old Mrs Dingle," responded the detective, sounding very police-like. "In his wisdom, the chief inspector has left the issue of what is to be done with Baxter to me."

Detective Huntress went on to say that all this talk of dogs turning into vampires and witches casting spells was simply far too outlandish for her as a police officer to take seriously. Much of the old lady's story, she surmised, was implausible at best and downright preposterous at worst. Saying all that, something very strange had certainly happened to Baxter, and the detective reluctantly admitted she was unable to account for this. It was a known fact that he had already attacked at least four people, and this meant he was not only dangerous but a menace to every resident of Dragonbutt. Because of this her decision to keep Baxter locked in a cell would remain for the time being.

"But Detective Huntress, it's Christmas," pleaded Old Mrs Dingle, with tears forming in her eyes. "Does he really have to stay in a cell? I can keep him locked up at home until Baverstock's can supply me with more kangaroo blood for my blend number twelve. Once Baxter gets that inside him, he would be no trouble to anyone."

"And if you cannot obtain more kangaroo blood, what then?" demanded the detective, who had folded her arms and did not look like she was about to yield to the old lady's plea. "Face facts, Old Mrs Dingle, by your own admission, without your blend number twelve Baxter will continue to escape and attack more of the residents in the village."

"Why does it have to be kangaroo blood?" questioned Bingo, as he helped himself to another chocolate coin while joining the heated conversation.

"Bingo, I've already told you that pig's blood alone is just not strong enough. Yet a blend of pig and kangaroo blood seems to do the trick and Baxter likes it almost as much as human blood," uttered Old Mrs Dingle, who was wiping away a lone tear that had been rolling down her cheek.

"So why don't you use something that is like a kangaroo but is not a kangaroo?" rebuffed Bingo, looking deadly serious. "You know, like a rabbit."

"Thank you for that invaluable input, Bingo. However, kangaroos and rabbits are quite different types of animals," proclaimed Detective Huntress, as she rolled her eyes again, impatient to end the tiresome conversation.

"Wait a minute!" cried out Trumper, who suddenly slammed his fists on the large desk and abruptly stood up. "Maybe Bingo is on to something. Bingo, why do you think kangaroos and rabbits are alike?"

While everyone's eyes were momentarily transfixed on the young boy, Bingo just stared back at them thinking they all must be thick-headed or something like that. And so after a short pause, he placed the last chocolate coin into his mouth and quite casually stated, "They both jump of course."

Trumper thought for a moment or two and then smiled before exclaiming, "Dragonsbutts! Bingo's right, and it just might work. Old Mrs Dingle, have you ever tried blending pig and rabbit blood?"

"Come to think of it, I don't believe I have," answered the old lady, who was now looking decidedly happier.

If rabbit blood could indeed work as a substitute for kangaroo blood in Old Mrs Dingle's blend number twelve, Trumper knew that Bingo could well have succeeded in coming up with the solution to Baxter's unfortunate plight. Even though Dragonbutt had no kangaroos, except the few dead ones imported from Gunduhwindy by Chomper Baverstock Senior, rabbits, as every resident of Dragonbutt knew all too well, could be found almost everywhere.

Knowing that if they were going to help the funny-looking dog, Bingo's idea was their only hope, the excited Trumper urged the detective to drive Old Mrs Dingle over to Baverstock's right away. Once there, they would need to buy both pig and rabbit blood so that the old lady could make a fresh batch of her blend number twelve and feed it to him before sunset. Without blend number twelve, he reminded the police officer; as soon as darkness falls, Baxter would undoubtedly turn into a vampire again. And of course, no one wanted that to happen.

Although the sceptical detective did not really believe that feeding Baxter any type of blood would make an iota of difference, she was new to Dragonbutt and eager to make a positive impression. So after a few seconds of thought, thankfully, Trumper's request received a favourable nod of her head.

"Does that mean Baxter can come home with me for Christmas?" implored Old Mrs Dingle, who was already thinking of the feast she had planned to eat with her funny-looking dog the following day. "If the rabbit blood works, detective, he won't be a threat to anyone."

Despite the fact she was still thoroughly baffled as to the cause of Baxter's horrific transformation; Detective Huntress took pity on the old lady and agreed to release the funny-looking dog if he behaved himself for one more night in a police cell. However, she insisted that his dangerous fangs, which mysteriously grew longer and sharper once night fell, would have to be removed.

"Dragonsbutts! You want to pull his teeth out?" gasped Old Mrs Dingle, who could remember the time not so long ago when she still had her own set of teeth.

"Only his fangs," affirmed the detective, unwilling to budge even an inch on this issue.

"Don't worry, Old Mrs Dingle, I can do it," volunteered Bingo, with a grin on his face as he thought of the pair of pliers sitting in his uncle's toolbox at home.

"Oh no, you won't," asserted Detective Huntress, as she shook her head. "I'll have Doris call Dragonbutt Dental Surgery so that one of the dentists can perform the procedure this afternoon. And there's no need for you to get concerned, Old Mrs Dingle, as Baxter will never feel a thing."

As time was marching on, Detective Huntress led the others through to the main office, where Doris Clutterbuck sat staring at her laptop with a vacant and rather bored expression on her face. The detective explained to Doris that she would be out of the station for no more than a couple of hours, and Old Mrs Dingle would accompany her. She then asked the office administrator to call Dragonbutt Dental Surgery and request an emergency fang extraction for Baxter. And, she stressed, it had to be performed that afternoon and definitely before sunset.

Never one to question an officer of the law, Doris Clutterbuck just nodded her head and smiled before saying, "Of course, Detective Huntress, and wrap up warm everyone."

Once they were dressed for the chilly afternoon and Bingo had slung his Dr Who backpack over both shoulders, they said their goodbyes and the customary Merry Christmas to one another. While Doris remained in the warm police station to call Dragonbutt Dental Surgery, the other four hurriedly made their way outside. Whereupon Detective Huntress marched over to her favourite police car, the BMW M5. After hastily ushering the old lady onto the backseat, she jumped into the driving seat and turned the key in the ignition before giving a farewell wave to the boys. Immediately the engine roared to life, and after a tumultuous rear-wheel spin, she tore off in the direction of Dragonbutt High Street leaving a forlorn-looking Trumper and Bingo alone in the cold.

"She could have at least given us a lift," complained Bingo, as the boys watched the police car speed down Old Dragonian Way.

"Never mind, Bingo, it won't take us long to walk home to Counting House Lane," reassured Trumper, while giving the younger boy a spirited pat on the shoulder.

Nineteen

MAOS

⚬⚬⚬⚬⚬

As they were impatient to apprise Uncle P of the Dragonbutt Witch's Institute and how a dark magic spell had turned Baxter into a vampire, Trumper and Bingo did not hesitate for a second and promptly began their trek back home. Yet again, the boys trudged down Pigswill Alley and past the all too familiar sight of Dragonbutt pond. But instead of continuing by way of the muddy footpath that ran behind the little old house, they chose to walk along Hunnickle Drive. Happily, it wasn't long before they could see the familiar sign at the end of their street, which had the words Counting House Lane printed in bold black letters with cul-de-sac written just underneath.

At full stride, they marched past Old Mrs Dingle's sadly neglected house and then not wishing to bump into Bertie Bovington and Flitcher Jenkins, the two boys expeditiously scurried past the large Bovington house with the chocolate brown coloured door. Standing at the front door of the little old house, the bright red one with the shiny brass number twenty-two that the old lady always polished so well, Trumper took out his key and unlocked the door before the both of them eagerly darted inside.

"Boys, is that you, I can hear?" called a rather boisterous sounding Uncle P, from somewhere inside the living room.

"No, it's the little vampire," yelled Bingo, while slapping Trumper on the back and laughing hysterically.

"Hello, Trumper, and you too, Bingo," greeted Barry, as the two boys entered the living room after sensibly taking off their outdoor clothing and muddy wellington boots by the front door. "Congratulations again, everyone at the Smoker has been talking about how Bingo caught the little vampire last night. So have you uncovered anything else during your visit to Dragonbutt Police Station?"

"We thought you would have been home some time ago," remarked Uncle P, who had been warming his feet in front of the fire. "It's not like you two boys to miss out on lunch."

"Not really," replied Bingo, as he slapped his tummy, just in case he was wrong. "We had a bite to eat at Dragonbutt Police Station and so I should be alright until it's time for our afternoon snack."

"Dragonsbutts!" exclaimed Trumper, while trying his best not to laugh. "You had three mince pies, four slices of The Beast and I lost count of how many Bovington's chocolate coins you polished off."

"Four slices of The Beast!" repeated Barry, looking at Bingo in amazement. "You must have been hungry."

"This one is always hungry," chuckled Uncle P, as he walked over to Bingo and ruffled his head of messy blonde hair.

Unhappy that everyone was making fun of him on account of his healthy appetite, Bingo muttered under his breath, "It was only three slices of The Beast and not four." And then he looked at the conspicuous flushed face of his uncle and said in a mocking tone, "I guess you had lunch at the Dragonbutt Arms again."

"As a matter of fact we did stop by the Dragonbutt Arms to notify Angus and Boosey Dooley the little vampire had been captured. And out of courtesy, we stayed for one of Flanna's delicious pies and a few pints of Dragonstone Fire to wash them down," responded Uncle P, who was reddening further by the second. "But how on earth did you know that?"

"It was just a lucky guess," professed Bingo, while rolling his eyes in Trumper's direction. "I assume the reason you had to visit the Dragonbutt Arms in person was that Angus and Boosey Dooley don't have phones?"

Instead of sparring with Bingo any further, their red-faced uncle quickly changed the subject by saying, "Boys, come and sit down on the sofa so that you can tell us about your morning with Old Mrs Dingle and what you discovered about Baxter, or should I say the little vampire."

"Not me, Uncle P, I have something urgent to do before it gets dark, so Trumper will have to fill you in," informed Bingo, as he walked towards the living room door. "By the way, do you still have some pots of paint in the garage?"

"What in the world do you want with paint? Is it something to do with Christmas?" inquired their uncle, thinking Bingo never struck him as the artistic type.

"Something like that, Uncle P, but it's a secret," answered Bingo, with a mischievous grin on his face.

"Alright then, I have several pots of paint sitting on the first shelf on your left as you walk into the garage. There are a few different colours, and you should find plenty of paintbrushes lying next to them," instructed Uncle P, who was more interested in hearing about the little vampire than the young boy's painting. "And Bingo, try not to make a mess."

"Thanks, Uncle P," shouted Bingo, as he ran out of the living room and into the hallway, slamming the door behind him with a loud bang. He then hurriedly pulled on his coat, along with his DPS woolly hat and picked up his wellingtons before walking over to the back door. After opening the door, he slipped his feet into the muddy boots and ran towards the unlocked garage to gather everything he would need.

Once he was inside, the young boy switched on the light and looked for the shelf containing the paint, which he found without any trouble at all. As his uncle had pointed out, there was quite an assortment of colours; black, blue, bright red and two large pots of white. It was the bright red paint that Bingo sought, the one used on the front door of the little old house. And with it, a paintbrush that was neither too wide nor too narrow but just right for what he had in mind. Not wanting to get wet paint on his woollen gloves, because that would have certainly annoyed his aunty, he left them in his coat pocket and then picked up the pot of paint and one of the paintbrushes.

Delighted that he had found the paint he was looking for and a suitable paintbrush; the only other thing Bingo needed to complete his task was a stepladder. This, he could clearly see, was hanging from the wall at the far end of the garage, and although it looked a little rickety, it would be ideal for what he had in mind. Consequently, the young boy carefully lifted up the stepladder with his free hand, grateful that it weighed very little, and then trotted off down the long garden path with the pot of bright red paint and the paintbrush, all the way to the red-brick shed.

Meanwhile, in the living room, Uncle P and Barry were listening to Trumper's gripping account of the mysterious Dragonbutt Witch's Institute. This was followed by the enthralling story of how Elvira Wyvern and her apprentice had for the past few months been meddling in dark magic. And, Trumper expounded, this was how the unfortunate Baxter became possessed by a long-dead spirit that caused him to transform into a vampire after sunset.

"Well, I'm glad to hear that you have ascertained the reason for Baxter's astonishing transformation. Although what concerns me is this Dragonbutt Witch's Institute or DWI as they like to call themselves. Naturally, we need someone who is Dragonbutt born that believes in the old legends to thoroughly investigate this strange organisation. And of course, that person needs to have an unrelenting disposition and exceptionally inquisitive mind. Don't you agree, Barry?" asserted Uncle P, as he looked towards the young reporter and then gave Trumper a sly wink.

"Oh yes, I'll be onto it right away, that is as soon as Christmas and the New Year celebrations are over," assured Barry, whose mind at that moment was a little preoccupied with the rapidly approaching week of merrymaking.

"Dragonsbutts! I didn't mean this minute, Barry," laughed Uncle P, while stoking the fire and tossing another log into the flames. "This is Dragonbutt after all and nothing gets in the way of a Dragonbutt Christmas and New Year. Not even a bunch of incorrigible witches."

"So what does Detective Huntress intend to do with Baxter?" asked Barry, who was thinking like a reporter once again. "He can't remain in a cell at Dragonbutt Police Station for the rest of his life. And if he continues to turn into a vampire every night, the detective can hardly free him because every resident of Dragonbutt will be in jeopardy."

Trumper disclosed how Old Mrs Dingle had created her blend number twelve as a substitute for human blood. And this had successfully if only temporarily prevented Baxter from turning into a vampire after sunset. He then attempted to explain her problem with supply and demand. But this merely flummoxed the two adults, especially when he started talking about kangaroos. In the end, he simply told them that the old lady just couldn't get enough kangaroo blood from Baverstock's. However, Bingo had come up with the ingenious idea of using rabbit blood instead.

"That's brilliant," commented Uncle P, looking noticeably pleased. "And does it work?"

"We don't know yet, but we're hopeful. Detective Huntress drove Old Mrs Dingle over to Baverstock's this afternoon so that she could make a fresh batch of blend number twelve using rabbit blood," confirmed Trumper, as he glanced at the old carriage clock on the mantelpiece. "By now, they should be back at the police station. I just hope Bingo was right, that rabbit blood works like kangaroo blood."

Before the adults could question Trumper further, the front door opened with a protracted creaking sound, and Aunty J's voice rang out, "I'm home."

And then the loud bang of the back door being closed far too energetically could be heard, and Bingo shouted back, "So am I."

"Dragonsbutts! What have you been up to, young man?" barked their exasperated aunty, from the hallway.

"Painting," retorted Bingo, rather bluntly.

A moment later, Aunty J abruptly opened the living room door and escorted Bingo through to where Trumper and the others were sitting. The young boy had indeed been painting, although instead of heeding his uncle's words that were spoken earlier, he had undeniably made a bit of a mess. Even though his clothes were still clean, his face and hands were covered in large blotches of thick bright red paint. And this, to his aunty's ire, had already dried forming a shiny crust on his pinky-white skin.

"Perygrin, if you were going to let Bingo paint then he should have been supervised," fumed Aunty J, using a scolding tone that her husband dared not question.

"Yes, of course, dear. But I'm sure it will wash off with a bit of soap and hot water," reassured Uncle P, with an unconvincing and somewhat feeble smile. "Bingo, what were you painting?"

"It's better if I show you," replied Bingo, who had a broad grin creeping across his face. "Come on everyone, you need to follow me to the red-brick shed. And it's already dark outside, so bring a torch."

Curiosity certainly got the better of each one of them because without a word passing their lips, they hurriedly pulled on their coats and boots before following the young boy down the long garden path. As they neared their destination, Uncle P shone his torch so that everybody could now feast their eyes upon what Bingo had been up to with a stepladder, paintbrush and pot of bright red paint. In big bold capital letters, about six inches above Trumper's head, he had painted the word 'MAOS' on the white door of the red-brick shed. And while the word was clearly visible for all to see, the thick red paint had run just a little, forming several drips beneath each of the letters.

"What does that mean?" beseeched Trumper, pointing at the word that Bingo had painted on the white door.

"It says mouse," responded Bingo, looking rather pleased with himself.

"Dragonsbutts! That's not how you spell mouse," groaned Trumper, as he rolled his eyes in the direction of the three adults.

"I don't mean that sort of mouse," snapped Bingo, who was now getting quite incensed that Trumper thought the letters he had written were just a juvenile mistake. "You pronounce it 'mouse', but the letters stand for something important."

"And what's that, Bingo?" interjected Aunty J, seeing that the young boy was getting a little irritated at Trumper's line of questioning.

"MONSTERS ARE OUR SPECIALTY," he revealed, smiling once again as his annoyance with Trumper was almost forgotten. "It's the name of our new organisation that specialises in eliminating Dragonbutt's monster problems. And the red-brick shed is now MAOS headquarters, the place where we store the Entwhistle journals and our monster dispatching equipment."

"Outstanding, Bingo. I like it, I like it a lot," declared Trumper, as he slapped the younger boy on the back. "We've already caught our first monster, the little vampire, and if the Grand Witch and her apprentice keep dabbling in dark magic, then who knows what sort of monsters may return to Dragonbutt."

"Trumper, I think we need a little less of this frivolous talk of monsters, and instead we should all return to the house for a mug of hot chocolate and some warm mince pies," implored Aunty J, while giving the older boy a cautionary frown. "It's far too cold to be standing around out here and talking about nonsense."

Upon entering the little old house, Aunty J promptly made her way to the kitchen just as the others headed into the warm and pleasantly agreeable living room. Except for Bingo that is, who had been ordered to wash the blotches of bright red paint from his hands and face or there would be no hot chocolate and mince pies for him. Fortunately, their aunty still had a dozen mince pies stored in an airtight tin that she had baked the previous day. And so all she needed to do was warm them in the oven for a few minutes while she made five large mugs of hot chocolate.

"Hot chocolate and warm mince pies everyone," announced Aunty J, as she entered the living room with a smile on her face.

Bingo, who had not done a very good job of washing the blotches of bright red paint from his hands and face, was the first to reach for one of the mince pies. Alas for him though, with a burst of speed that rivalled Old Mrs Dingle, Aunty J quickly slapped his hand away.

"You know that guests are always served first, Bingo! And we use plates in this house, young man," scolded Aunty J, while placing a mince pie onto a small plate and handing it to Barry.

The next mince pie did actually go to Bingo, and although he was relieved, the young boy was not at all happy that he was second. Trumper and Uncle P came next and then finally their aunty allowed herself one of the warming Christmas treats.

"Thank you, Jemyma," acknowledged Barry, who still managed to speak even though his mouth was full of mince pie. "This hot chocolate is perfect for a cold Christmas Eve, and you know how much I love your homemade mince pies."

Aunty J gave a modest smile, and then Uncle P and Trumper joined in to thank her as well. On the other hand, Bingo, who was finishing off his first mince pie and helping himself to a second, just nodded and stuck his thumb into the air. This was his way of saying thank you without wasting any precious eating time on unnecessary words, or so he claimed.

"Oh, Aunty J, I nearly forgot but did Doris Clutterbuck call the dental surgery this afternoon about defanging Baxter?" queried Trumper, who, like Bingo, was now gleefully munching on his second mince pie.

"Yes, as a matter of fact, she did," answered Aunty J, while placing her unfinished mug of hot chocolate onto the coffee table. "That's why I was so late returning home. Azalia Blenkinsop drove down to Dragonbutt Police Station to perform the procedure, and I was left to deal with not only my own patients but Azalia's as well. It was such a strange and highly irregular request; nevertheless, I guess Detective Huntress knew what she was doing."

"Was it a success?" appealed Trumper, sounding rather impatient as he drank the last of his hot chocolate.

"Just before I left the surgery this afternoon, I did speak to Azalia on the phone, and the procedure was a complete success. Baxter will be a little sore after the anaesthetic wears off, but apart from that he will be right as rain in no time at all," explained Aunty J, who doubted the funny-looking dog really needed to be defanged in the first place. "Oh yes, and Azalia did have a message from Old Mrs Dingle for the two of you that I really couldn't make head or tail of. She said they had obtained all the ingredients from Baverstock's and administered the new blend to Baxter. Then she went on to say, he likes it and so far it appears to be working, though she asked for you boys to keep your fingers crossed anyway. And one more thing, the old lady is calling it 'blend number thirteen', and by all accounts, she thought that was quite hysterical."

"Of course! Thirteen is a witch's lucky number," laughed Trumper, pleased that the new blend was a success.

"I told you it would work," grinned Bingo, as he bit into a third mince pie to reward himself. "Kangaroos and rabbits both jump and so it had to work."

"Oh, is that the time? I'm afraid I have to head over to Old Privy Bottom now because Doris Clutterbuck is hosting a Christmas party this evening and it should be a blowout. So I'll say my goodbyes and will finish writing this jaw-dropping story after Boxing Day. That'll give me more than enough time to have it ready for next Saturday's edition of the Smoker," pointed out Barry, after finishing his hot chocolate and two of Aunty J's gratifyingly moreish mince pies.

"Yes, of course, Barry. You have a Merry Christmas and let's meet on Boxing Day at the Dragonbutt Arms to discuss the story," winked Uncle P, sporting a roguish smile as he escorted Barry to the front door.

"The Dragonbutt Arms, again!" uttered Bingo, chuckling as he rolled his eyes in Trumper's direction.

"Boys, it's Christmas Day tomorrow, and if you want Father Christmas to bring lots of presents tonight then you will need to be in bed and fast asleep by nine," stressed Aunty J, with an immovable expression on her face that meant this was not a friendly suggestion. "So I want both of you to have a hot bath right now, and when you come downstairs, your dinner will be ready and waiting for you on the table."

"What's for dinner?" demanded Bingo, who, after eating three mince pies, wasn't particularly hungry. Yet he knew in no time at all his tummy would surely disagree with him.

"I'm frying fish and chips tonight, and we are having them with plenty of my homemade mushy peas," smiled Aunty J, as she knew that Trumper and Bingo both loved eating fish and chips, especially when they were doused in lots of salt and vinegar.

"Whoopee! I could eat fish and chips every day," yelled Bingo, rather loudly as the two boys walked out of the living room to climb the stairs, only to bump into their uncle.

"Hang on a minute, boys, I need a quick word before you take your bath," requested Uncle P, in the softest tone he could muster so that their aunty would not overhear. "My ancestors wrote their journals about the monsters they encountered during the dark days and how they defeated them. As you have taken the Entwhistle Oath that responsibility now rests on your shoulders. And so I would like you, Trumper, to write a journal about how you and Bingo caught the little vampire."

"Certainly, Uncle P," affirmed Trumper, pleased that he had been given such a prestigious charge at such a young age. "But what should I call it?"

"How about 'Baxter the funny-looking dog who turned into a vampire'," suggested Uncle P, thinking that off the top of his head he had come up with quite a catchy title.

"Boring!" chimed in Bingo, looking downright ecstatic because he believed his proposal was much better. "It has to be 'Brave Bingo Malloy with his Monster Obliterator captures the bloodsucking vampire of Dragonbutt'."

Shaking his head, their uncle offered a second, and he modestly thought quite splendid suggestion, "I have it, what about 'The Little Vampire of Dragonbutt'."

Trumper considered this for a moment and then said, "I like it, Uncle P, although the little vampire wasn't just from Dragonbutt, but from

251

right here on our very own Counting House Lane. So I have a better title, I'm going to call my very first journal 'The Little Vampire of Counting House Lane'."

Trumper Gallant and Bingo Malloy will return in

The Dragonbutt Itch

www.ingramcontent.com/pod-product-compliance
Lightning Source LLC
Chambersburg PA
CBHW030127180626
46812CB00002B/590